THE FATHER'S SON

PETER McPHIE

This book is a work of fiction. The characters, incidents and dialogue are drawn from the author's imagination. Any resemblance to actual events or persons, living or dead, is purely coincidental.

PUBLISHER: PETER MCPHIE

CONTACT: petermcphie.com

OR: petermcphie@hotmail.com

THE FATHER'S SON/Peter McPhie—1st edition

ISBN 978-0-9952877-4-7 (Paperback)

ISBN 978-0-9952877-5-4 (e-book)

VISIT : https://petermcphie.com

FOR HELGA

CHAPTER ONE

1961

It had been dark for hours, an October rain lightly falling, when Albert Macky hurried up the steps of the Hotel Continental, stopping under the entrance overhang to take a final drag. Macky was thirty-three, short and slight, and plain of face. He didn't stand out in even a small crowd, which, in his line of work, was an asset. For he was a master pickpocket, a virtuoso of the bump, the buzz, the two-fingered lift, the palm dip, the thumb hitch.

But as talented as he was, he was on the lam. If he was ever arrested he'd be returned to Buffalo to prison, and he never wanted to do time again. More beatings would kill him.

With satisfaction he noted the expensive cars parked nose to tail all down the street, the rain lightly drumming the roofs, shiny under the streetlights. He tossed his cigarette and entered the hotel, crossed the chandeliered lobby and followed the long marble corridors to the Starlight Room, the hotel's glitzy ballroom.

There was no name-check attendant, no watchful doorman. The room was low-lit, dusky. He could see it was a full house, five hundred of Philadelphia's business elite in well-cut suits and stylish gowns. The staff was preoccupied in filling endless wine glasses, the servers circulating silver platters of smoked salmon. A small orchestra backed a soulful black woman who caressed the lyrics of Etta James's latest song, 'At Last'. The dance floor was crowded with couples swaying in close embrace.

Macky wore a black suit like everyone else so he blended. He was unremarkable, uninteresting. If any incident should occur, he wanted very much to be unremembered.

He scanned the crowd as he walked, a shrewd observer, careful to note the silent communications of the face, the eyes, the hands, reading attention level and mood. Now, with hours of food and drink behind, most were less than alert.

Near him a white-haired man and his wife were distressed by a sniping argument between a young couple they were with, the young wife protesting to her husband, her finger raised. Macky made his move, an imperceptible nudge faster than a blink, and the older man's slim wallet slipped invisibly into Macky's pocket. He removed the bills by feel as he moved on. He would discard the wallet once out of the room.

Thirty feet away in a black dress stood a tall, statuesque blonde, eyes bright, a diamond choker on her slim neck. She was deeply attracted to the man she was with, giving him delicious smiles, smoothly insinuating her body forward. The man was focused on her, his back to Macky, a lucrative opportunity.

Watching her, Macky moved to within four feet, standing

behind him. The orchestra finished the song and the ambient sounds suddenly quieted. He caught the man's voice clearly, uttering comment on the singer's performance.

The man's voice had a rich tone—distinctive, memorable—and disturbingly familiar.

Macky didn't know anyone in Philadelphia, but a warning bell began to clang. He moved steps away and looked back. The woman put a sensuous finger to the man's lips and in mock avoidance he turned his head.

A pang of fear drove through Macky and he looked away, his heart racing. The man's bearing, his face, his eyes as they shifted past Macky, all struck a chord.

He chanced another look. They had moved, eclipsed by the crowd. As very uneasy as he was, a potent curiosity was building.

He threaded his way until he spotted them. Again the man presented a rear profile, shorter than the woman, but his wide shoulders expressed strength. That, too, seemed familiar. He worked his way closer, this time from the other side to see his face. The man was regarding the woman intensely, listening to her speak. He didn't recognize him exactly, yet somehow he was insistently familiar, that face that communicated intelligence, or more precisely shrewdness and composure, a man used to wielding unquestioned authority.

Suddenly it all fit.

Like taking a blow to the stomach, Macky shuddered, struggling with disbelief. But there was no mistake; he had witnessed a terrible magic. The man had risen from the dead.

Macky saw him put his mouth to her ear for several moments then walk away, swallowed in the crowd. Macky felt himself absorbed by the shock and stood as if cemented to the floor, comprehending with a deepening fear that this was a man who, above all else, did not want to be recognized. Ever.

He watched the woman who now stood alone, a graceful air about her, her eyes casually taking in the room. A minute passed. She began to walk, somewhat in his direction, her face calm and beautiful. She passed by him, ten feet away, but then unaccountably stopped. Her back was to him. With deliberation she turned slowly, her eyes lighting directly onto his and staying, her gaze a laser.

The sickening realization flooded him—he'd been discovered, and now suckered.

His eyes darted about the room as he hurried for the exit. He rushed along the corridors and through the lobby, straight-arming one of the wide front doors and bounding down the wet front steps, glancing behind.

He hit the sidewalk in a sprint, ran a half block, turned into a narrow dark lane between tall buildings and ran to its end. He looked back, breathing hard, grimacing from the exertion, too many cigarettes.

The rain had subsided, a light patter now. He kept glancing behind as he trotted down a dimly-lit street, stately old houses with deep yards, big trees, thinking that if he were pursued he could find concealment in one of those yards. A car slowed and passed him, its tires sounding on the rain-slicked asphalt.

A block ahead a black Thunderbird turned onto the street in his direction, its lights bright. It traveled a quarter of the block then slowed and pulled to the curb, the engine running.

Watching the car warily, Macky crossed the street to the other sidewalk. The driver's door opened and a tall man stepped out, lifting his coat collar against the spitting rain. The man crossed the street half way but stopped, calling back to the car, "What? Yes, it's in the trunk."

Macky relaxed a little, walking on as the man went back to the car and opened the trunk, retrieving a shoe box. Macky watched him close the trunk, watched him hurry across the street and suddenly look up at Macky as if just registering him coming along the sidewalk.

Macky glanced to the car. There was no one inside! The man was approaching quickly, the shoebox raised, pointed.

Macky turned and ran. Two quick shots came from a silenced pistol, the second shot catching him and he fell to the gutter, clutching his side. The man came up and held the shoebox close to Macky's chest. Macky's eyes widened with horror. "No."

The guttural sound of a souped-up car suddenly erupted from two blocks down as it turned onto the street, its lights sweeping. The man glanced to it, then fired into Macky's chest and his head slumped. The man pocketed the gun and grabbed Macky by the feet, dragging him toward his car as he watched the lights of the oncoming car, Macky's head bumping along the asphalt.

The car came quickly, its headlights lighting up the whole scene. It braked to a screeching sideways stop just twenty yards away. All four windows were down and teenagers gawked from each one. "Take a picture with the instamatic," one yelled.

The man heard it and dropped Macky's feet. A picture is harder to beat than an eyewitness. He leaped into his car and its engine roared, the tires squealing, the car fish-tailing a whole block, then gone.

Macky lay motionless in the running gutter, in and out of consciousness, sinking in a black pool from which he couldn't surface. The sound of sirens now penetrated the pool, getting louder, stirring deep fears. Sirens had never meant anything to him but bad luck.

CHAPTER TWO

THE YELLOW SCHOOL bus slowed to a creaking halt on the empty country road and the front door swung open. The lone remaining passenger, seven-year-old Andrew Locke, came down the two steps and jumped off, his knapsack bouncing on his back. He watched the bus lurch away in a grinding of gears and lifting dust.

Surrounding him were vast fields, the October wind rustling the rows of empty corn stalks. The nearest neighbor, the one who farmed the land, was a half mile away.

He walked the long gravel lane leading to his small house and thought of the birdfeeder he and his father would make, the picture-book of instructions tucked in the knapsack. His teacher said the almanac predicted a hard winter so the winter birds were going to need help.

He heard a faraway throb of protesting engine and looked to the sky and watched an open-cockpit biplane struggling in the distance, its wings unsteady, its progress slow. He knew the biplane, a neighbor down the road who had a grass runway. His eyes followed it until it was swallowed in bulky clouds, but in his mind he still saw it, saw the brown leather helmet, the snug goggles, the determination in the pilot's face.

The engine's drone finally faded to silence.

He climbed the back porch steps and knew with confidence that one day he would be a pilot and fly with determination through clouds in a gray sky.

He took a key from his pocket. He had attached it to one of his belt loops with a string so no one could ever take it and make a wax impression like he had seen in a comic.

He was glad to be able to come home after school today and not go to the sitter's. His father was home days because he was working nights. But he would still be asleep and so the door would be locked. He turned the key until he heard the bolt slide free and pushed the door open.

In the mud room he un-slung his knapsack and hung it on a hook. On another hook was his cowboy gun belt with a silver revolver in the holster. He lifted the gun belt and strapped it onto his waist.

He swaggered into the kitchen and walked toward the fridge.

He stopped dead in mid stride and spun around, the revolver leaping into his hand. He pointed it straight at the wall and his eyes narrowed. "So there's two of you," he said in his best drawl. A small smile crept on his lips. "Well there's two of me, too. Behind those rocks is my dad. Maybe you've heard of him—Detective Paul Locke." He nodded slowly, letting the point sink in. "That's right. Best shot in the territory. So just lay down your guns and back away, *real* slow."

With flair he holstered the revolver. He took a glass from the cupboard, opened the fridge, and poured a glass of milk. He stood in the middle of the kitchen taking a slow drink as he watched a narrow shaft of sunlight that reached almost to the floor. His father had called them sunbeams. He had seen them in the Cathedral in Philadelphia at his mother's funeral stretching from the highest stained-glass windows down to the shiny marble aisle. He wondered if angels really did glide down sunbeams to take a mother when she died.

He took another sip.

He heard a sound, faint, then again, the pitch higher. It was the back door, the yaw of the hinges. Someone was opening the door but trying to be very quiet about it.

He stood perfectly still, straining to listen, staring toward the mudroom, the glass tight in his grip. His heart quickened. No one except his father and he ever came in by that door. His father would have given it a hearty push, but all he heard was a creeping slowness.

A different pitch now, ever so gentle. Someone was in the mudroom carefully closing the door. Anyone entering there had to pass through the kitchen. He found he couldn't move, his legs numb and unconnected. He opened his mouth to call out but his throat was tight and no sound came.

Then he saw them.

He dropped the glass and it smashed on the wood floor.

Two men as big as bears, each with a black pistol in black-gloved hands. They walked into the kitchen looking at him, their eyes steady and cold.

He heard his father's movements upstairs, heard his father's voice, "Andrew?" He heard his father coming down the stairs, calling again, "Andrew, what was that?"

The men made no move, their faces showing not the least fear even though his father was coming. He couldn't seem to utter a sound. His father was in the hall, but still he couldn't move.

His father entered the kitchen and saw them. Andrew stumbled to him and grabbed him around the waist. As much as he wanted to, he couldn't seem to cry.

Neither of the gunmen took their eyes from his father. One spoke flatly. "Detective Paul Locke?"

He heard his father take a deep breath, a terrible sigh. His father nodded.

"Anyone else here?"

His father shook his head slowly. "No."

"Anyone expected?"

He shook his head again.

The gunman assessed him a moment then nodded to the other gunman who went to the window and made an 'all-clear' sign. The first gunman stepped to the phone on the corner table and severed its cord with a quick knife stroke.

Shortly the back door opened. A man appeared dressed in a full length black coat, his head and face concealed in the frightening black hood of an executioner. Only his dark eyes could be seen looking out from the two holes in the black hood.

He was shorter than the gunmen and broad shouldered and walked with calm. He came close to his father and the eyes carefully examined him, deeply curious.

"Have them put the guns away," his father said quietly. "They're not necessary."

"No, Mr. Locke. I live by caution. I take no unnecessary risk. More correctly, I eliminate risk." The voice was relaxed, confident.

The hooded man walked down the hall and paused at the closed

French doors to the living room. He pushed them open and signaled all to follow.

Andrew and his father entered the living room, the gunmen remaining in the hall. Andrew clutched his father and watched the hooded man who was studying a framed family portrait sitting on a cabinet, a picture taken at the county fair—his father, and Andrew age five, each in old homespun clothing, each smoking a corncob pipe. Seated between them was Andrew's young mother in flowing period dress, a radiant beauty with long dark hair smiling at the camera.

The hooded man turned to his father. "I was vulnerable last night." The man's eyes searched his father's. "We thought he was dead, two bullets up close. He lived a little too long. And now I'm put in this position."

Andrew buried his face in his father's waist. His father slowly knelt and hugged him closely.

Andrew whispered, "What are you going to do, Dad?" He could feel his father trembling as he hugged him. But he knew it was not fear because his father feared no one and no thing. It was the trembling he had felt when they hugged at his mother's funeral.

"You're a fine, fine son, Andrew," his father whispered. "I love you so much."

He felt the stroke of his father's hand on his head.

He looked at his father and began to sob. "No, Dad. What are they going to do?" He squeezed his father tighter, never taking his eyes from his father's.

His father stood and released the hug and held him at arm's length. He locked his eyes on Andrew and spoke firmly, calmly. "You must go to your room. The sitter will come for you later. Do as I say, Andrew."

Andrew's tears streamed. He turned and looked at the hooded man's eyes in the two holes in the hood, holding the man's gaze until his father led him to the hall and released his hand. "Do as I say, son."

Andrew could see from the intensity in his father's face that he must do as he was told.

The gunmen were so large and the hall so narrow. One led him by the arm, but he stopped at the bottom of the staircase, gripping the banister, turning to see his father. Through tears he said, "I love you, Dad."

His father nodded and smiled. "Go, son."

The gunman led him up into his bedroom and left, closing the door behind him. The gunman tied one end of a cord around the outside handle of Andrew's door and secured the other end to the handle of the closed door across the hall. He tested the hold and quickly clumped down the stairs.

Andrew tugged but couldn't open the door. He put his ear to it crying silently, listening to the voices down in the living room, low and muffled. He could tell when it was his father speaking. Often, when his mother was alive, he would lie awake at night and listen to them talking in their bedroom, his father's deep tones intersecting with his mother's light ones, her soft laugh. They were often the last thing he remembered before drifting warmly off to sleep.

He heard the back door open and ran to the bedroom window. He saw his father being led across the lawn, a black sack covering his head tied close at the neck, his hands tied behind his back.

He opened the window and screamed, "Dad!"

There were two cars, one black, one green. A gunman opened the trunk of the green car and guided his father inside.

An uncontrollable anger seized Andrew. "No! Don't do that!"

The gunmen and the hooded man looked up at the window. One slammed the trunk shut.

Andrew shook violently and clenched his fists. "Stop! You can't take my Dad."

The gunmen got into the black car and started the engine and their car moved away. The hooded man waited at the side of his car.

Sobbing, Andrew remembered something and quickly reached under his bed and grabbed the coil of thick rope. His father had shown him how to do it if there was ever a fire downstairs in the night and the stairway was blocked with flame or smoke. He tied one end of the rope onto the steel bed leg and hauled the rest of the rope to the window and tossed it out. Gripping it firmly he stepped out of the window and propelled himself backwards down the wall, the rope swaying, his feet bouncing off the brickwork. When he was halfway down he saw that the green car was starting down the laneway.

"Dad!"

Four feet off the ground he let go of the rope and dropped and ran. "Dad!"

Now thirty yards away, the car slowed. He was gaining on it, his legs churning. But when the car reached the end it turned quickly onto the road with a roar and surged powerfully. The engine bellowed as it picked up speed and climbed and crested the ridge.

He stopped and watched it soon disappear completely from sight.

Silence was all around. He fell to his knees on the gravel, his body shaking, his eyes brimming with tears looking at the empty road. His mouth trembled so terribly that not even a bird could hear him call, "Dad."

CHAPTER THREE

TEN YEARS LATER

1971

HE HAD BEEN riding the Greyhound bus for two hours, and even though it was late evening the heat in the bus was stifling, the heat wave in its third day.

But it didn't matter to him. He was away from the hell of the reformatory where he had lived an eternity although it was only six months. Four hundred young men—sixteen and seventeen year-olds—a brutal place where primitive feelings, primitive fears, primitive behaviors, ruled.

The beatings he took from others in the first month had added a valuable reminder to the lesson he had been struggling for ten years to learn: that life just isn't fair, so get over it. He had bulked up, trained hard, and survived. In fact, he had excelled, becoming the senior boxing champion. At 6' 1" and a muscled 190 pounds, nobody pulled his chain anymore.

At the Board hearing this week he'd worn a suit, his hair neatly trimmed.

"Andrew Locke," the chairman had said, "you should never have been here. You were a young man adrift for a time, you lost your way, lost your grandpa, but you should never have been here. You have the intelligence, the exceptional intelligence I might add, and the capacity for hard work and the good temperament to be anything you want to be. And you have displayed the desire these months here to lift yourself to be who you truly are. Your early release is your chance to prove it."

"I understand, sir. I won't disappoint you."

The chairman had looked him in the eye. "Or yourself."

Even though it was now twilight, his eyes drank in the passing country scenery as if he had been blind until now. The simplest of things was so impressive—a tractor turning silently in a field of golden hay stacks, a snaking stone fence, an old concrete bridge arching over a brooding river.

He studied the people in the seats near him, bored faces, hot, fanning themselves with magazines having given up trying to read. Some were sipping a drink. Although he was getting very thirsty, he would save his water until he got off the bus and started his long walk.

As he watched them he knew they didn't appreciate the gloriousness of their freedom. He would never give up his freedom again. He would never do another stupid thing. He was grateful, released early to complete twelfth grade out in the community. He would toe the line every day, never deviate, never forget that he was grateful.

The thought floated into his mind as it had so many times before—how crushed his father would be to know his son had spent time in a reformatory, even a short time. The only consolation—his father had never had to know.

When he had first come to the reformatory six months ago, the psychologist and he had talked at length.

"The day those men took your father, is it something you remember well?"

"Well enough."

"Is it something you think of often?"

"Sometimes it's just… there. I realize, even without thinking…it's there."

The truth was he lived with it, the dark eyes of the man watching him through the two holes in the black hood. When he was younger the eyes were as big as baseballs, black balls that engulfed and squeezed the life out of him. The nightmares—the cold sweat, the shaking—were less often now. Sometimes he woke shouting. He told no one about the nightmares, not even his grandpa who had too much depression of his own to ever help. And certainly he wouldn't tell this psychologist whose opinion might waver about his emotional stability and jeopardize his early release, even his whole future.

"You then had to live with your grandpa."

"Yes."

"And how was that?"

"He tried his best for me. But…my Mom, she was his only child. He never got over her dying. Just couldn't beat it. He drank more and more over the years, more and more depressed. No supper on the table."

"You had to be a very strong boy for a very long time."

Andrew considered the comment.

"Your school marks didn't suffer."

"I found school easy, but I still worked hard. If one day my Dad came home, I wanted him to be proud of me."

"You held out hope…"

"Yes, when I was young, I held out hope. There was still a chance because nobody knew what had happened, where he was taken. Maybe he was still alive."

"But that hope stopped."

"I hoped for so long it became… like a state of mind. But one day when I was twelve I remember realizing that I didn't hope any more. He was gone forever. It was just Grandpa and me. We were like two drowning swimmers."

"You began to get into trouble, small stuff."

"I made some friends whose family lives weren't great. We understood each other, knew what it meant to go home at night, be alone, not like other kids. I began to make some bad decisions."

"You presented an odd dichotomy. Even in high school you were an excellent student but getting into enough trouble to come to the attention of the Courts."

Andrew nodded. "And then Grandpa died."

"And the judge believed that you needed intervention, structure and discipline, like this reformatory."

"Yes."

The psychologist had then surprised him, jumping backwards. "Let's go back to you losing your dad. Does it bother you not to know why it happened?"

He had breathed deeply, taken a few moments. "Sometimes I feel it inside me, a riddle. Yes, sometimes it bothers me."

"Does it make you angry?"

How could it not? My life went completely off the rails, was destroyed, because of some evil man. I was only a boy! But he had spoken calmly. "I do feel a kind of intensity sometimes. But I can live with it."

"You sound philosophical. Where's the anger?"

He didn't want to engage on that with this psychologist, or anyone else. They would never understand. "You can't change what's already happened. It took me a long time to stop looking back, sir. Looking back is what got me into this place to begin with. But what you *can* do is consider what you *have*, what you can *do*, what you can *be*. And go for it. Take no prisoners."

"Take no prisoners?"

"It's just an expression."

"Sure. Sounds good, rational, inspirational. But we're emotional creatures, not mental machines."

"I've read biographies of people who've gone through hell on earth and they are stronger for it, better for it. And I intend to be one of them."

The psychologist had sat back and looked at him for long moments, studying him, saying nothing. Andrew had held his gaze, long wordless moments, each taking the measure of the other.

He had felt himself quieting inside. "It's simple, sir. You said structure and discipline, like this reformatory. And that's good, that's important. But that's only on the outside. You also need something on the inside. I know that my father and mother loved me. I know it, and I feel it. I have no one else. Even though I messed up, I want my life now to be something I can be proud of, that they would have been proud of. That gives me direction, gives me strength."

The bus was slowing to a stop even though they were still in the country. It pulled to the side of the highway at a crossroads. The driver called out, "Andrew Locke?"

"Yes?"

"This is your stop."

He grabbed his knapsack and hurried to the front. "Thank you," he said and stepped off. He watched the bus pull away, a deep growl from the engine, a stench of diesel filling the night air.

It was oppressively hot and the supervision house was four miles down the side road. He realized he was parched, his throat as dry as sawdust. He reached into his knapsack for his bottle of water, his hand working around and around.

Damn. Where was it? He thought for a moment, then remembered—he had left it on the bench at the bus station when he rearranged his pack. How unbelievably stupid was that? he thought.

All around was darkness and quiet fields except for a low brown building down a ways that looked like a tavern, a neon sign flashing STACEY'S, a string of white lights stretched across the front eaves, a 'Cold Beer' sign in lights hanging in the window along with a picture of a shimmering glass of beer, condensation running down its side, beckoning.

He had no money. He would be allotted some at the supervision house. He would never drink a beer anyway, but maybe he could get a drink of water. He was on conditions and shouldn't be in a drinking establishment underage, but with his size, he didn't look underage. Anyway, he would just ask for water. It would just take a minute.

He crossed the road, walked the couple of hundred yards along its shoulder, and crossed the tavern's gravel parking lot. Three guys and a girl were coming out of the tavern. He heard one guy saying to the others, "Fuck that shit."

He drew his baseball cap lower and pushed open the door. The tavern was shabby in the murky half-light, a long dark bar, heavy dark wood tables, dark wooden chairs, dark wide-planked flooring, everything dark so you wouldn't notice how cruddy it really was, he guessed. The smell of spilled beer wafted in the air. Through the sound system, Three Dog Night was saying, "Mama told me not to come".

He didn't see anyone serving at the bar. He saw four customers, only four, all sitting at one table shoved into a back corner, bikers—tattoos, long unkempt hair, muscle shirts, thick arms. They were talking loudly, laughing, empty beer pitchers on their table.

A waitress in a miniskirt and a T-shirt that said STACEY'S across her chest was serving them more beer. He saw one of the bikers put his hands on either side of her waist as she placed a round of drafts on the table.

"Why don't you sit in my lap?" the biker said.

He saw that another waitress who was clearing up glasses from another table was watching the biker.

A bartender, thinner and old, appeared from somewhere behind the bar. Andrew tugged at his cap again and went to the bar. "Could I possibly get just a glass of water? It's awfully hot out there."

The bartender didn't look at him, his eyes only on the bikers. "Water's in the restroom," he said, his finger pointing to a far corner.

Relieved that he wasn't turned away, he made a beeline to the corner and followed a long narrow hallway to a door that said 'GENTLEMEN' and went in. He wondered how many actual gentlemen ever came there.

*

The biker wouldn't let the waitress go. He forced her into his lap. "I want you to sit on it." The others were laughing, good fun here.

"Stop it," she yelped, trying to balance her tray. Another biker slid his hand up her exposed thigh.

"Stop that. Don't," she squirmed. The bikers leered at her twisting body.

The other waitress who had been clearing the empty table was now at the bar and smacked down her tray of empties, shoving them across the counter at the bartender, anger on her flushed face. But she kept her voice low. "What the fuck are you going to do about it? They're not going to stop and you know it."

"I don't want trouble…"

"They told me they want one of us to go for a ride. They're getting rough about it. They're animals."

"They'll drink up and be on their way…"

"You are so fucking stupid. I'm not letting Kim get hurt." She glared at the bartender but kept her voice low. "I'm making the call." She disappeared into a back room.

In the corner, the bikers chorused to the struggling Kim. "Show us what you've got." One was reaching, tugging at her top.

*

There were two wash basins. The handle of one spun aimlessly without producing water. The water from the other ran in a tiny stream. But it was clear and cold and wet, and Andrew watched as it slowly fill his cupped hands. Twenty times he filled them and slurped it down, the process prolonged by the slow tap. He washed his face, too, and unbuttoned his shirt and washed his chest and under-arms to cool off. He wished he had deodorant to help make a good impression when he checked in at the supervision house. He slurped a final mouthful, wet his hair and carefully combed. He looked in the mirror and smiled—he wasn't in the reformatory anymore. Alleluia.

He stepped out of the washroom into the narrow hall. The waitress he had seen serving the bikers was running down the hall toward him weeping, her T-shirt in her hands, clutched across her chest to cover her bare breasts. She slipped by him, her makeup streaked with tears. She ran through a door at the back.

He was dumbfounded and his heart raced. There was big trouble here. He had to get out quickly or he might be implicated. Whenever there was trouble at the reformatory and you were anywhere near it, you were implicated. Damn, just being in the tavern at all now could completely screw him.

At the end of the hallway he stopped and poked his head out just enough to see into the tavern room. He saw the bartender looking white as a ghost. At their table in the far corner, three bikers stared across the room toward the front door, angry. He saw a young policeman standing in the room near the front door. Someone must have called because of the trouble, Andrew thought, maybe sexual assault charges.

He felt huge panic—him in a beer tavern, and underage. Not good.

The policeman was only mid-20s, a boyish face. Andrew sized up people quickly, a skill honed in the reformatory. He saw no toughness in the officer's face, no steadiness, no firmness of conviction, the bikers staring defiantly at him from across the room. Clearly the officer needed backup. His hand went to the mini-radio on his shoulder.

But there was a fourth biker. He came silently from behind and smashed a beer bottle over the officer's head, the bottle shattering and spraying beer. The officer's eyelids dropped, his body toppling forward, his forehead slamming with a crack as it bounced off the edge of a slab tabletop before he thudded on the floor.

Andrew was stunned. The policeman didn't have a chance.

The four bikers gathered over him, sneering, smug. The biker who seemed to be the leader looked at the bartender and his eyes iced over. "You didn't see anything, right?"

"Nothing," the bartender squeaked. "I was in the back."

"Then get the fuck there," the leader barked.

The bartender didn't hesitate.

The officer let out a low painful moan.

A biker said, "You didn't hit him hard enough, Roddy. Maybe we better make this pig's memory so fuzzy he don't remember who he seen here."

"Yeah," another said. "A few boots to the fucking head would do it."

They looked to the leader, grinning with the clever boldness of their plan. He showed no sign of disapproval.

Fury was building in Andrew, deep, deep fury, the young policeman helpless on the floor, the biker's heavy boots near his head. His insides tightened and power surged in his body and his head cleared of all other thoughts.

"Stand back," the first biker said, boastful.

CHAPTER FOUR

LIKE A STEEL spring unloading, Andrew charged. The surprise and force of his tackle carried the kicker into a wall so hard his head bounced off of it like a ball and he crumpled to the floor, his lights out.

Andrew spun and ducked a swing from the enraged leader, replying with his own lightning punch like a powerful piston driving into the leader's stomach. His eyes bulged and he dropped to his knees puking beer.

Andrew jumped away from the other two bikers to where he could move freely and where his footwork might give him some edge. He hoped his timing would be better, his hands faster. But one thing was for sure—he could never let them get him down; they would kick him in the head until he stopped moving, then kick it some more.

The two came quickly. He would work their bodies or his bare hands wouldn't last long. He kept his feet always moving according to his training, bobbing and dancing. He made two swings concealing his real hitting speed, assessed their reaction time, saw their favored hand. His eyes never left theirs, recording their every move of hand and head to see any pattern. He made them believe he was on the defensive.

The first one threw a roundhouse swing which Andrew read. He avoided it and unloaded a solid left into the floating rib area. Although he was right-handed, he had worked hard to develop serious power in his left. He heard a crunch and a gasp. A fleeting feint with his left to the same spot brought the biker's face-protecting hand down a fraction, just as Andrew knew it would. His right flew into the now unprotected nose. Then a quick left feint high and Andrew's powerful right drove into the stomach taking the air away and as he danced to the right, the biker fell clutching and sucking for air. It all took only seconds.

The fourth biker, heavy muscled, had hung back, smarter. Andrew saw resolve in his look. He would make Andrew pay. He would adjust himself, aware of Andrew's skill.

He threw two quick punches, one getting to Andrew's cheek, a glancing blow. Andrew had longer reach, penetrating back with a flurry, left, right, left, good body blows to the bread basket, one to the nose in the unguarded moment. Blood spurted.

But it seemed to mean nothing to the biker, a smile creeping on his lips.

Something wet on the floor, spilled beer, and Andrew's footing slid out. The biker landed a blow to Andrew's stomach then a solid right to his forehead and two rapid blows to the cheek and ribs delivering huge pain.

Andrew danced quickly away, fighting the shakes, registering more pain than he had ever felt boxing anyone. He was only seventeen, his opponent a muscled powerhouse ten years his senior, and a smart fighter.

Andrew realized his life was really on the line. He had to stay disciplined, focused, because if he went down…

He delivered another solid hit to the stomach but the biker didn't flinch.

Okay, everything has to go to the head now, only fakes to the body. He hoped his hands would hold up. He let a flurry at the biker, faking to the body, trying to penetrate to the head. But the biker surprised him, connecting a stomach shot that staggered him. He reeled back to get breath. He had to dig deeper into himself, into his core, believe in himself, but accept that he would take punishment.

He feinted low twice but the biker didn't buy it, protecting his head. The biker threw a fist back that caught Andrew's cheek. But this time Andrew launched a flurry, faking body blows, delivering shots aimed at the head. But only one penetrated.

But he had learned something. The biker was not committing to defending body shots, really blocking only head shots.

He saw a way. It would take only a split second. But would it work?

The liver punch is delivered with a left hook. It's devastating and can paralyze a man who isn't trained to protect against it. But it's hard to do well. And you have to be in very close so it's very risky, especially with a strong opponent. But if the biker hesitated, thinking it only another fake body shot…

Out of the corner of his eye Andrew saw that the leader was getting off his knees, rage in his eyes.

Andrew picked up his foot speed, faked to the biker's body

twice, faked to the head which the biker bought keeping his hands there, and in the split second of that buying, Andrew shifted forward, throwing the left hook with the commitment of a pile driver, the liver punch.

The hook drove unimpeded, the biker's face contorting in a grimace and he staggered, hands lowering a fraction, legs suddenly heavy. Andrew landed a locomotive right into the jaw. Square contact!

But he felt an explosion of pain in his right hand. Damn! It was broken!

The biker wobbled, his eyes unfocused, falling against the table, then fully to the floor.

The leader was now up and coming, hate-filled eyes. A switchblade snapped open in his hand, the long blade gleaming even in the half-light. "You're going down."

He lunged and slashed at Andrew but Andrew jumped behind a table and grabbed up a chair with his left hand, balancing it on his right forearm, his right hand limp. He held the chair like a lion tamer, the legs forward, thrusting it at the leader's head and chest, again and again, forcing him backwards, forcing him to keep his eyes on him to avoid a crushing leg in the face.

Andrew maneuvered him so he was almost in front of a pillar. He made a quick lunge forcing the leader to move left, lining up with the pillar. The leader sensed the pillar, but too late. Two chair legs punched him full in the chest and the chair's cross piece pinned his knife arm against the pillar. Andrew threw all his strength behind it and the leader shrieked with pain, his right arm being crushed.

The switchblade fell from his hand and Andrew kicked it away and scooped it up himself. He jumped back, his chest heaving with exhaustion. The leader clutched his mangled arm.

The officer gave a whimpering moan like a dog hit by a car, rising in tragic pitch, still unconscious. Andrew backed up to stand over him, shaking with rage, waving the switchblade at the bikers, hatred now in his own face. He screamed, "Any of you come near him and I'll slit your fucking throat!"

The tavern door flew open and three policemen ran into the room, guns drawn, immediately seeing their colleague on the floor, a desperate moaning, and Andrew brandishing a switchblade.

"Drop it! Now!" the lead officer shouted with anger, pointing his gun at Andrew, the other two officers flanking him, guns swiveling to the bikers. "Everyone on the floor! Facedown! Now!"

All were handcuffed, including Andrew.

*

Two hours later he was brought up from the holding cells still handcuffed and placed in an interview room alone. His right hand was swollen, purpled. Ugly red welts showed on his forehead and cheeks.

The door opened and a man in his fifties entered reading a file. He closed the file and looked at Andrew for several moments.

"Andrew Locke?"

"Yes, sir."

"I'm Chief Hennessy."

He took a chair beside Andrew and carefully began to take the cuffs off. "You're a little young to be in a tavern."

"Yes, but…"

Hennessy smiled at him. "You can relax." There was affection in Hennessy's voice.

Andrew was surprised.

"I've learned the whole story. The bartender said you asked only for water. A waitress was hiding, saw everything, heard what they were going to do to my officer, the bastards. One hell of a time you had."

Andrew looked at his hand.

"You put a lot on the line. Like possibly your life. Why?"

The cuffs were now off and Andrew held his swollen right hand carefully in his left to relieve pressure. "I just reacted."

"I don't know many people who would do what you did, four tough bikers."

Andrew nodded. "I got to meet each one."

Hennessey smiled at that. "I was puzzled, shocked really, when I learned about you, released today from the reformatory, on conditions. You had every reason and every opportunity to run out of there, stay in the clear. But you put it all on the line."

Andrew was quiet, gently rubbing his hand, not looking at Hennessey.

Hennessey took a slow, deep breath. "I checked you out more, learned your dad was a cop. I read what happened there. I'm very sorry, Andrew. What you did tonight, I can tell you, he would have been proud of you, very proud."

"Thank you, sir."

"I want to thank you for the decision you made. If you hadn't been there, my officer might have been killed, or maybe disabled for life. He just became a father, a baby girl a few weeks ago. Thankfully the word from the hospital is he's going to be okay."

"That's good. I'm very happy for that."

"I'm going to see something's done for you here in your new town, starting with supper at my house when you get settled."

Andrew looked surprised. "Thank you, sir."

Hennessey held his hand out to shake. Andrew looked at him and smiled, and shook with his left.

The account of what happened made him a hero in the town. Learning he was without family or support, the town took up a donation to assist him with his future college expenses, collecting several thousand dollars. The story even made it into the big Philadelphia papers.

Then came a stunning anonymous donation—$15,000, enough in itself to pay for two full years of college.

For ten years he wondered who would do that for him, and why?

CHAPTER FIVE

TEN YEARS LATER

1981

ALONE IN HIS corner office on the top floor of the FBI building in Philadelphia, Wesley Lawrence stirred a morning coffee and pondered his soon-to-arrive visitor.

As the Special Agent in Charge, the SAC, of the Philadelphia field office, Lawrence directed more than a hundred agents and two hundred support staff. He had been the SAC for two years here since his transfer from Phoenix.

He was forty-seven but looked older, lines imprinting a weary face, all of his hair gray. His once muscled build had long ago lost definition. He was well-liked by his agents and staff, well-respected as a leader and diligent investigator. They accepted that he was very private, often withdrawn, and didn't socialize. They knew he lived alone.

He was waiting for Senator Booth who had earlier this morning requested a confidential meeting. Lawrence learned that Booth's wife had died only a week ago after a fight with cancer. The request for an interview so soon after seemed odd. Was there any connection?

There was a rap at the door and Lawrence's assistant, Fiona Cummings, ushered Booth in, made introductions, then left.

Senator Booth was about seventy, white-haired, and distinguished looking. But today he looked haggard, anxiety etched on his drawn face.

"I'm very sorry to hear about your wife," Lawrence said.

Booth nodded slowly. "Thank you." His voice was quiet.

Booth took a seat in one of the leather armchairs. Lawrence resumed his seat behind his desk.

Booth's eyes turned to the window as if taken by a thought, and Lawrence noticed his hands were trembling. With reverence Booth said, "For forty years Anna was my love, my rock. Life holds little for me now."

His eyes came back to Lawrence. "She knew nothing of this. She would never have believed it." His fingers trembled more, an involuntarily tapping of the arm of the chair. "I couldn't tell anyone. I was afraid for her."

He paused and took a deep breath. "I don't say this with any exaggeration. I'm in the grip of a killer. I've never met him, don't know who he is. He keeps himself unknowable. He calls himself 'The Watcher'. He's been extorting large sums from me for years."

"He has something on you?" Lawrence said.

Booth nodded, "My crimes. Shameful crimes." Lawrence saw

the hands shiver. "Beginning many years ago, and continuing each year thereafter, I received hundreds of thousands of dollars deposited to secret offshore accounts so I would arrange for certain corporations to get lucrative government contracts. In the same way, I received generous and very illegal campaign checks in return for other favors. I was much younger when it all started, weaker."

He took a moment to compose himself. "When The Watcher first contacted me fifteen years ago, he demanded four large payments a year. If I didn't pay, my crimes would be made public. In politics you get threats. But this was different. He had detailed, accurate, provable information against me. The money he wanted was far less than the money I took in from my crimes, so I paid it, and said nothing. I stopped my illegal activities a few years ago, but, nevertheless, I had to keep making the payments."

"Those details can wait," Lawrence said. "I want to know why you say he's a killer."

"I quickly learned that The Watcher would do far more than only make my crimes public. He would cause me to disappear. 'Always make your payments, and never, never, go to the police, or you disappear.' That's what the communications always stated."

"Could these have been only idle threats?"

Booth leaned forward, his eyes firm. "No idle threats. When the victim doesn't pay, he disappears. We—the other victims and I—get a letter explaining his disappearance as a warning. And when a man disappears, he's never found."

He reached into his suit pocket and drew out four envelopes. "Here's what's key—the letter is always postmarked the day *before* the disappearance, processed through the post office the day *before*. The Watcher wants to prove to us beyond doubt that he did it, that his threats are not idle. They're highly motivating."

Lawrence brought his hands together, concentrating, nodding to Booth to continue.

"I looked into the reports on several of these missing men. Each was last seen the day *after* the date the letter was processed."

"The Watcher that supremely confident in his capabilities," Lawrence said.

"Yes. None of those men has ever been found."

He slid the envelopes across the desk to Lawrence. "Five men over the last few years, different cities—New York, Washington, and three here in Philadelphia. All vanished. All unsolved disappearances. How many others like me live under this man's threat?"

Lawrence examined the postmarks. "You're sure these arrived by the regular mail, the usual mail? Not a covert delivery with a mocked-up postmark?"

"No. I was in my front yard the day one of those was delivered by the mailman. I know him to see him. But you'll want to have the postmarks verified."

Lawrence nodded. "Of course." He opened one of the envelopes and took out three pages of typed print and began to read.

Booth said, "The sender identifies itself as Extract Enterprises, a private joke. They purport to be a mining company. You'll find the address is nonexistent. The letters always begin with the usual solicitation of investment monies for a supposed venture. A lot of boilerplate intended to disguise the real content. Anyone else looking at it wouldn't notice anything. But look at the middle of page two. That's where they speak directly to me and the other victims."

Lawrence turned to page two. He read until he found sentences that appeared to be unconnected to the rest of the letter. He read aloud. "He declined to honor his payment obligations under our arrangement. He made empty promises, tested my patience. Note the envelope's date and watch the news."

Lawrence looked up at Booth and nodded. "I see. Now…you said *five* men. You gave me four envelopes."

"Yes." Booth drew another envelope from his pocket and set it on Lawrence's desk. "This is the fifth. I got it two weeks ago, regular mail. The victim is another man here in Philadelphia. You'll find there's an ongoing search for him. But I know he's disappeared, and I'm certain he'll not be found."

"That's three men from Philadelphia? That you know of?"

"Yes."

Lawrence was silent for moments, looking at nothing, seeming distracted. "Very bold," he said almost to himself, still thinking.

"He can snatch a man and make him disappear without leaving a trace," Booth said. His gaze again drifted to the window. "It's time for me to do the right thing. Anna deserved better from me." He looked back to Lawrence. "Time to make amends, even though it means giving up… everything. My quarterly payment to The Watcher is tomorrow which is why I came today…and because Anna's gone." He looked stoically at Lawrence and took a noticeable breath. "I'm prepared to be your bait."

Lawrence considered Booth for several long moments. "How exactly are payments made?"

"Always cash, divided into three separate envelopes, mailed as instructed. The address is a P.O. Box, but the number and the place changes each time."

Lawrence tapped a finger on the table. "If everything you say checks out, then this Watcher has real reach and is, I suspect, completely anonymous. Collects damning information and extorts the victim to the limit without ever exposing himself."

"Correct. And intimidates and murders and never gets caught." Booth sat back and released breath.

"You haven't told *anyone* else about you and The Watcher?"

Booth shook his head. "No one."

"And you haven't told anyone you were coming here today?"

"No one."

Lawrence sat back in thought. He finally looked at Booth. "What we're going to do is make your payments for you, mail the cash in three envelopes as directed. We'll track the money, see where it goes, see who deposits it, see whose account it goes into."

Booth nodded, "Good."

"As for your crimes, I'll take your statement but I don't propose arresting you yet. You know that your full cooperation will go a long way to mitigating your eventual sentence. You've taken significant risks to come to me."

"You have my full cooperation," Booth said quietly.

"I'm concerned about this Watcher's reach. If he sniffs something's up, it seems likely he wouldn't stop at anything to get you. So I want you in a safe house starting tomorrow night."

CHAPTER SIX

ANDREW LOCKE LISTENED intently to the gurgle of the idling Continental engine, a sound to him better than music. Satisfied, he opened up the throttle and the open-cockpit biplane began to race across the grass runway. Gaining speed, the tail came up and the grass blurred beneath him. As he pulled back on the joystick, the wheels gently lifted off the ground.

When he had graduated as an FBI agent and was posted to the field office in Minneapolis, he had taken out a bank loan and bought the classic Waco UPF, an aerobatic biplane with two seats, one behind the other in separate, open, leather-trimmed cockpits. It had needed a lot of work but he had tended to it lovingly. To him it was not a thing of metal and wire but a creature, a living extension of himself.

It was a fine day at two thousand feet, the late-June sun warm, the sky clear except for some wisps of cirrocumulus powdering the blue, the wind whipping in the wires. It was more enjoyable still because Madeleine, in leather flying helmet and goggles, was seated in the separate open cockpit directly in front of him. She was leaning out to watch the forest slide by below. He loved when she came along, and it was the first time in a long time she had come with him.

When he was in his sophomore year at college he had stopped in the gymnasium complex to watch a beautiful woman with long thick chestnut hair playing squash. He smiled every time she laughed at missing a shot because her laugh was so inviting and lighted her warm and friendly face. He had wanted to meet her so badly, and she was kind enough to let him. (Later, when new acquaintances asked how they had met, he would always say, "Oh, in some grungy bar. She picked me up." Madeleine would always laugh at that same old joke then whack him on the shoulder.)

He saw her every day after that and every day was filled with elation, his life suddenly richer, bigger. Over the months he felt his past losing its grip, his mind ever more forward-looking, the future ever more bright, the nightmares of thirteen long years plaguing him less and less.

They had married when they were both only twenty-one, still in college. A year later, Christopher came along. Now he was five.

Madeleine worked as an educational diagnostician with the school board, testing children who showed difficulty in learning, interpreting the test results and recommending the most effective teaching strategies to the teachers. She loved working with children, especially the younger ones struggling with challenges.

This morning when they woke, Andrew had seen tears in her eyes.

"What is it?" he had said. But he already knew. Their baby,

Olivia, lost at just two months. Crib death they called it, a terrible blow. The days and weeks and many months following had been so dark, and he so helpless to help her.

"She would have been ten months today," Madeleine said, fighting tears. "Our little girl, smiling to me, laughing. Sometimes it just catches me."

He had held her close. "I know, Maddy. I know."

Her eyes brimmed with tears. "She didn't get to know how much we love her."

"I know… I know." He had cried with her, squeezed her tight.

At breakfast she was still quiet, circling the loss, the sadness.

It was a weekend. He had gently pointed out the perfect sky, the warm air, and said he would love to have her come flying. "And after that," he said, "I was thinking we could pick Chris up from the sitter's and go to that pet shop you were talking about, the one with the hamsters. He'd love that."

She had looked at him. "I thought you weren't that keen on getting one."

"Well, I was thinking, you know, it would be good. Teach him some responsibility, having to care for something. As long as you agree it would be his job, not yours."

"Yeah, I know."

"I have an idea. He could name it 'job'."

She had smiled.

"You know, as a kind of constant reminder of it being his job. He could even tell friends, I really love my 'job'."

She laughed. "Andrew, you're crazy sometimes."

He laughed too. But he saw her smile continue in her eyes as she looked out the window at the perfect morning sky. And he worshiped that smile.

They were cruising at a hundred miles an hour, the loud bawling of the biplane's engine muffled by the audio headsets built into their leather flying helmets allowing them to communicate. But still, they had to yell.

The biplane gained altitude to 3,000 feet and Andrew yelled into the microphone, "I'm expecting a little turbulence soon."

"Okay," he heard her say.

He waited a few moments, then executed a perfect snap roll, a quick, complete rotation of the plane, upside down, then right-side up. He heard her voice sarcastic over the headset, "Sure, a little turbulence."

Then he put the plane into a barrel roll, flying a horizontal corkscrew, slowly turning upside down and continuing to roll until it righted again, one complete turn.

He heard her laughing. "Okay, okay, enough with the turbulence already."

"How's that indigestion?"

There was a pause. "Hey, it's gone! Just what the doctor ordered."

They flew another twenty minutes when Andrew received a beep on his FBI pager—an emergency. He told Madeleine and banked sharply and swung back to follow the railway track that would lead them directly back to the airfield. He eased off the throttle and pushed the joystick slightly forward. They gently descended, now feeling their speed as they flew low over the faint rises and contours of the hills on approach to the runway.

When they landed, they were met by an FBI agent who had brought Andrew's equipment. "Need you in the air. Three older teenagers with high-powered rifles did a bank in Fergus Falls. Their car was spotted pulling into a barn a dozen miles north of there. They're holing up at the farm house. Don't know they've been seen."

*

'Surveillance' derives from the French, meaning 'to watch from above'.

Andrew had been flying surveillance for almost a year, one of the few investigator agents who could do that. He was also a trained sniper, often joining SWAT team operations.

Now he was flying alone in an FBI Cessna surveillance plane on his way to the coordinates of the remote farm house, about 180 miles north-west, an hour and twenty minutes flying time. The Minneapolis FBI field office served a very large area which included three States, a lot for a medium sized office. A bank robbery, being a federal offence, required the FBI's involvement.

In many situations it's impossible to conduct ground surveillance without being noticed, whereas Andrew was far less noticeable at 4,000 feet. He could get to locations quickly and make close observations through stabilized binoculars. The plane's three cameras also produced photographs not obtainable any other way.

He would stay high and do a fly-by of the farm property and surroundings from a couple of directions. The close-up pictures would assist in making plans for the take-down that would be conducted in the middle of the night tonight to catch them asleep, there being no present threat to the public if the teenagers stayed put. The FBI SWAT team in Minneapolis would be getting assembled and briefed and transported but he knew they wouldn't arrive for a couple of hours after he touched down at Fergus Falls.

As he flew he thought about Maddy, hoping she wouldn't be worried for him. She had always worried when he was out on a take-down anyway, but her feelings were especially tender these days. She knew he wasn't only doing surveillance on this one. They wanted his sniper skills, wanted him on the ground and in place in case the kids decided to make any move from the farm house before the SWAT team arrived.

When he touched down he was met by a local trooper who informed him that things had gone sideways. "The kids saw one of our cars. We had to move in, take up periphery positions. They fired on us. We're worried they'll try to run."

Andrew changed into SWAT dress. The kids had long-range high-powered rifles, so if a real fire-fight broke out, a sniper backing up the local police could make all the difference.

They drove at high speed for fifteen minutes, the cherry twirling, the landscape becoming more and more barren. The trooper dropped him five hundred yards from the lonely, ramshackle, red bricked farmhouse set amid low rolling poor grassland and a few spindly trees, two lines of old gray split rail fencing going off in different directions, grazing pasture in better times.

About three hundred yards to the south of the farmhouse was a forest. But there was no decent cover anywhere as you got close. He had observed and photographed the property from the air not thirty minutes earlier.

Two black-and-whites were parked in a field about 300 yards from the house, just off the long narrow lane leading to it. A policeman and a policewoman crouched behind one of the cars. The sheriff squatted behind the other. An unmarked cruiser had driven wide out over the grassland to cover another side, also out 300 yards from the house. Two troopers kneeled low behind that car.

By Andrew's calculations, the police here didn't have the numbers or the firepower they would really need, especially with standard-issue rifles, if the kids started firing and made a run for it. And the SWAT team, they would still be another hour getting here.

As he crawled forward in a zigzag pattern, a shot rang out.

He stopped, head down, waiting. He saw nothing, heard nothing more. He continued another fifty yards to the Sherriff's car.

The Sheriff was kneeling behind his car talking with forced calm into a radio phone. "Look, Bernie, you got carried away. You didn't mean to take things so far. We know that. And it will go a lot better for you if you just come out peaceful. You don't want to get into a firefight with us."

Bernie retorted, "We've got better firepower than you." The radio phone's receiver was on maximum volume. Andrew could hear everything clearly. The voice was young, cocky, and seemed fueled on something unnatural, Andrew thought.

"But we're trained in how to shoot," the Sheriff said.

"You can't shoot nothing but the breeze, at Dunkin' Donuts." There was a chorus of high-energy cackling from the other two kids. Then Bernie hung up.

The Sheriff gave a look of despair. He turned and saw Andrew with his sniper rifle. "Glad you got here. Them taking shots. Nervous as hell how this thing's going to end. They're just stupid kids."

"I understand."

"What do you think?" the Sheriff asked.

"You're deployed well, a good 'L' formation, no crossfire issues for us. But what about to the south if they try to make a run for those woods?"

"Yeah, I'm worried about that. Sooner or later they'll try. I've got to make them understand they're going to get themselves killed."

Andrew had never killed anyone. But if he had to, he sure didn't want it to be some scared kid. He had been one himself for many years.

He viewed the house carefully through his binoculars. He

picked up his sniper rifle, a Remington 700 with a Leupold scope. He peered through the scope long moments.

"I have an idea," he said. "You might say I had a light-bulb moment."

"What is it?"

"A light-bulb."

"So?"

"The living room window is open."

"Yeah, that's where they've been shooting out of."

"In the living room there's a bare light-bulb dangling from a cord about 5 feet down from the ceiling. The kids think they have a chance in a shoot-out or breakout. I want them to see they don't."

"How're gonna do that?"

"Tell them I'm going to shoot that tiny light-bulb. Make them realize what I can do if they poke their big heads out again, or make a run for it."

"Okay, good."

The Sheriff grabbed the radio phone and waited for the connection.

The phone was answered. "What do you want now?" Bernie said.

"Like I said, Bernie, I don't want anyone getting hurt here. I want you to look at the light-bulb there in the living room. I have an FBI trained sniper here. You can't even see him. He's almost 300 yards from you, more than a football field away. But he can hit it."

"Yeah, sure," Bernie said. "Like I'm gonna fall for that."

The Sheriff put his hand over the phone and said to Andrew, "One-shot?"

"With a lot of luck."

The sheriff removed his hand. "One-shot, Bernie, light-bulb gone. Now think about your head, big as a balloon. Or your big body if you take one step out of that house. You'll be dead before you hit the ground. You get me?"

No answer.

"Think about it, Bernie."

Still no answer.

The Sheriff looked at Andrew and shrugged his shoulder. "Well, I'm hanging up. Keep your heads down in there."

He hung up and nodded to Andrew. "The show's all yours."

In the military, a sniper aims for the torso. In the FBI, the sniper must shoot a head shot because a hostage taker might be holding a gun to a hostage, so you only get one shot and it must totally disable. So the FBI shooting benchmarks are extremely exacting. At a hundred yards, the best graduates can put five rounds into a dime. At two hundred yards, its five rounds into a business card. Andrew had been the top shooter of his group.

But he was worried. The light-bulb was only a dot at this distance, even in high-powered optics. He assessed the weather conditions: about 75°, faint breeze southerly, humidity not an issue. Overall, they were good shooting conditions. He had already begun relaxation exercises. Breathe in, hold it for seven seconds, exhale for seven seconds. Repeat and repeat.

He moved out from behind the sheriff's car, working his way forward almost fifty yards until he found the ground he wanted. He positioned the rifle in front, resting it on the bipod. He lay out his full length.

FBI gunsmiths fit the rifle to the individual. This rifle had been made for Andrew and was accurate in the extreme. He eased the stock into his shoulder and tugged it snug. It wasn't true of all rifles, but with his rifle, the first shot, known as the cold shot, was absolutely dead on. Then as each successive round was fired and the barrel got hotter, he knew the bullets would hit lower and lower. But he desperately wanted the cold shot to do its work.

He continued the breathing exercise as he adjusted his legs to better stabilize himself, digging his right foot back against the earth. He looked through the scope and acquired the target. The light-bulb was bobbing up and down which meant he wasn't relaxed enough. He also felt tension in his left shoulder. He had to be still, perfectly. He did the breathing sequence twice more, slowly releasing his breath until his lungs were empty. He knew his heart had calmed to a gentle fifty beats a minute.

He eased the trigger until there was no more play. One more breath in, hold, exhale slowly.

The bulb was as still as a picture. He pulled the trigger.

The recoil punched his shoulder and the explosion carried across the open landscape.

"Did you get it?" Andrew heard the Sheriff calling.

He couldn't find the bulb in the scope. Dangling from a cord, it would be moving if it were hit. After a moment, the cord stopped its swaying. He traced down the cord with the scope. The metal socket slipped into view, completely mangled, and not a shard of bulb left. He had hit the socket, not the bulb.

"Close enough," Andrew said.

"Hot damn," said the sheriff, his voice cracking with tension.

Two minutes passed and the front door of the farm house opened slowly. A white shirt wrapped on top of a broomstick appeared first, then three teenagers came out in single file, hands up, looking toward the police cars, waiting for somebody to tell to tell them what to do next.

*

By the time he flew himself back to Minneapolis, got to the field office, debriefed, and got home, it was after midnight. He had made a quick call to Madeleine from the airport hours before just to say he'd be late, not to wait up.

But when he opened the front door she was there in the living room in her housecoat.

"Hi there," he said. "You didn't need to wait up."

"So it went okay?" she said.

"Fine. The kids surrendered. We were able to call off the SWAT team."

"Was there shooting?"

"They tried to scare us a bit, that's all. The local guys were up to it. The kids saw they'd be overpowered."

She was quiet, looking at him, worry lingering.

"I was never in any real danger, Maddy. I get to stay way back now remember."

"I know. But you were hit once."

He had been shot at close range with a handgun but the Kevlar vest had stopped the bullet.

His eye caught something on the floor in the hall, like an opened bag of ...wood shavings?

"Hey, did you get the hamster?" he said, surprised.

"Yeah we did. Chris was very excited. It's in his bedroom."

"Was he okay with the name 'job'?"

She smiled. "No. That didn't fly, that's for sure. I told him we'd just brainstorm for a name tomorrow when you're home."

"Okay."

"But he said no. I think he was worried what you'd say. He decided he wanted to call it 'Brainstorm'."

"Brainstorm? What kind of name's that for a hamster?"

"He thinks it's better than 'job', and I said okay. So it's non-negotiable."

He laughed. "Okay, okay. At least he didn't want to call it 'Non-Negotiable'.

She chuckled. "Yeah, lucky."

"I'm feeling kind of gritty. I've got to have a quick shower."

The shower was downstairs in the renovated basement. When he finished up, toweled off, came upstairs and walked the hall and turned the corner to go up the stairs to the bedroom, he stopped.

She was standing against the French doors to the living room, a black silk nightgown clinging, her long full chestnut hair combed out and flowing over the front of her shoulders. Her lips and eyes were lightly made up, and her eyes were on him. She didn't say a word.

He walked to her, not taking his eyes from hers. He kissed her then lifted her and carried her upstairs.

CHAPTER SEVEN

IT WAS EARLY in the morning of the fifth day after Senator Booth had met with Lawrence that dozens of letters were posted in four different cities, all the letters exactly the same, all carrying the same regrettable communication that Senator Booth had fundamentally and irretrievably breached his arrangement with The Watcher in going to the authorities. In doing so he had brought the dire and imminent consequences, fairly warned of, entirely upon himself.

It was now late evening of that day, very dark, a light rain falling, when a black '79 Lincoln drove through an old residential neighborhood in Cedar Park in West Philadelphia, passing a stately and large two-story yellow brick house set well back on a generous treed lot. More lights than were tasteful illuminated parts of the spacious grounds.

It was the second time the Lincoln had passed the house this evening, to give more opportunity to orient the five men in the car. The man in the front passenger seat, known only to the others as 'Leader', had briefed them that afternoon in a hotel room. "He never comes out of the safe house. His phone calls are forwarded there to give the appearance he's at his own home. The calls are answered by a policewoman, the calls recorded and traced. Two FBI agents are inside around-the-clock, well armed."

In the two drive-bys tonight, Leader had observed that all the windows were curtained, as expected. But key to his observations were two smaller windows on the west side wall on the second-storey. Curtained, of course, but also with lights out, it appeared. That was good.

The Lincoln drove on, went around the whole block, back to where there was a good view of the safe house a block away. The car pulled to the curb. Leader glanced down a side street and saw the payphone booth a hundred and fifty feet away, just where he had been told it would be. He looked at his watch. 10:05.

The lazy sweeping of the windshield wipers was the only sound in the car as Leader peered down the street to the safe house. The street was empty, no walkers to consider, rain having that beneficial effect. He could see that the safe house would not be visible from the payphone itself so he would wait in the car until he got their signal.

He turned and spoke quietly to the three men in the back. "Okay, let's go."

Kell, Franks, and Smithy, wearing black trench coats and thin black leather gloves, left the car one at a time, thirty seconds apart. Smithy hustled on ahead around the block to approach the house from the far end. Kell and Franks walked on opposite sides of the street.

Two minutes later, Leader saw Smithy's flashlight go on and

off twice signaling that the perimeter of the property was clear and they were in place. Leader got out of the car and walked to the payphone.

On the west side of the safe house, Kell crouched at the shadowed brick wall, a two-way radio in his hand. He was well away from the ground floor windows, their curtains shut. On the second storey of that wall were two smaller windows, one up and to his left, one up and to his right, curtained and dark.

Leader had told them that Booth took his calls on the second storey in a den facing this street. The window of a den would be smaller than bedroom windows which were farther along. Kell knew that one of the two closest windows was the likely den candidate.

At the payphone, Leader switched on his two-way radio and said, "Clear?"

Kell whispered, "Clear."

Franks and Smithy stayed at the property's periphery, fifty yards from each other, watchful of any movement anywhere.

Leader punched in the phone numbers with his thin-gloved fingers. He held the radio close to the telephone speaker so Kell could hear the conversation.

*

Inside the safe house, the phone rang downstairs and upstairs. The two FBI agents were in the living room reading a newspaper and eating Chinese food. They continued, taking no obvious notice. A uniformed police woman passed through the living room and quickly climbed the stairs. She entered the den and snapped on a light. A ringing phone sat on the desk with recording equipment hooked up underneath. She hit a button on a recorder and picked up the phone.

*

Kell had been watching the two second-floor windows directly above him. He saw a sliver of light suddenly appear at the edge of the curtain on the window on the right, just as if a light had turned on. Bingo. The Watcher's information was, as always, bang on.

He heard a woman's voice faintly over his radio. "Hello?"

He heard Leader's voice, "Is Senator Booth in? I'm a friend from college days, Gerry Fowler. I just heard the news about his wife's passing and was hoping to pass on my condolences."

Kell heard the policewoman, "I'll get him for you."

He motioned to Franks and Smithy. They sprinted over into the shadows to join Kell who moved to his right to put himself directly under that second-floor window. From under their trench coats, Franks and Smithy each drew a short Uzi submachine gun that was snap-strapped inside.

Shortly a new voice was on the radio. It was Booth. "Hello, Gerry?"

Leader's voice was muffled. "Harold, yes, it's Gerry. I'm so sorry…"

Franks and Smithy hoisted Kell and he stood balanced on their shoulders braced by their arms. He was now six feet directly below the window. His left hand leaned in against the wall for balance. With his right he pitched a brick-sized explosive device set on a three-second delay. The window smashed and Kell hit the ground. The three scrambled from the wall.

A horrific explosion blasted outward hurling huge chunks of brick and mortar onto the lawn leaving a gaping hole where the den wall had been.

In the living room the two agents grabbed for their rifles. One hit a switch and a dozen outdoor floodlights washed the property grounds in glaring white light.

Franks, Smithy, and Kell were almost across the lawn as the Lincoln approached. Franks and Smithy dropped behind different stout elms twenty yards apart to cover Kell and the Lincoln.

They saw the outside door push half open, an agent kneeling in the doorway quickly scanning the property. As planned, Franks already had his Uzi trained on the doorway and squeezed the trigger for two full seconds riddling the agent who slumped forward.

Smithy was covering the second floor and saw a window smash and the policewoman jabbed her rifle through to aim at Franks' position. Smithy's position was a complete surprise to her and the firepower of half his magazine danced her like a rag doll.

The Lincoln slowed to a roll picking up Kell and sped on another half block to be out of firing angle from the house. Shots from the remaining agent began from a ground-floor window. Franks and Smithy fired simultaneous bursts from their divergent angles hitting the agent and sending him spinning back into the room.

Franks and Smithy sprinted the half block to the Lincoln, jumped in, and it sped away.

*

Lawrence was at home when he got the call from his assistant.

"Senator Booth's been killed," she blurted. "A bomb through the window in the telephone room. Both of our agents and the policewoman were killed in gunfire immediately following the blast."

Lawrence felt like he had taken a fist to the stomach, his body shaking, his mind racing. The news supported his worst fear, a conjecture that he had been secretly harboring from the day Booth had come to see him, a conjecture absolutely to be kept from everyone. But all he said to her was, "They made a phone call…got him to come into the telephone room."

"Yes. We're having AT&T check it and source where the call came from."

He knew that wouldn't get them anywhere. The call would be from a phone booth. The Watcher would be far too clever to leave any useful trace.

"The Watcher had to know Booth came to us," she said, "learned of the safe house, knew the set up, everything."

Lawrence's voice was unsteady. "Of course he did. He has insiders, informants. Probably has had for a long time. We have leaks; our information isn't secure."

"A damn situation, sir. What are our next steps?"

Lawrence felt nausea gripping him. He wanted to get off the phone quickly. "I don't know right now. Let the team do its work tonight. I'll want a full report in the morning."

When he hung up he ripped at his collar button, snapping it off, gulping at air. But it wasn't just that Booth and two FBI agents and a policewoman had been killed. It reached much further for him. Like an avalanche cascading down a mountainside, his long ago past thundered toward him. A girl's face screamed at him, 'Why did you have to do it?'

Guilt freshly clawed at his insides and he went to the bathroom and threw up. When he finally lifted his head and looked at himself in the mirror, the tormenting thought again fixed in his mind— 'if people only knew…'

CHAPTER EIGHT

LORNE NIX WAS fifty-four but still carried his tall and solid frame like a twenty-year-old.

He stood at the immense window in the living room of his 30th floor penthouse suite contemplating the Delaware River below, an inky band winding its way through Philadelphia as the twinkling lights of the skyline brightened against the darkening sky.

Nix was an attorney who specialized in corporate law with a decidedly international flavor. He had an office in downtown Philadelphia, but no secretary. He had only one client, a client who owned a dozen corporations registered in several tax havens—Panama, Barbados, the Caymans, Switzerland. The real ownership of those corporations was untraceable, identity shielded in secrecy through trusts. The real business of the corporations was unknowable.

For the moment he considered the laundering of the $125,000

in cash that had been collected that week. All cash was always laundered because the bills, even some, might be marked as part of a police investigation. Better in that case that the bills turn up somewhere where nobody was looking. This time, he decided, that somewhere would be Panama.

He poured himself a double of Islay single malt scotch and walked into his teak-appointed study. He hit the rewind button on the voice-activated, reel-to-reel tape recorder on the credenza. The reels spun just two seconds which told him there was only one message from the radio house.

Messages came in to him on four short-wave radios that faced the recorder, each radio set to a different frequency. The network of secret insiders spanned the police departments of several cities along with the FBI offices in Philadelphia and New York, as well as departments in the IRS that contained boatloads of uniquely leverageable information. The network also reached into private industry and finance where early insider-trader information could quickly become sleek gold bars in the basement.

The money offered to the insiders was so good, the anonymity so secure, that recruiting them was never difficult. Sometimes it wasn't even for the money. Sometimes it was to keep a dark secret quiet, unexposed. His client was excellent at excavating dark secrets.

An insider would first encode a message then radio it to the radio house so he never had to pass any paper or ever meet anyone. It meant the insider didn't know anyone else in the entire organization.

At the radio house the encoded message was transcribed into plain English then radioed to Nix in two-word snippets using the four different radio frequencies in revolving sequence. Anyone eavesdropping on one of the frequencies would be unable to glean anything meaningful from only two words out of every eight in a message.

Nix hit the play button and settled into a deep leather sofa and listened to the recorded voice of one of the radio house people.

> **'BEGIN MESSAGE…A343…BOYD KENNEDY… DYLAN KIPLING…THE NEW…YORK TIMES… SEEKING VINTAGE…STOPWATCH PARTS…SEEKS ALERT…PHILLY PD…PHILLY FBI…END MESSAGE.'**

The tape recorder reels stopped turning.

Here was a potential new customer. Nix always brightened at the prospect.

The message came from A343 who was a cell member whose specialized job it was to peruse the want ads in The New York Times every day watching for any ads seeking vintage stopwatch parts. Some of those who placed such an ad were purely legitimate enquiries. But for others, it was, in fact, the covert method of seeking a service from his client. Nix would receive such a message only after the person who placed the ad had been vetted to be certain there was nothing afoul, no rat lurking, no police set up, no entrapment.

A three-page background report on Boyd Kennedy and Dylan Kipling would be waiting for Nix at a secret drop. Then Nix would meet his client.

*

Salvatore Velez was the same age as Nix, fifty-four, but with his smooth olive complexion he looked younger.

His tall blond Finnish-model girlfriend leaned over the purple felt of the billiard table, her silky tanned arms carefully positioning the cue. "Is this going to work?" she asked with a noticeable accent, her clear blue eyes surveying the billiard balls before flashing up to him for an answer.

She was his latest acquisition and new to pool. "See for yourself. You'll learn faster. Pool is like life," he mused aloud, "a game of angles, best learned by playing."

Facile games' room philosophy, he thought, but he wasn't exactly in conversation with Aristotle. "You've got the curves," he said. "Now acquire the angles."

"Oh, Alfred, you're so mean," she laughed and leaned forward, concentrating on her shot, her long blonde hair splaying across the rich purple felt.

She had called him 'Alfred', not Salvatore or Sal. On his driver's license, on his citizenship papers, on all official records, to all the world including her, he was Alfred Armano, an immigrant to the U.S. from Argentina twenty-three years ago. Nix was the only person alive who knew who he really was—Salvatore Velez, born and raised in Buffalo, New York, a man who had never set foot in Argentina.

The grounds of his sprawling Georgian house in Philadelphia abutted the Delaware River for a sweeping two thousand feet, the twelve acres of treed property ensuring ample privacy. From the games room he looked out past the hundred yards of softly night-lighted lawns to the river where his 75-foot Benedetti yacht, *Miss Nomer*, was docked, its glittering lights defining its shapely lines. A glow emanated from the master cabin where one of the house staff was preparing the cabin for later. His girlfriend always wanted their nights there, the motion of the water in bed.

The telephone in the games' room was ringing. Velez picked it up and listened for a few moments then said, "Certainly. Come right over." He hung up.

She was watching him. "Is something wrong, Alfred? Is someone coming over?"

He had been away until this afternoon and tonight was to be theirs. He looked at her. Even when her face was wrinkled in disappointment it was sublime.

"Nothing's wrong. A little business, that's all. It may take a while. You'll have to entertain yourself on the yacht."

"But I thought we—" She stopped herself. She had learned never to question him when it came to matters of business. She didn't know what he did exactly, but whatever it was it was supremely successful, and his first priority.

She walked to him, taller than he, lightly stroking her cue, her generous lips making a pout. "But I shall be lonely, Alfred."

"You'll live. And I'll make it up to you."

Her eyes brightened, her disappointment dissipating like soap bubbles in a wind. "Oh", she said playfully, "a diamond perhaps?"

He smiled at her. She was unflinchingly greedy. But, of course, that was why she was here. And who was he to disparage unmitigated greed?

*

A bright fire crackled in the field-stone fireplace in Velez's living-room, fire-light bouncing off the dimmed baccarat chandeliers.

"There are seven, and they're among the most prized paintings in the world," Velez was saying to Nix, "and one day I will have one, maybe two. Why not?"

Velez was in an animated mood, stirred by telling Nix that he had been to the Museum of Art downtown on his return home that afternoon. It wasn't that Velez was an art lover, at least not in the conventional sense. He only respected the great piles of cash that some art could bring, in this case one of van Gogh's 'Sunflower' canvases. Velez sometimes visited Philadelphia's Museum of Art as one would make a pilgrimage to a religious shrine.

"I stood in front of the 'Sunflower' for fifteen minutes wanting it to speak to me. It's astonishing really. At the last auction of one of those seven paintings, the final bids rose at the rate of $50,000 *a second.*"

"Sure spoke to somebody," Nix said. "Finishing at what price?"

"Six million. A painting of simple fucking sunflowers on a piece of ordinary canvas, thirty-nine by thirty."

"And he painted seven of them? The same one thing over and over?" Nix said. "Sounds like something Henry Ford would have done if he could paint."

"Not just seven—twelve! But the first five he did in an earlier period and they're less valuable. The other seven he did a year before he committed suicide. Shot himself, at thirty-seven."

"Cranking out a succession of sunflowers then shoots himself. Sounds crazy."

"Could be he was. He spent a lot of his last two years in an insane asylum."

"Yet still producing works of supposed genius? I think the buyers are as crazy as he was."

"Maybe he was a genius. I don't know. His friend was Gauguin. Maybe he knew. Or maybe people are just buying into the tormented soul of a genius thing."

"I don't get art."

"You don't need to. I don't either, in case you didn't notice. You just need to get your hands on some, one or two pieces like a van Gogh and watch the price skyrocket. You know, the irony of ironies, the paintings were worthless in his lifetime. I think he sold like… one. Needed his brother just to cover his day-to-day bills. But today any one of those seven sunflower paintings would command $10 million."

"Turning out priceless paintings but getting no money, no love. I'd shoot myself, too, especially if I knew I was a genius."

"You are a genius, just not in the world of painted sunflowers. One day I'll show you my very own van Gogh. Maybe it'll stir something in both of us."

"Unlikely. But it'll make money."

Velez laughed. "Which is the point. So anyway, tell me about this new customer."

Nix lifted a brown envelope from where he had placed it on a side table when he first got there. "His name's Boyd Kennedy, an enterprising drug king. And there's Dylan Kipling, his gunman. Kennedy was manufacturing meth on a large scale in Texas for street sale all over the country. But he got caught. He already had a rap sheet that reads like the criminal code so he knew he was going away forever. Halfway through the trial, that's a month ago, the Judge in the trial happens to get assassinated."

"I guess Kennedy didn't like how the trial was progressing."

"Seems so. So the trial brakes to a stop. The jury's dismissed. And while a new trial is awaiting rescheduling, Kennedy escapes from the local lockup under a pile of dirty laundry they figure."

"With inside help."

Nix nodded. "He's got the money to buy it."

He took a sheet of paper from the envelope and read a moment. "Here's what the Dallas Times Herald said three weeks ago: 'Dylan Kipling is being hunted all over the southern U.S. When you kill a federal circuit Judge in cold blood and then try to burn his wife alive, the law pulls out all the stops.'

Velez said, "Really? Burn the wife alive? Kipling sounds like a real bastard."

"Kipling goes into the judge's house late one night, sees the judge's wife in the kitchen and shoots her. Goes upstairs and shoots the judge. Although she's wounded, the wife manages to hide herself in a locked pantry. Kipling can't break into the pantry, but he had brought five gallons of gasoline along to burn the house down anyway, destroy the evidence. So he sets the fire, sees it's blazing well enough, and scrams. But the wife crawls through the fire, barely survives. Kipling was known to be Kennedy's gunman so the law suspected he might have been the one and they show her pictures of him. She gives a positive ID."

"So let me guess. Kipling and Kennedy aren't in the southern States anymore."

"Right. They're around here somewhere. The request we got is from Kennedy but he names Kipling, too. So Kipling's with him. Kennedy doesn't want to be alone without his gunman. We presume the law doesn't know of any of this at this moment, of course. Kennedy knows the heat is on high on both of them everywhere now, not just in the south. Better he stay put, keep his head low, a small needle in a very big haystack. Kennedy's asking us for an alert, an early notice, if Philly PD or the Philly FBI picks up his scent and gets onto his whereabouts."

"Easy enough."

Nix nodded, "So what's the price?"

Velez considered a few moments. "I presume both Kennedy and Kipling are now on the country's most-wanted list."

"They are. Steepens the price, I know."

"Kennedy was already looking at life. Now he's looking at chemical injection, and his gunman, too. How do you price life?"

Nix smiled. "Our service is like art, sometimes impossible to price."

"But I'll try. I think their lives, taken together, are worth about a small Cezanne. There's one I'd like to acquire that I'm told can be had for half a million. So that's the price, half a million, for our priceless information, but only for three months. If he wants our help after that, we talk again."

"I'll make that offer, then follow up with our inside people."

"They'll be the same people who helped us with Booth. That wasn't an easy one, and was so recent their nerves may still be tingling. I don't want any of them getting cold feet. So keep them happy. Put out extra money."

"This one should go easy anyway," Nix said.

"Sure. No fishing around, just ears-to-the-ground easy," Velez said as he walked to a corner cabinet. "Scotch?"

"Sure." Nix went to the window and looked toward the river, admiring the lines of *Miss Nomer*. A white light turned off in the master cabin. In its place, a soft purple light came on.

"How's what's her name, Miss Helsinki, or whatever she was?" Nix said.

"Not quite that stature, a lesser city, but nevertheless still tall, blonde…and greedy."

Velez came to Nix and handed him a scotch. "You need to get a girl again, one whose deepest virtues are selfishness and greed. Keeps them focused."

Nix raised his glass. "To just such a girl. And, of course, to Kennedy and Kipling."

Velez raised his. "To Kennedy and Kipling, and one day soon… to my van Gogh."

CHAPTER NINE

LAWRENCE KNEW THAT the leaked information that led to Booth's killing at the safe house had to have come from within either the Philadelphia PD or the Philadelphia FBI field office, or a spouse or close acquaintance of someone there who enticed the information. An internal investigation had been started in both the Philly PD and FBI offices, concentrating first on those who would have been in possession of the information regarding the location of the safe house and its workings.

But Lawrence had no illusion that the investigation would be easy. The problems were many. Not only was there the inner ring of people who had knowledge of the safe house, people such as all the officers who had *ever* worked that detail, but there were the outer rings, the supervisors, the clerical support staff who had some access to that information on a day to day basis, and even the administrative staff responsible for managing all aspects of the safe house property itself. The tentacles were myriad. And that did not include those who just might hear something at a water cooler.

More, it was unlikely that it was a case of a *single* insider informant in either the Philadelphia PD or the FBI field office. There would likely be several, but unaware of each other. But their information, their individual small pieces, like the pieces of a puzzle, would be fed to the Watcher to be collated by him to form the whole accurate picture. So finding even one informer, itself a feat, could possibly mean little. Secrets could continue to pass.

But ever since Booth disclosed the existence of the anonymous phantom Watcher and described his method of operation, Lawrence had been tormented by a bigger problem that required a bigger plan. He had been struggling to bring himself to accept that its time had come. He just had to be sure of that, and sure of himself, sure of his own readiness to face it, because ultimately it could bring about his own end.

He had been mulling it, undecided, his mind clouded with anxiety, when an investigative request came to him from the Dallas FBI office, classified and top-priority.

Title:

DYLAN KIPLING;

JUDGE THOMAS BARNES (Deceased) - VICTIM;

ELEANOR BARNES - VICTIM

UNLAWFUL FLIGHT TO AVOID PROSECUTION;

MURDER; ATTEMPT MURDER; ARSON

Synopsis:

Request to locate and arrest subject DYLAN KIPLING

Subject KIPLING is wanted for the murder of the deceased, the attempted murder of the second victim, and arson, all occurring on May 15th, 1981 in Dallas, TX. According to a confidential source, KIPLING may have fled to the Philadelphia area.

Conduct logical fugitive investigation to locate and arrest subject,

DYLAN KIPLING, ARMED AND VERY DANGEROUS

A month earlier, Lawrence's office and all other FBI offices across the country had received a brief on what had happened to the Judge and his wife in Dallas. They well knew the name of Kipling and Kennedy, both men now in the top ten of America's most wanted.

Lawrence wanted more information now so he called the Dallas field office and spoke with an agent named Morton.

"A $10,000 reward was offered to anyone who supplied information leading directly to the arrest of Kipling," Morton said. "A one-time cellmate of Kipling spoke up. The guy's name is Sharp. He was recently arrested for armed robbery, looking at twenty years. I've got his statement here. He said he had heard about Kipling and the judge in Dallas. He wasn't interested in the reward. Instead he wanted some leniency and felt he had a bargaining chip."

"Like what?" Lawrence said.

"One day when they were in the cell together a few years ago, Sharp says that Kipling, and I quote, 'in a moment of sentimental forthrightness said he had a place just north of Philadelphia that nobody knew about. Kipling said he had been real smart, careful never to take anybody there and it wasn't even registered in his name. It was by some water, like maybe a pond or something, because Kipling complained about the damned ducks quacking and driving him crazy.'"

"Maybe just jail house talk," Lawrence said.

"The agent put that to Sharp and he said, and again I quote, 'Oh no, it's true alright, because Kip later said it wasn't, that it was just bullshit, that he just had the jailhouse blues. But I knew different. Kip wasn't one who daydreamed about nothing.'"

"So maybe Kipling dropped his guard in a weak moment," Lawrence said.

"Exactly."

"Is there any other evidence to say he might be in this area?"

"None, that's all we've got."

"And Kennedy, anything on him?"

"No sightings, no clues. But he may be with Kipling. It's likely."

"I understand. Okay, thank you."

Lawrence considered what to do. Wanted posters for both Kennedy and Kipling had already been posted in Philadelphia and everywhere else in the U.S. for weeks, but no other concrete steps had been taken. There had been nothing more to go on until now.

If Kipling were indeed in the area, and maybe Kennedy, too, what new steps did this new information suggest? Kennedy and Kipling would surely not move from wherever they were if they believed their current location was safe. Movement attracted notice, more risk, especially if it was to set up home somewhere else. Staying put would be the smartest thing.

Was Kipling at a place 'just north of Philadelphia… by some water, maybe a pond or something, because Kipling complained about the damned ducks quacking, driving him crazy'?

'Just north of Philadelphia.' What did 'just' mean—ten miles, fifty miles?—especially when you're sitting in a southern jail a thousand miles away. And how much water did ducks need to call a place home, even for a night?

He decided he would keep the investigative request and what he had just learned on the telephone confidential for now, not make any move that might tip off anybody even in his own department, until he knew how best to utilize this new information.

*

Two days later, two events occurred.

A woman arrived at the reception saying she wanted to 'make a report based on a wanted poster. It said contact the nearest FBI office.'

Reception said she was extremely nervous and wouldn't say much. She wanted confidentiality. In light of the obvious information leak on the Booth matter, Lawrence had set several temporary protocols in place, one being that he alone would interview any member of the public purporting to have made a sighting of someone wanted by the FBI, a relatively rare occurrence anyway.

She was middle aged, a proper sort, and gave the appearance of being credible.

"If he's ever caught because I spotted him, well, it could be lights out for me," she said. "He's an America's most wanted, that's what I'm worried about. So I don't want it out there that it was me."

"I understand," Lawrence said. "You have complete confidentiality with me. Your name and address are safe with me, me alone."

She told him that while she was filling her car with gas at a gas station north of the city, a man, 'tough looking', was two pumps over filling his car. "What caught my attention was how often he would glance to the highway, both ways, like always checking for something, seemed really odd." She was nervous and needed to catch her breath.

"Yes, go on."

"When I was in the store paying for the gas, he was in there, too, and I got a good look at him from behind the candy rack. He kept sniffing, like a nose problem, like maybe a cocaine user or something. The next day when I was in line at the post office to mail a parcel, I saw the row of pictures on the wall, America's most wanted. I gasped—he was one of them. I almost shouted, but stopped myself. Like I said, I don't want anyone to know I know."

"And who did you see?"

"Dylan Kipling."

Lawrence felt a shiver. He leaned forward. "Are you sure?"

"I'm sure. I'm good with faces."

"Where was the gas station?"

"Kind of west, I think it's west, of Doylestown."

"Can you describe the car he was driving?"

"A light-green, newer car. But not European or Japanese. American, I'm pretty sure. Not as good with cars. I'm a lot better with faces."

"Did you get a look at the license plate?"

"No. I wasn't looking."

The second occurrence was a teenager, Randy Taylor, who hoped to be a policeman one day and liked to memorize wanted-posters. Randy brought along his girlfriend.

"Thank you for coming in," Lawrence said, offering them seats. "So tell me what you saw."

"We were driving between Doylestown and New Hope following behind a light-green, 1977 Monte Carlo, two-door hardtop that I took an interest in."

It immediately intrigued Lawrence because he had not yet put out a description of the car to anyone and here was the 'light-green' description again, and a reference to Doylestown. That location would put them about twenty-five miles north of Philadelphia, Lawrence knew. And Randy also seemed to know his cars.

"So why take an interest in that particular car?"

Randy hesitated, shyly glancing to his girlfriend.

She spoke up. "As we were driving behind it, he said that it was the most beautiful he had ever seen. And I said to him, 'That's odd, why?' And he said, "Because it's exactly the color of your eyes."

Lawrence noted her eyes were a beautiful light-green. Randy's face was now a ripe-crimson. "Okay, then what?"

The girlfriend said, "I said, 'why don't you pull over. I want to give you a very nice kiss.' He did. And I did."

Randy should be a policeman, Lawrence thought. And the girlfriend could write romances. "Okay, so what happened to the Monte Carlo?"

"It got way ahead of us," she answered.

A very nice kiss, Lawrence concluded.

"But then we caught up to it again. I saw it pulled up at a country convenience store, nearer New Hope, and pointed it out to Randy."

Randy said, "We were only doing about fifteen miles an hour as we passed it. I looked at the guy as he walked from the store to the driver's door. At that moment, I knew I had seen his face somewhere but couldn't remember where. It was only later that I put two and two together. Dylan Kipling."

Lawrence said, 'Was there anyone else in that car?"

They both agreed they hadn't seen anyone else.

"It's vital neither of you says anything to anybody about what you saw for now. Can you do that? It could mean saving lives."

They nodded seriously.

When they had gone, Lawrence considered that Kipling had

likely been in hiding here the whole time since his murder of the judge more than a month ago. He would believe his hideout was secure so would stay hunkered. And Kennedy…what safer place could he find?

He sat and stilled himself. He realized he had been presented with something that could fit the much bigger plan he had been developing ever since Senator Booth told him of The Watcher—the interlocking pieces, the tell-tale pieces.

His mind traveled back. Who would believe it, that the pieces connected to him, the respected Wesley Lawrence? But the pieces did connect to him, intersected with him, sliced right through his life.

Like a razor-sharp knife.

CHAPTER TEN

A WEEK AFTER Lawrence had interviewed the witnesses who believed they had seen Kipling, Andrew walked into his home in Minneapolis at the end of a day's work, an envelope in his hand. "Maddy," he called, excited.

She came downstairs. "What is it?"

"Fabulous news! When I got back today, my SAC told me I'm being reassigned. He handed me a sealed letter. We're going home!"

Her eyes were wide. "Philadelphia? Really?"

"Yes."

"But why? How did that happen? You didn't even apply."

"No, didn't think there was much chance. But it's happened," he was waving the envelope, "out of the blue. It's a special assignment, at least at first. Maximal classified."

"What's that mean?"

"It means my SAC here can't tell anyone where I'm being transferred for now. And you can't either. Seems I'm going underground."

"Underground?"

"Surveillance, without anyone knowing about me, not even other agents in Philadelphia. There's an internal problem."

"Oh."

They sat themselves on the sofa. "But here's the amazing thing," he said, "for the next while I'm to have contact with only one person in the Bureau, the SAC in Philadelphia, Wes Lawrence."

"Isn't he —?"

"Yes, the guy I told you about. He knew my father. After my Dad was gone, he always came to Grandpa's just before Christmas and brought me presents, always model airplanes. He would stay for hours and we would make them, fly them. But I haven't seen him or heard from him since I was twelve."

"What a wild coincidence."

"I checked and found out he was made the SAC in Philly two years ago. I get my assignments from him, report only to him. No contact with other agents."

"So no office, I guess."

"No."

"Must be a very serious problem in the Bureau there. But why you, Andrew?"

"I've been wondering that myself. Over the last year I put it out to the powers that be that I'm really hoping to get into complex investigation work. This assignment sounds like it could be just that, a close mentoring with Lawrence."

But even though he said it, he still really questioned why he had been selected, and without any discussion. His long-ago connection to Lawrence figured in the plan somehow; the coincidence was just too high. Was he getting favored, Lawrence pulling some strings to let Andrew return to his hometown, something he and Madeleine always hoped for?

"So weird he never communicated with you in all that time," she said. "He knew you were in the FBI, had to know, obviously."

"I know. Weird, I agree."

Excited though, she said, "But anyway, going home! Nadine is going to be thrilled! And I know I can get a position with the school board there for September. They're desperate for experienced diagnosticians."

*

Another confidential letter arrived a day later.

Andrew was to report to Lawrence, but to maintain secrecy they would not meet at his office, or at any office, but at Lawrence's very remote lake house. Andrew was to get himself there by plane, and not a Bureau plane, but in his own plane, landing at a grass airstrip on some farmer's field a mile from the lake house.

The arrangements seemed exceedingly odd, taking secrecy to a whole new level. But Lawrence was a SAC with twenty-plus years' experience while he was only a junior agent. So who was he to question?

CHAPTER ELEVEN

THE BIPLANE WAS cruising at two thousand feet in a taut blue sky over Schuylkill County eighty miles north of Philadelphia, the engine burbling with loud joy in the otherwise vast and empty quiet.

Wearing his brown leather helmet and goggles, Andrew closely scanned the ground ahead, soon seeing the tiny tell-tale lake he knew to look for. He looked north and spotted the wind-sock atop a thirty-foot red pole, right where it should be, lightly waving in the westerly ten-knot breeze. The grass airstrip ran parallel to a long field planted in crop.

He eased the joystick forward and dropped to five hundred feet. Lawrence had made arrangements with the farmer, and as Andrew dropped further and made a quick pass, he observed that the grass runway had been cut low.

But he didn't want to land yet. He pulled back on the joystick, gained altitude, banked sharply and turned south. In a few moments he saw Lawrence's green-roofed lake house a mile south of the airstrip in a clearing of about three acres. The lake house fronted close to the tiny lake.

No other lake houses or buildings were visible for miles, just unbroken woods. Lawrence apparently owned two hundred acres. Andrew could see his private gravel lane snaking its way a half mile in from the public road.

He descended and flew low over the lake house making a tight circle. It sat back about a hundred feet from shore, a large verandah facing the water. Lawrence had the whole lake to himself, all very private.

He flew the mile back to the grass strip, made an easy landing, then walked fifteen-minutes along an old tractor path to the lake house. He knocked at the door and it opened immediately. They looked appraisingly at each other. Lawrence, smiling warmly, offered his hand. "Welcome, Andrew." They shook and went inside.

"Any trouble finding the place?"

"None at all. Everything just as you said," Andrew said.

"Good. Good. Can I offer you a drink? A beer?"

"My plane doesn't like it when I drink. Anything else would be fine, Sir."

"No need to call me 'sir'. Please call me Wes." He got a pitcher of lemonade from the fridge. "So, you're settled into a house?" Lawrence asked.

"Yes. All happened so fast. A real estate agent knew of a cardiologist setting off to sail around the world and wanted someone to care for his house for seven months. He was very taken with Madeleine. The place is beautiful and furnished, so our stuff can stay in storage."

Lawrence poured the lemonade into tall glasses. "And your plane, does it have a home?" He handed Andrew a glass.

"I got hangar space and flying privileges at an aerodrome just north of the city."

"Good. Good." Lawrence held up his glass to Andrew. "Here's to working together."

Andrew smiled and raised his glass. "To working together."

Lawrence motioned Andrew into the living room where they took seats. Its walls and ceiling were pine-planked, its view of the lake magnetic.

Lawrence said, with a note of sadness, "Andrew, you were only twelve when I saw you last."

Andrew was surprised that Lawrence would remember that so exactly. "Yes. We made two planes that day. I see one of them sitting on your bookcase there, a Sopwith Camel."

Lawrence smiled. "You insisted I take one home and that I come back in the spring and we fly them together. And now you fly a real biplane." The smile shrank and he said, "I'm very sorry, Andrew, that I didn't make it back to see you again."

"That's okay. You had your own busy life. I really appreciated that you visited me those years. Other than a few social workers, you were the only adult who visited after my dad was gone."

Lawrence looked genuinely sorry. "I should have visited you more, done more."

"No, I'm grateful. You were someone I could look up to, someone who …reached out to me back then."

Lawrence seemed to want to dismiss the compliment. "I remember you asking on that last visit whether there were any leads in your dad's case. Five years had passed since he'd been taken. I knew you still held out some dim hope that he would be found. But I had to tell you there were no leads, nothing. You were older then, understood more. You were gravely disappointed."

"You knew that at the time?"

"I felt it." He contemplated his glass and his voice slowed, a sorrow creeping. "You don't know how much I wish things had been different for you…and for me."

After moments he looked at Andrew and his face cheered. "But you've turned out to be such a man, the spitting image of your father. He would have been proud."

"How well did you know my father?"

"Well enough to know that you meant the world to him."

"Did you socialize together?"

"No, but we worked together a lot. I was the liaison man at the FBI field office in Philadelphia, coordinating with their P.D. Your dad worked a lot of cases. We were on a number of joint task forces together." His hand moved the glass in a small circle, his eyes on it, his voice solemn, honoring a memory. "He was an excellent detective, an excellent man, an excellent father." He looked up. "But tell me about your wife and son."

"We're very happy. Madeleine's ecstatic to be back in Philly. Her younger sister, Nadine, is here. They're very close."

"I had some idea."

"We're very grateful to you. She would love to have you over to meet you, to thank you."

"That's kind. Tell her I'm happy for you both, but for now that can't be arranged. But also be clear, there is nothing to thank me for. This isn't about favoritism or any such thing. You are uniquely qualified for the task I have for you, the best candidate."

"I wasn't even applying for the job."

“Which made it all the better. This isn’t a job one applies for anyway.”

“I have to say I’m feeling very much in the dark.”

“That’s the nature of some secret assignments. But let me…illuminate. A short while ago Senator Booth of Philadelphia came to me in confidence to say he was being extorted by an anonymous organization called The Watcher. He knew that others who were being extorted, but who failed to pay as demanded, just…disappeared. I checked things out and he was right, many men over many years, all unsolved disappearances. We had had no idea those disappearances were all connected. I set up an operation to make Booth’s payment to The Watcher, to follow the money, see what we could learn. Fearing the possible consequences to the Senator if The Watcher smelled a rat, I put Booth first in a safe house.”

“I read about that, the bombing,” Andrew said. “Didn’t look good on the Bureau.”

Lawrence was quiet for moments. “No, not good at all.”

“The Watcher had to have inside information.”

Lawrence got up, a slow pacing of the room. “Yes, we’re being sold out, informants in our offices, or the Philly PD, or both. The money I had sent as Booth’s payment…The Watcher never picked it up, knew not to. There’s an internal investigation underway in both our offices and the Philly PD. The most optimistic view—identify an insider informant, learn how he communicates, follow that up the chain until we reach The Watcher. But I’m pessimistic about our chances. So I’ve devised a parallel strategy completely outside the reach of The Watcher and his informants.”

Andrew had been concentrating, watching him. Lawrence turned and looked at him. Andrew took a breath. “You mean…me?”

“You.”

"How?"

"By working at the problem from the opposite end—finding The Watcher."

Andrew stared a moment. Maybe Lawrence was having him on. "I see. Simple. Take out The Watcher… and the insiders no longer have anyone to leak to. Problem solved."

Lawrence was smiling. "A very effective result, wouldn't you say?"

"But how do I, acting alone, find him?"

"You're not alone, of course. You'll have my help. I'll have ongoing access to information, much of it that only you and I will know. Tight as a drum."

"I understand. No leaks," Andrew said.

Lawrence sat back down and set his glass away and leaned forward, his hands clasped together. "But finding The Watcher's only one component of the job. I want to maintain secrecy in some other key investigations. You see, someone like The Watcher, with access to inside information, can use that for the benefit of others, others not directly in his organization, but who are willing to pay handsomely to get confidential information."

"You've seen it happen other than on Booth?"

"I've been the SAC in Philly just two years, but I've seen a few odd things that could be explained by information leaks. We were in the final stages of seizing a commercial bank account that had ten million in it, but it was as if the account holder got word just in time. The account was cleaned out an hour before we got our seizure order. We put it down to very bad luck. But there have been other occurrences, surprises to us."

"But because of what happened with Booth, there's no guessing anymore. You *know* you've got a big leak."

"Yes. So the more information stays only between you and

me, the better. And that's especially true of high priority cases. So I needed someone working alone with me, someone not known in my office or in the Philly P.D., someone capable of independent action, someone with whom I share select information."

"So I'm not directly a part of any internal investigation?"

"Not for now. You'll carry out surveillance in high priority outside work."

"I see."

"You and I, Andrew, are never to be seen together. We cannot be known to talk together. No other agent here must ever know of you. I want you totally insulated. It's just you and me. Nobody but Washington knows you're here."

"Exceptional measures," Andrew said.

"Exceptional problems. Success depends on our secrecy."

The basic question was still weighing on Andrew. "But why me, Wes? There are others more qualified. Frankly, I'm still puzzled."

Lawrence smiled. "I would be disappointed in you if you weren't. I've kept track of you, Andrew. I've watched your progress, read the Bureau reports, activity summations. You're very capable, and you've expressed an interest in complex investigations."

Andrew was surprised again, wondering why Lawrence would have done that, and wondering also why, in the four years Andrew had been with the FBI, Lawrence had never reached out, just to acknowledge him.

"Coming back to your question, you fulfill many requirements. No agent here knows you. You know the city. You know this part of the country. You are SWAT trained."

"I didn't know my SWAT skills were being called on."

"They're, let's say, a bonus. Also, not many agents are pilots.

Even fewer own their own plane, particularly a stunt plane. Nobody would ever suspect you're law enforcement."

"My plane?"

"It's only one aspect of it, and maybe occasional only. I have a pressing case right now that could benefit from your plane. Also, hereafter, we meet only here at my lake house, and I insist you fly. There's only one road in and one road out, but I don't want you ever to be on it. You'll always come here as you did today, by plane and walking the mile at the back through the woods. No one will know you're here."

"Wes, I'm unclear. I can see you wouldn't want to be seen with me in the city around work situations to keep me anonymous. But I still ask myself, who would even be watching you to see who you're with? And that's especially true here, at your private lake house. Why would it matter?"

Lawrence took a perceptible breath, his eyes lowering a moment. "There are hypothetical possibilities that I want to protect against. I won't get into those now. You'll understand more as we go."

Andrew felt no clarification but knew he shouldn't press the point. "You said you already have a case where my plane could be of use."

"Yes. Have you heard of Dylan Kipling and Boyd Kennedy?"

"I think everyone has. The Minneapolis field office gave us an informational briefing a few weeks ago."

"I have evidence his whereabouts are near Philadelphia. Only you and I know this, no one in the Bureau, so no leaks. And I think it likely that Kennedy's with him."

Andrew was impressed. "Really? I can understand holding that info very close."

"I'm playing it safe. I could set a dragnet of twenty agents, but that would involve a lot of chatter, a lot of coordination, and possibly loose lips. I still may have to do that, but for now I want to try something different. I think Kipling's staying in a fixed location. You and your plane are going to discretely plot some things for me over a significant area north of the city. I'll give you details later."

Andrew nodded, inwardly amused his biplane was being recruited.

"Covert aerial surveillance could make a difference in some investigations. That's partly how I sold Washington on your transfer here with your plane. If you and I succeed on the Kipling matter, that alone will have made your transfer worthwhile."

Andrew had to smile. "Flying my biplane."

"That brings me to the final criterion I had." Lawrence studied Andrew. "I needed someone I could trust implicitly, without question, without fail."

Andrew felt honored. "Yes, of course…Wes."

"Thank you, Andrew. You know, I'm even more impressed with you than I had hoped to be. I feel this assignment's going to go well. Although one of the rules is we never be seen together, I've just decided I can make a small exception, for just one occasion."

"Oh?"

"I would like to see Madeleine and Chris. Not meet them, just see them, to see you three together. You must not acknowledge me whatsoever. They must not know we have any connection. I eat at Franky's in the Bella Vista district on Thursday nights. Why don't you take a table near me at 6:00?"

Andrew grinned at the notion. "I would love you to see them. Just *see* them. And I think between you and me, we could pull off just such a covert action."

Lawrence laughed and slapped Andrew on the back.

CHAPTER TWELVE

THE CARDIOLOGIST'S HOME they rented was a Cape Cod style with large dormers in the mature neighborhood of Chestnut Hill, its streets lined with majestic red oaks. The property boasted a deep tree-studded backyard backing onto a green belt. Madeleine was smitten.

When Andrew got home the sun was pouring through the living room window, the stereo cranked high, Madeleine dancing with a broom to a Supremes' song. She saw Andrew but kept dancing, eying him romantically, mouthing the words, pointing her finger to him in tempo.

He went to her and they danced out the song clutching one other, indulging a long kiss. Chris, watching from the hall, was embarrassed for them.

"How did it all go?" Madeleine asked as she turned off the stereo.

"Good."

"Can you tell me more?"

"Later," he said.

She looked at him. Ah, when Chris was asleep.

"And how about you?" he said.

"I went to the Board offices, dropped my resume and application. I already got a call back this afternoon. An interview. Looks 'very promising' they said."

"That's so great, Maddy, everything falling into place for us."

She smiled and headed for the kitchen. "Dinner's almost ready."

Andrew called out, "Where is that buckaroo?"

"Right here!" Chris poked his head around the corner.

"Time for bucking bronco?"

"Yes!"

Andrew got down on all fours. Chris clambered onto his back lashing his arms under his chest and squeezed his legs around Andrew's middle. Andrew started slowly, a lazy, uninspired bronco.

Chris spurred with his heels, "Come on, horsey. Go!"

Andrew sped the action, heaving up and down, Chris squeezing to stay on.

Madeleine came in. "Where's your lasso?"

Chris managed to raise a hand above his bouncing head and made a twirl.

Andrew laid it on now, snorting and bucking, his hands popping off the floor, his back rearing.

Madeleine was laughing. "You sound like a frantic pig."

He intensified the herky-jerky, Chris mostly airborne with little hope of hanging on.

Madeleine laughed. "I've got to finish rustling up some grub for you cowboys," and went to the kitchen.

Chris finally bounced off. Andrew rolled over on his back on the carpet and stretched out, breathing hard. "Horsey… needs a rest." He closed his eyes and lay still, catching his breath.

Chris walked in a big circle, then went over to Andrew. Chris straddled him, one leg on either side, then sat down on Andrew's stomach. Andrew grunted.

Chris's demeanor had changed. "Dad," his voice carried concern, "Did your dad play bronco with you?"

"Yes, he did."

"Mom showed me a picture of you when you were seven, standing with your dad."

Andrew knew the picture more than perfectly, the only one he had of his dad other than the family picture taken at the county fair. He and his father had walked the woods looking for signs of rabbit and deer. They had found fox scat. They target-practiced with crossbows that his father had made, his father's an oak crossbow he had designed for deer. In the picture, they each held their crossbow in a mock-serious pose on the front lawn, standing on either side of a hay bale draped with a colorful bull's eye target, two arrows firmly dead center, side by side, one from each.

He had fingered the picture a thousand times.

"Could your dad hit a can off a fence post with the crossbow like you do?"

"Yes, he could."

There was new emotion in his Chris' voice. "Did your dad love you like you love me?"

Andrew opened his eyes and looked at Chris. "Yes."

"You aren't ever going to leave me, are you?"

He lifted Chris off his stomach and sat up. "No, Chris. I would never leave you. Don't you ever worry about that."

"But your dad left."

"With my dad, it was different. It was like… an accident…he couldn't avoid."

Madeleine yelled, "Dinner!"

Andrew rolled Chris over onto the floor and got himself up onto all fours again. "Hey, this horse is getting mighty hungry. Let's make some tracks, partner."

Chris mounted with a grin, gave a kick, and off they rode into the kitchen.

*

That evening, after Chris went to bed, Andrew and Madeleine talked in the living room.

"Lawrence emphasized absolute secrecy, and I mean really," Andrew was saying. "As far as communication, Lawrence and I are never to meet face to face anywhere except at his lake house. Our only other contact is by phone, but the thing is I can never call his office from our home phone because all incoming numbers are recorded and can be traced. So I have to use a payphone. Also, I'm never to call him at home except from a payphone because, again, there must be no traceable link between us.

"My heavens."

Our home phone is to be listed in your name alone, your maiden name. He wants us to install a second phone in the house with an unlisted number, registered again in your maiden name. An answering machine is to be connected to that one. That phone is never to be answered. And no calls are ever to be made out from that phone; it's one-way communication only. If Lawrence needs to reach me, he'll phone from a payphone and leave a message on that second line."

"Wow. You really are going underground. Can you still be my husband or what?" she laughed.

He laughed, too. "I think we could manage that. Basically I'm doing textbook surveillance on important cases, but nobody but Lawrence will know I'm doing it. And this part's really wild—sometimes I'll be flying my plane."

"What? On assignment?"

"Yeah, it's all part of the covert aspect. It seems it helped us to get here, my distinguishing feature. Over the next few days, he wants me to outfit cameras on it and do a few other things before we meet this Friday. Then I get my first assignment."

"Wow, Andrew, this is all so interesting, in a weird way actually."

"I know. But he says it's because of 'extraordinary circumstances'. So listen, people we meet around here, like neighbors and others, can't know I work for the FBI. So we've got to come up with some simple cover we both know, but keep casual about it."

"Real cloak and dagger. I feel like I'm living with James Bond. Martini, Sir? Shaken, not stirred, of course."

Later, at bedtime, Andrew was already in bed watching Madeleine in her nightgown standing at a mirror undoing her earrings when she said, "Okay, I've figured it out."

"Figured what out?" he said.

"Your cover. You work for the government as an analyst. Usually that's enough to make anyone's eyes glaze over and they go away. But if anyone asks more, I'll just say that you're working on a project for the US Department of Commerce, *Bureau* of Economic Analysis. That way, if one of us accidentally mentions 'Bureau', it's *that* Bureau. And if that doesn't deliver the knock-out punch, I'll say, 'Well, I don't understand what gross domestic product is. Do you?' And they'll say, 'No.' And I'll say, "So, where can I get good pad thai in this town?"

She turned to him with the earrings now in her hand. "Did I pass?"

He was looking at her, an admiring smile. "You're really very good, you know."

CHAPTER THIRTEEN

IT WAS THURSDAY, and Andrew, Madeleine, and Chris entered Franky's for dinner.

Andrew quickly saw where Lawrence was seated and had the waiter get them a table two over, feeling it distinctly odd not to be able to say 'Hi', or say anything to Madeleine about it. Once seated, he surveyed the room taking no extra time gazing in Lawrence's direction. He saw that Lawrence was already finishing his meal, but showed no sign of noticing Andrew. Good training.

"Okay, Maddy, let's order drinks. What would you like?"

She was studying the menu.

Andrew said, "I'm going to have a whiskey sour, something different for a change. How about you, Chris? Do you want a lemonade?"

"Yes, please."

Andrew looked to Madeleine. She lifted her eyes from the menu and gave him an odd smile.

"What would you like to drink?" he said.

She looked back at the menu, still smiling inexplicably. "Maybe some water."

"Water? Don't you want that Bahama Mama colorful thing with the cherry?"

"Ohhh," she said, stretching it out like elastic, then another Mona Lisa smile.

"Maddy, you're acting a little strange. What's going on?"

"I don't think I should."

"What do you mean? Have a drink. We're having a little celebration outing."

"I know that. But I shouldn't be drinking." That smile again.

"What do you—?" He stopped himself. His eyes searched hers. She kept looking at him, her eyes unwavering. He leaned forward, staring at her. "You're not kidding me, are you?"

She held his gaze, but a tear came, her eyes joyful but measured now by the sad memory.

"You didn't say anything. Really? We're expecting?"

She reached her hand to his. "I wanted to surprise you." Another tear.

He felt his emotions welling, the long grief of Olivia. They so wanted another baby. He took both of her hands in his and kissed them. He got up and walked around to her. She stood and they hugged.

People close by stopped eating and watched.

Aware of the attention, Andrew announced quietly, "She just told me we're expecting."

There was a round of applause, some even raising beer glasses.

He saw Lawrence walking toward the exit.

*

That night in his house in a quiet, mature, suburban neighborhood, Lawrence sat very still in an armchair in the living room in semi-darkness, one small lamp projecting a dim yellow light in a far corner. He was alone, as he always was, a deliberate choice.

His mind followed a too familiar path. He had worked hard to be a good cop, harder than anyone. He had solved many crimes, brought many to justice, more than most. He had put everything into his work—no family, no hobbies. He was respected, admired, received high praise. None of which he deserved.

He had done everything he could to serve justice.

Except turn himself in.

All the good work he did, all the accolades, counted for nothing. For they did not know who he really was. He had betrayed the uniform to the core, and worse.

He had, of course, thought to do the right thing, to make a clean breast of it, to take his punishment—prison for a very long time. Not that he would survive long there anyway.

How do you live with guilt every day from the time you're only twenty-one?

He had hidden, immersing himself in a demanding job, building a wonderful shell around himself. He had tried to cease to feel, but he couldn't. Sometimes the shell cracked, the pressure from within too much, and the lava of hot feeling flowed and burned. And there was only one way to assuage it he had found. Surrender to the white magic.

With a delicate key, he unlocked the small desk drawer. His

hand reached blindly to the back of the drawer, past the small handgun. Might he one day surrender to the handgun?

He withdrew the tiny clear plastic packet of white powder. His hand reached in again, felt for and found the needle.

CHAPTER FOURTEEN

WHEN ANDREW ARRIVED the next afternoon at the lake house, Lawrence said "How's the plane looking?"

"All outfitted now. Three cameras under the fuselage, configured like in the plane I flew out of Minneapolis. Each has a different telephoto lens so I get long, medium, and close shots, all operated by a remote-control unit on the dash. Each camera shoots four pictures a second."

Lawrence nodded with satisfaction. "What about range?"

"I had a supplementary fuel tank installed. Flying time is now two and a half hours, a range of over 350 miles."

"Your enthusiasm for the plane is obvious."

"Maddy tells me it's a jealous mistress."

Lawrence smiled at the comment as he brought a thick accordion file to the kitchen table. "Have a seat." He pulled several documents from the file and began to open and spread them on the table. "Maps," he said, "covering an area of about 250 square miles."

With a pencil he drew four straight lines that made a large square in one of the maps. "This is the area I've chosen for you to search within."

Andrew saw that the other maps were enlargements of the area within the square.

Lawrence explained what he had gleaned from the two interviews of the possible sightings of Kipling, the woman who believed it was him at a gas station west of Doylestown, then Randy the teenager and his girlfriend who followed the light-green '77 Monte Carlo on the road between Doylestown and New Hope.

He also told Andrew about Kipling's cell-mate and Kipling's property not being registered in his name, and the property being close enough to water that the damn ducks' quacking drove him crazy.

"The first task is to identify house properties that have a pond or marsh close by, or anything that you think amounts to enough water that ducks might land in. I expect the property would be something not too close to neighbors, probably not expensive, maybe a cabin even. I'm guessing Kipling didn't spend a fortune on a hideaway."

"An interesting challenge."

"Just use your best judgment. You know everything that I do at this point."

"Okay," Andrew said, folding up the maps.

"I made some tuna sandwiches for our lunch. Is that alright?"

"Sounds delicious."

Lawrence passed him a sandwich on a plate from the fridge,

took one for himself, and they went into the living room. Andrew sat on the sofa. Lawrence took a chair.

Andrew said, "I've been wondering, did you happen to be involved in the investigation of my father's disappearance?"

Lawrence seemed to hesitate. "…No."

"Were you acquainted with the facts?"

"I followed the case closely."

"In hindsight, do you believe that everything was done that could have been done?"

Andrew was surprised at how slow Lawrence was to answer. He seemed disturbed by the question, his eyes casting toward the lake, a look of agitation. Regardless of what Lawrence might say now, Andrew felt the full answer would not come out.

"A specialist team was set up, followed every lead however small. Produced nothing."

Andrew pressed. "Do you recall the essentials?"

Lawrence's finger rapped absently on the arm of the chair. He cleared his throat and began slowly. "Your dad's abduction was believed linked to the murder of a pickpocket named Macky. The thinking was if you found Macky's killer, you found your dad's killer."

Andrew detected something in Lawrence's voice. Was it reluctance, or just sadness? Or was it guilt? But why would he feel guilt?

"Macky was shot twice, close up, with a silenced 9 mm pistol on a dark residential street the night before your dad was taken. Some teenagers in a car saw a tall white man, solid build, dragging Macky toward a parked Thunderbird. The man took off in his car, leaving Macky on the street. They didn't get a good look at the man's face."

"Plates?"

"They got the numbers, but the plates were stolen, the

Thunderbird never traced. Two officers were on the scene almost immediately. Your dad was there minutes later. Macky was barely conscious. Your dad kneeled to him to try to get him to talk while they waited for the ambulance. The officers didn't hear anything. Macky died in minutes."

"Macky didn't talk?"

To Andrew, Lawrence seemed oddly grim and uneasy. His voice was quiet. "There was nothing in your dad's report to that effect."

Lawrence shifted in his chair like he was mustering resolve. "Robbery certainly wasn't the motive. Macky had lots of money on him. Your Dad checked Macky's background that night and learned he was a master pickpocket and on the lam, wanted by Buffalo P.D. from years earlier. I know the team looked into anyone who might have been motivated to kill Macky, but nothing turned up."

"But that doesn't explain someone taking my dad, and taking him the very next day."

Lawrence looked at Andrew. "No. It doesn't." He paused and got up and walked to the window, his face drawn. To Andrew he seemed oddly moved by the recollection.

"A stolen wallet was found on Macky," Lawrence said. "Its owner was located the next morning. He had been at a gala at the ballroom of the Continental Hotel the whole evening before, a swanky affair, a lot of Philadelphia's business elite, expensive suits, stylish gowns, good food and drink, an orchestra. The owner was certain he had his wallet as late as 10:20 because he had bought drinks and checked the time, worried about drinking too late, he said. Thirty minutes later Macky was dying on the street six blocks away from the Hotel with that wallet in his pocket."

"I'm surprised that you recall things to this degree."

Lawrence gave an awkward smile. "This conversation wasn't exactly unexpected, Andrew. I did a little homework."

"I really appreciate that, as you can imagine."

Lawrence nodded. "I can imagine." He began to pace slowly. "So the wallet naturally led to the theory that Macky had been at the gala, although not as a guest. The organizers and hotel management put together a list of all the guests and hotel staff working that night. Over the next days a picture of Macky was shown to everyone. Nobody recalled seeing him, not even the man who had lost the wallet."

Andrew was thoughtful. "A good pickpocket knows better than to walk six blocks with a stolen wallet. You take the money and get rid of the wallet quickly."

"A good observation, Andrew, and that was considered. No one else at the party had anything stolen. Macky lifted only the one wallet which led to the theory that something unusual there made Macky leave, and distracted him enough that he forgot to discard that wallet."

"And very soon after, he's shot. He must have seen something, sensed danger."

"The coincidence was very high."

"How many people were there?"

"Almost five hundred. Over three hundred were men, well-to-do businessmen mostly. None on the list had left before 11:30. Everyone was thoroughly questioned. Full background checks were done, but they turned up nothing."

There was sudden sympathy in Lawrence's face. "But you offered something. You were a brave boy. You said that the hooded man who came to your house was shorter than your Dad, his eyes level with your Dad's chin, making him no taller than about five and a half feet. You said his voice was lower, too. Intense surveillance was conducted on all men at the gala who were shorter than average and had a low voice. Phones were tapped, hidden microphones, forensic accounting. Nothing connected anyone at the gala to Macky's murder or to your dad's abduction. The wallet led to the gala, but the gala led nowhere. If someone there was behind it, he had an ironclad cover."

Neither spoke for moments. Then Andrew said, "I've long wondered why the man who came to our house wore that black hood. What would he care if my Dad saw who he was? He was going to kill him anyway. I used to think he just didn't want *me* to be able to give a description. Then something else occurred to me. Did even the two gunmen not know who the hooded man was? There were two cars, not one. And the hooded man, with my father in the trunk, drove away in an opposite direction. Maybe the gunmen didn't even know where the hooded man was going."

Lawrence said nothing, seeming suddenly weary. Maybe he had been over it all too many times before, Andrew thought.

"I still see my father and that man. It haunts me, why my father had to die. He knew something no one else did."

Lawrence nodded in acknowledgment but said nothing, going to the living room window and looking at the lake, his back to him. It was clear he didn't want to talk about the matter further.

Andrew stayed seated, wondering what effect those memories had on Lawrence. Was he that close to his father?

"There's a totally unrelated matter I meant to mention when I was here before," Andrew finally said. "Ten years ago, when I was just released from the reformatory, I helped a policeman who was knocked out in a bar. A college fund was set up for me in appreciation. The town raised several thousand dollars. But there was also an anonymous donor who gave $15,000. That alone was two years of college paid."

Lawrence remained at the window, his back still turned. Andrew continued, "I made a lot of inquiries to find out who it was. But I never did find out."

Andrew waited, watching. Lawrence finally half turned and Andrew caught a wary flicker in his eyes.

"Was it you?" Andrew said quietly.

He saw uneasy hesitation.

"It *was* you."

Lawrence looked uncomfortable.

Andrew stood up. "Why didn't you ever say? All this time? You helped change my life."

Lawrence's voice was tight. "It was something I felt was right, an opportunity to help. I didn't want any attention."

Andrew saw that the discomfort was genuine, not a simple modesty. "Well, I really want to thank you. It was so generous. It made such a difference for me."

Lawrence's smile seemed forced. "You're welcome, Andrew. And you know, I haven't even congratulated you on the news that Madeleine's expecting. I'm happy for you both. She's a lovely woman, and Chris, a fine boy." Then a wistful note. "You're very lucky."

"Thank you. I feel I am."

An awkward silence followed. Andrew said, "And you, you never married?"

"Never married."

Andrew tried to sound light and casual. "Never that right girl?"

Lawrence's smile faded. "Never that right girl."

Andrew sensed he had overstepped.

Lawrence walked to the kitchen table and picked up the accordion file folder and went to a corner cabinet and opened a door and set the file onto a shelf. Andrew thought he saw Lawrence's hands shake as he stood there a moment.

"There was, in fact, a girl," Lawrence said, not looking at Andrew. "She died."

"I'm sorry, sir. I shouldn't have brought it up."

Lawrence lifted his eyes to the window and as he watched a breeze ripple the surface of the lake, he seemed about to say something more. After a moment he said, "It's okay, Andrew. Think nothing of it."

CHAPTER FIFTEEN

FLYING A DAY and a half, Andrew covered about eighty square miles north of Philadelphia, charting properties that had possibilities, out-of-the-way properties with a house or cabin, and very near to enough water, even a pond, to accommodate ducks.

Now he was back at the lake house to give an update. At the kitchen table they reviewed high-magnification maps, and Andrew explained the areas he had flown and provided the coordinates of specific properties of interest.

"Good work," Lawrence said.

Andrew proposed the next two day's search coordinates and Lawrence nodded as the information finished, saying again, "Good work."

But Andrew noticed him now becoming distracted, something obviously on his mind. He finally said, "Is there something I didn't explain clearly?"

Lawrence cast him a nervous look and his lips moved without speaking at first. Then, "That girl I mentioned the other day—."

Surprised, Andrew felt a pang of guilt, sensing he had unearthed a painful memory. "Yes?" he said.

"Why don't you have a seat in the living room?"

This sudden twist was unsettling, but he knew he had no choice but to hear Lawrence out. He sat on the sofa, but Lawrence remained standing.

"I was twenty-one that year," he said, "a rookie cop with the Buffalo P.D. Her dad was a cop on the force, a very tough guy, the kind you wanted to see coming through the door when you called for backup."

He rubbed absently one hand on the other. "Her dad hosted a barbecue at their house for some of the guys from work. I was the new cop, still wet behind the ears, everybody kidding me. She was there, cute, slight, quiet. I thought shy. We talked a bit, a nice girl. Her name was Sylvie."

He began to pace slowly. "Not long after, she dropped into my place one night, an apartment I had in a big old house. I hadn't spoken to her since the barbecue. She seemed to be very interested in me and wasn't too shy about showing it. I figured that when her father wasn't around, she came out of her shell. She told me her dad and mom didn't know she was visiting me. In fact, nobody knew, and she wanted to keep it that way."

Andrew was mystified. Why was he telling him all this?

"We talked a lot, had a couple of drinks, enjoying each other's company, laughed at stupid things. You know how it is. Some hugging and kissing."

Lawrence walked to the leather easy chair and sat down. The room dimmed and Andrew was aware of clouds blocking the evening sun. He knew he had to get going soon to have enough light to land.

"A few days later she came by again. She said nobody knew she was there, not even her girlfriends, otherwise her father might find out. She said he was over-protective, wouldn't let her go out to do things other girls did, even though she was eighteen."

Lawrence tapped the leather arm slowly. "I felt uneasy, her dad being my colleague. But we had a few drinks, some kissing. She told me she thought she loved me. Passion ran away with us." He stopped tapping. "One thing led to another."

Lawrence paused a moment, his eyes restless. "She came by days later. She said we should end it now before anything more happened. She was abrupt, agitated. I didn't understand. I said, 'Before anything like what happens?' She was very quiet, looked away from me and said, 'I'm only fifteen.'"

He got up, his voice louder. "It hit me like a hammer. Fifteen! I was stunned. She had deceived me. I yelled at her. But then my feelings turned to dread. Here I was, twenty-one, a cop, and I had had intercourse with a very under-aged girl. The act had occurred only once, but there it was, statutory rape. Then it struck me, there loomed a *much* worse possibility. We had been drinking a lot that night. To a Court, drinking like that would take statutory rape up to forcible rape, prison time, the end of my career. The end of my future."

He looked at Andrew and Andrew thought he seemed to be deciding how much he should say. "Of course, nothing would happen if she never spoke of it again. We agreed on that. I told her I could never see her again. She left."

He paced back and forth like a prisoner in a cell. "But I lived in continuous fear. She was so young. If she ever felt compelled to tell someone sometime, a girlfriend maybe, it could get out. It was a sword hanging over my head. Her father would push the charges all the way… if he didn't kill me first."

He stared out at the lake. "Weeks went by. I didn't hear from her, just as we agreed. Then one night, a knock at my door. She looked ghastly, washed out."

He turned and looked at Andrew. "She told me she was pregnant. Fifteen and pregnant. Everything was going to come out now. My head was spinning with fear. She was very scared, one minute wanting to talk to her mother, the next minute wanting to kill herself. She hadn't slept in two days, hadn't gone to school. I was afraid of what she might do, she was so unstable. Her mother and father had just gone to Florida for a week and only her older brother was at home. He didn't know anything, she said. Nobody knew but us. I hugged her to calm her down. I told her that she could have an abortion. I would make private arrangements. It made sense then, in my young mind."

Lawrence wrung his hands. "Can you imagine my fear, Andrew? Twenty-one years old. I had the whole world in front of me, my whole life, and it was going to tip one way or the other."

Andrew felt tremendous unease. Why was Lawrence telling him this? It was obviously hard for him, so personal, and Andrew hardly knew him.

Lawrence continued, "She said yes, she would do it. Naturally we couldn't go to a doctor, not at her age without her parents involved. And anyway, abortions weren't even legal then, still criminal, especially the back alley kind. I told her that I would take care of things. I had heard at the station about a woman who was charged with performing an abortion, but the charges were dropped before it got to court. I looked up the file, found out where the woman lived, and I went to see her. She agreed to do it."

He looked at Andrew, remorseful.

Andrew felt he had heard all he should hear. "And it went badly," he said.

Lawrence nodded. "We do things when we're young, Andrew, that haunt us, that follow us like a beast."

"She…died."

"Yes. I can't forgive myself for what happened, for what I did."

"You didn't mean harm to her. And it was a long time ago."

But Andrew was very uneasy. It felt to him like Lawrence had never told this to anyone, but he didn't want to ask. It was all too strange, such a revelation, and to him. And more, what Lawrence had done was arrange for a criminal act that had resulted in the death of a young girl. He found himself unsure what to say or do. But he said, "I'm very sorry, Wes, a terrible thing. It was a long time ago."

Lawrence's face was somber. He looked away from Andrew, his hands clenched.

Andrew quietly said, "I should get underway. The light's falling. I need the light to land."

They both put on a good face and Andrew left.

As he walked through the woods to the grass airstrip, he pondered on the deep dark currents flowing in Lawrence. Was his life so without friendship, so without trust, he had told no one else?

He also couldn't shake a nagging worry that something important was missing. Lawrence had carried this burden far too long, and Andrew felt there had to be more to it. And also, why tell it to *him*?

*

When he arrived home, very late evening, his mind was still mulling it over. Madeleine met him at the door in a light-hearted mood. "Welcome home." She wrapped her arms around his neck and gave him a warm kiss.

"I was thinking," he said, "if a young girl died having an abortion twenty-five years ago, there would be an autopsy, especially if the abortion was illegal."

"Well, you're all fun and games. Yes, there would be an autopsy either way if she died. And the doc might be charged and his license yanked."

Andrew paused, "Yes, particularly if it's *not* a doctor but some woman in a back alley. It could be manslaughter or worse. But here's the thing. If the whole thing was set up by someone else, the police are going to search out that someone else. The prime suspect is going to be the guy who got her pregnant."

"Presumably," she said with growing indifference and started for the kitchen. "By the way, you really know how to kill a mood."

Andrew followed her, saying, "The woman who did the abortion, she's going to want to cough up the identity of the guy who set it up, to get a better sentencing deal for herself because the cops are going to really push hard on this one."

She opened a cupboard and grabbed a bag of cookies. She didn't want to encourage this conversation, but said, "And why especially on this one?"

"Because the dead girl's father's a cop. But the guy who got her pregnant and who set the abortion up, he said no one knew what he had done. How is it they didn't get him?"

She bit off a large chunk of cookie. "I admit this is just fascinating, Andrew, but…want to do something else?"

He looked at her. She was looking back at him less than amorous now, chomping with unseemly vigor. And they weren't even hard cookies.

"Hey, Maddy, I'm sorry." He took her in his arms and kissed her neck and nibbled her ear.

She reached for another cookie. "Glad you're back." She bit into it and made loud eating sounds. "Don't forget the other ear."

CHAPTER SIXTEEN

HE WAS FLYING ninety miles an hour, the wind whipping around him in the open cockpit, a chill in the air at 3000 feet even in late morning. He was maintaining a grid pattern without being obvious, not flying in straight rows. To anyone looking he would appear to be a stunt flyer, every couple of miles practicing an aerobatic maneuver.

He had been up two hours, covering thirty square miles, and now felt himself getting punchy. It took a lot of concentration to fly the open-cockpit biplane, keep track of where he'd been, do the aerobatics, ignore the heavy engine drone, and carefully survey the ground for hours. He pushed his aching shoulders back and twisted his head up and around, back and forth, trying to work out a growing kink in his neck. Then he did a slow barrel roll.

He had decided he should enhance his strategy, add efficiency. Rather than just identify and photograph properties that had the possibility of being Kipling's hideaway, he should get a much closer look at any property that really caught his attention. He would avoid suspicion from the ground by doing a few extra tricks.

*

In the screened-in back porch of a wood-sided older frame home badly in need of painting, Kipling watched the biplane in the distance. Beside him, Boyd Kennedy played with a thick-bodied, massive-headed pit bull. About 150 yards away, just past the tall-grassed rear yard, was an elongated sizeable marsh with bulrushes. A stubby dilapidated garage stood well back from the house.

"Look at that," Kipling said, pointing to the biplane as it did a barrel roll about two miles away. "Some stunt flyer. Every so often he does some stunt. Maybe teaching someone how to pull stunts," he laughed, getting his own joke.

"Here, Ace," Kennedy called to the pit bull and threw two hunks of cooked hamburger patty. Kennedy looked up at the plane and watched. "Not my preferred way of travel. Zero in-flight service."

Kipling said without expression, "Coffee wouldn't stay in your cup anyway."

Kennedy grunted, "Not even in your stomach."

*

Andrew had seen the older frame house and the marsh a half mile from any neighbor. To deflect suspicion he had done two aerobatic maneuvers miles out then swooped in low over a farm half a mile away.

Still low, he slowed the plane and skirted this property, staying well away, studying it through stabilized binoculars. His interest was in any cars. A garage stood to the side of the house at the end of the driveway. He saw that the garage door was open. There didn't appear to be a car inside.

There was a second garage, smaller, dilapidated, deep in the rear yard. Two brown tracks like car-tire tracks in the grass led from the driveway around the first garage and on into the rear yard and then to the rear of the rear garage. Anything parked in that garage wouldn't be seen from the road. Maybe that was the idea.

He flew on in a wide circle doing a slow barrel roll as he did. He righted himself when he would be in the best position to see the rear garage from a good angle. It was an odd feature, he thought, the door facing rear, unless it was maybe just an oversized tool shed, or somewhere to keep big boy toys. You'd have to be deep in the rear yard to see into the door of that garage.

He realized the door was open.

Something caught his eye, a glint of sunlight off something metallic. Grillwork? A car's front end?

Pictures taken with a telephoto lens would tell. But the angle of the sun was causing glare. He saw that oncoming scudding clouds would soon solve that problem.

He slowed and flew for another five minutes away from the property gaining altitude to 4,000 feet. He put the plane into a tight circle, its wings almost vertical. He leveled out and flew twenty degrees off a direct course toward the house. At two miles out, he saw that the clouds were now shadowing that area. The glare would be gone.

He eased off the throttle and dropped to 2000 feet. He looked hard through the stabilized binoculars. The metallic form was definitely a car, and light-colored. From a car-dealer brochure he had memorized what a '77 Monte Carlo looked like at all angles. He knew what the front would look like. This car had definite possibilities.

He did a quick barrel roll a half mile out.

He eased off the throttle more and banked, dropping in quickly, leveling at 800 feet, flying at a slow sixty miles an hour, positioned to get the very best angle for the multiple cameras. He held his thumb on the remote for five seconds as he approached, each camera whirring through twenty pictures.

Just over the house, he pulled up sharply into a spiraling vertical climb, the engine wailing in protest. Just as in the best of air shows, he held the vertical until he reached the apex then did a tail slide into a hammerhead stall. He kicked the rudder into a slow-spinning free fall, straight down, the ground coming up fast. He could feel the audience hold its breath. He hauled back on the joystick and eased out of the fall bottoming at a thousand feet, the engine loudly protesting.

He had done the formidable stunt for two reasons: first, he had seen a man standing in the shadow of a screened-in porch at the back of house and he was looking up. Andrew wanted to squash any notion the man might have that the plane was the law. And second, it was a jubilation ride because he got a very good look at the front of that car—a light-green Monte Carlo.

*

Kipling was still standing outside the porch, Kennedy beside him. Both had seen the biplane's dare-devilish spiraling ascent and the stall and the dive. As they watched it fly off, the engine noise now quieting, Kipling said, "That guy is *some* crazy."

CHAPTER SEVENTEEN

ANDREW GOT THE photos developed at a one-hour shop.

He sifted through them and selected thirty. Three very clearly showed a car's front-end and hood of exactly the correct description. Two others caught precise images of the man standing beside the screened porch. He appeared to be about thirty, solidly built, and similar to Kipling's general description. Andrew had no photograph of Kipling, but Lawrence did. The rest showed the layout of the house and property and the surrounding properties to 1500 yards, all for the orientation of the SWAT team.

He phoned Lawrence and at 4:30 touched down on the grass runway and made the mile hike to the lake house. When he got there he saw Lawrence's mood had greatly improved from the evening before when he told Andrew about Sylvie and the abortion.

Lawrence took the envelope of pictures from Andrew and quickly spread them on the kitchen table. They were crisp and clear. He studied them, nodding often. "Excellent, Andrew, absolutely excellent."

From a briefcase he withdrew FBI pictures of Kipling and Boyd Kennedy. He held them close to the pictures of the man by the screened porch. Blond hair, broad forehead, jutting jaw, powerful shoulders. There was no question. It was Kipling.

"You've done it, Andrew, the needle in the haystack, absolutely fine work. And there's a good chance Kennedy's there as well."

He studied the pictures of the property itself and the wider surroundings. "Three points of ingress and egress, a more complex takedown operation. I'm going to hold off sharing any of this until later this evening to delay any possible leak. I'll go to the office in a while and start on what logistics I can myself. I'll coordinate with Philly P.D. as late as possible, too. I can't use your photos, of course. Nobody can know you're involved, or that *anybody* else is involved."

"How are you going to explain how you know Kipling's at this location?"

"I'll say I got a credible tip. I'll say my concern about leaks means I'm playing my cards close. No one will question my actions. They're my decisions for my reasons."

Lawrence thought further, calculating the timing. "I'll arrange for the takedown to go at 3 a.m., but I'll not be saying where it is or who it is until as late as possible. I've got a lot of work to do. A dozen of our men plus coordinators need to be contacted, jacked up, and fully briefed, and a similar number from the Philly SWAT team and their coordinators for wide back-up, then State troopers to sort out roadblocks in every direction. That's a lot of hot communication and all done maintaining complete secrecy."

"But what are the real chances someone like Kipling is hooked up with any police insider?"

"Kipling maybe not. But Kennedy...just maybe."

Lawrence's mood was changing to annoyance. "It's a lot to keep quiet. Only takes that one rat on the take to let the cat out of the bag. In my cynical moments I feel I might just as well cable the sons of bitches, tell them we're coming."

He picked up the FBI pictures of Kennedy and Kipling and handed a set to Andrew. "Of course, I need to know they're still there tonight. Or that at least Kipling is. I want you on the ground there at 9:30, just after dark. Call me immediately at my house in the city if the Monte Carlo's gone or it appears no one's there. If I don't hear from you by ten, I'll know we're on, and that's when I pull all this together and release details to our people and Philly P.D. If someone's there, you stay put until they're settled in for the night, say until midnight."

"You want me to call you again then?"

"Yes, you clear out at midnight and call me at home to confirm. I'll not have any road perimeters set up or surveillance in until 12:30 to give you time to get away from the property."

*

The night was black with thick cloud cover.

Andrew positioned himself well at the rear of the property close by the marsh. Through his night vision goggles he could see everything with about the clarity of twilight. The Monte Carlo was still there. It looked like it hadn't moved an inch.

Andrew was dressed head to toe in black, wearing Kevlar protective gear and carrying a semi-automatic black Smith and Wesson 459 pistol and an M-16 assault rifle, the rifle he had trained on before becoming a sniper. At this close range, his scoped sniper rifle would be a liability, not that he expected he would need to use any weapon tonight.

The windows of the house were curtained shut but there were lights on in four rooms, too many rooms if they were just on timers. Kipling had to be there, and maybe Boyd Kennedy too.

The ground between Andrew and the screened porch at the rear was level and overgrown with wild grasses. There were no trees, no real cover, the distance—about 250 feet.

All was quiet. There was nothing to indicate Kipling was going to get up and leave. But he would wait until midnight as Lawrence had instructed. He settled on the grass, lying flat. He glanced at his watch: 9:45.

Ten o'clock came and went. He wouldn't be making a call to Lawrence, so Lawrence would know Kipling was still at the property. Lawrence would initiate the next steps in the takedown preparations which would, of course, include saying where the takedown would be and that the target was Kipling, and possibly Kennedy, too. The buzz at the Philly PD, the FBI field office, and the local State police would get very loud very quickly.

*

At 11:05 p.m., Nix got a message on his beeper. He went into his study and turned on the tape recorder. A five second recording: **'B322. URGENT. LOCATION OF DYLAN KIPLING KNOWN AND CONFIRMED. SUSPECT KENNEDY TOO. FBI/PHILA SWAT TAKEDOWN 3 AM.'**

Nix smiled. It was satisfying when things worked this seamlessly, especially when timing was this critical. B322 was a shift supervisor in the Philadelphia police department who had a tenacious gambling addiction and always needed money, and this was easy money. His information was top notch. Mr. Kennedy would be eternally grateful that he spent his money wisely, purchasing the priceless services of The Watcher.

He jotted a phone number from a file, threw on a light jacket, and grabbed the elevator to the underground parking where he got into his white Porsche 911. He drove only two minutes. Three blocks past a payphone, he parked and walked back to the phone. Wearing thin leather gloves, he dialed then glanced to his watch. 11:14.

After three rings, Kipling's voice answered sharply, "Hello?"

"The early bird gets the worm," Nix said, the code, and hung up.

*

Andrew had noted two of the four lights were turned off just before 11:00. What appeared to be the bathroom light had been turned on for five minutes, then shut off. What seemed a bedroom light then turned off. Only one light was still on, which Andrew figured was another bedroom. Things were winding down for the night.

But at 11:15 three lights in different rooms came on in quick succession. He heard a muffled shout from inside the house.

He felt his pulse quicken. What was happening, and why so quickly?

Clearly someone besides Kipling was there. If it was Kennedy, Andrew would know him from the FBI pictures: a squat build, a round sour face, jet-black hair, probably a stubbly beard, looking older than his thirty-nine years.

The back door opened only inches with obvious caution. A

man's head eased out, listening, quickly looking around. Andrew tensed. The man stepped fully outside. Through the goggles, Andrew saw a scowling Kipling, two hundred muscled pounds wearing only jeans and squinting into the darkness. After a few moments he went back into the house and the door closed soundlessly.

Why was he doing that? Andrew worried. What had caused the sudden lights in the house? In the still night quiet he heard what sounded like the door at the front of the house, the hinges yawing. Checking things out from the front door? Why now?

The obvious answer was a tip off. He felt his body tighten, cold shivers racing.

*

Inside his bedroom, Kennedy was moving quickly, throwing clothes into a suitcase, grabbing up shoes and looking for his wallet. Ace, the pit bull, was moodily watching from the hall.

Kipling walked down the hall and stopped at the open door to Kennedy's room. "Darker than the ace of fucking spades out there," Kipling cursed low and turned into his own bedroom. He grabbed a rifle and jammed in an ammunition clip.

Nerves playing, Kennedy whispered angrily out into the hall. "Well that's fucking great. Don't even know if somebody's watching us. If we're into a firefight, I want to know where it's gonna come from *before* it fucking comes."

Kipling threw on a shirt then zipped on a loose bulky coat. He dropped several ammunition clips into its pockets. He picked up a second rifle and swept a pistol off the dresser, dropping it into another pocket. He crossed into Kennedy's bedroom, "Well I just can't be sure either way." He leaned one of the rifles in a corner and said, "It's loaded." He threw a spare ammo clip onto the bed.

Kennedy's anxiety was more controlled now. "Have Ace check it out before we walk into anything. I'll grab all the other stuff."

"Alright."

With rifle in hand, Kipling led Ace to the front door, Ace smelling the growing fear in the air. Before opening the door, Kipling whispered angrily to the dog's ear. "Get him, Ace. *Get him.*" Ace fully understood, a growl deep in his throat and his body quivered.

Kipling opened the door slowly and whispered again, "Get him, Ace."

Ace raced out into the front of the property, his eyes searching for quarry. He ranged across the front of the wide property, dashing behind trees and along the ditch. He ran along the road, his head in the air smelling. Kipling could hear the angry growls.

Ace found nothing. Kipling moved out from the door and crept along the front of the house and around the side of the house to get to the back yard, Ace with him.

At the back corner of the house, Kipling knelt, holding Ace, looking into the blackness of the deep yard. He whispered, "Get him, Ace."

*

Andrew lay flat 250 feet back in the darkness, rifle aimed, watching Kipling and Ace through the night vision goggles. He knew with certainty there had been a leak. They were going to make a break for it. But they weren't sure if they were yet being watched.

It would be very useful to take Kipling alive and find out how insider informants were contacted. It could very well be through The Watcher. To learn how to contact The Watcher, to learn anything about The Watcher, would be a major break.

But there was also someone else in that house, maybe Kennedy.

Maybe he could take both alive. He didn't want to give himself away by killing the dog. And he didn't want to kill Kipling if he didn't have to. His heart was now pounding. He had never killed a man.

Ace rushed into the thick grasses, snarling, searching, seeking, dashing back and forth nearer the house, gathering more and more intensity in this odd midnight hunt. Half crouching, Kipling moved further out into the yard, peering into the darkness, his rifle pointed.

"Get him, Ace," Kipling whispered, encouraging.

Ace stopped a hundred feet from Andrew. His growl intensified, his nose feverishly working the grass. When Andrew had first arrived he had taken a position at that spot a hundred feet closer, but had soon moved back. Ace snarled as he detected the scent more fully. He sniffed the grass greedily. He lifted his big head, his nose working the air, eyes probing in Andrew's direction.

Ace saw the goggles. His killer eyes widened as he fixed on Andrew. His lips curled baring his fangs. One unbroken bloodcurdling growl came leaping from deep in his throat.

"Get him, Ace!" Kipling yelled and dropped to the grass.

Ace raced toward Andrew with the promise of flesh-tearing death. Andrew fired, hitting Ace's bounding shoulder. But it took the second shot, piercing his chest, to stop him. Ace toppled with the hard punch of it, his hurdling body rolling to a convulsing death stop within feet of Andrew.

Kipling fired two wild shots as he got up and ran back toward the house. Andrew yelled, "FBI! Stop! Put down your weapon!"

Andrew swore to himself as Kipling ducked into the rear garage instead, sliding past the Monte Carlo. He heard the front door of the house open again. Kennedy, or someone else, was out of the house now too!

Andrew yelled, "Kipling! This is FBI! Put down your weapon and come out!" His heart was racing.

He saw the other man—it was Kennedy!—dashing from a corner of the house and into the rear garage from the other side. They were going to try to make a break for it in the car.

Andrew barked. "We have you surrounded! Don't try to mess with us." It wasn't approved FBI text, but Andrew was angry, and afraid, because maybe they suspected they weren't actually surrounded. They would have a good chance of getting away if they could get the car maneuvered around and out to the driveway at the front.

He heard the Monte Carlo's engine start. Two shots came from somewhere in the garage, not well directed shots because Andrew was lying flat and almost impossible to see. But it was clear they weren't going to be intimidated. They were shooting with every hope to kill.

The Monte Carlo began to move out of the garage, Kennedy driving, ducked down behind the steering wheel. Andrew saw Kipling's head bobbing. He was outside the car, on the other side of it, keeping tucked low and using the car as a shield. Kipling would give cover fire, staying with the car as it moved out.

The headlights came on with a burst of light washing the whole yard, exposing Andrew. He fired once, punching out the left headlight. But Kipling also let go two shots aimed at Andrew's now known position.

Kennedy swung the car a sharp ninety degrees, the right headlight like a searchlight sweeping across the deep yard, the car not on the smooth tire tracks but bouncing over the uneven terrain. The light momentarily blinded Andrew.

He realized their plan. Kipling would keep using the car as a shield while it made the full 180 degree turn and got close to the house. Then he would dive into the house and run through it, shielded from Andrew's fire, then out through the front yard to join the car on the road.

He fired three quick shots into the side of the car, hoping Kennedy would give up. But the car continued forward, no surrendering. Kipling fired back another two shots from behind the car as he ran along with it.

The car's turn was now a steady arc to make another ninety degrees. Andrew took aim. He knew he wouldn't miss. He was going to kill a man. Three shots pounded through the driver's side window. The car rolled to a stop.

Kipling jumped away from the car and hurried along the garage wall in the darkness. Being a gunman and wearing a bulky coat, Kipling might be wearing chest armor, Andrew thought. He knew Kipling would make a dash across the yard a hundred feet to the house for protection then out through the house to the front. If he did, he might get away, clear away.

He saw Kipling's rifle swing up to take aim. Andrew was already aimed. He fired once, a headshot in case Kipling had body armor. He instantly fired a second round to the chest for good measure. Kipling's body slid down the wall and slumped, his back against the garage.

Andrew waited a full minute. He heard nothing from the car other than its quiet idling. He made his way forward to the car. Kennedy was slumped dead, one of the shots in the head.

When he was got close to Kipling he saw he was dead, too,

blood coming from his forehead, and also from his chest. No chest armor.

*

From a payphone outside a darkened country store two miles from Kipling's house, Andrew phoned Lawrence. It was 11:40.

"Are you sure both are dead?" Lawrence said.

"Very."

"You sound rattled."

"I am. I've never come this close to getting killed. And I've never killed anyone before."

"You did exactly as you had to, Andrew, and you did it well. A very good thing you were there."

"They had to be tipped off."

"As I feared might happen," Lawrence said.

"What are you going to do about the takedown?"

"I'll call it off and send a team out to the property to clean things up."

"They'll know you're working with someone now. The secrecy of my assignment is blown."

"It's a loss, but couldn't be helped. But your *cover* isn't blown, Andrew. No one is going to learn who *you* are. I want to keep that safe."

"What are you going to say?" Andrew said.

"That I took steps to countermeasure the serious possibility of a leak. That I brought in some outside help, and the details must remain confidential to me alone."

"There'll be a lot of questions…"

"None of that is your concern. Go home and get some sleep. But I want you to come to the lake house tomorrow."

*

It was after 1:00 a.m. when Andrew got home. He sat in the living room in semi-darkness, his mind hyper alert, waves of anxiety ebbing and flowing.

Tonight he could have been killed. And he had killed two men. And nobody was to know except Lawrence. He had been in Philadelphia only two weeks and almost been killed, and he had killed two men. There was no fellow agent to talk to. He was just to lock it up and throw away the key.

He heard the bedroom door open and Madeleine's footsteps on the upstairs hall. He had told her that evening that he was doing surveillance and that he would be very late getting home.

As she came down the stairs wrapping a housecoat over her nightgown, she said quietly, "You're back. Are you coming to bed?"

They had shot at him, wanted him dead. He would not have come home.

She came into the room and could see him better now, saw something was wrong. She sat beside him on the sofa and looked at him, saw his anxiety. "What is it?"

He looked at her a few moments. He leaned over and hugged her close. It was not at all like him to be so somber. After a moment, she gently pushed him back to see his face, her eyes fearful. "Andrew, what is it?"

He didn't know if he should tell her. He took her hand and stroked it. He knew he had to tell her, at least part of it. "I killed two men tonight."

She clutched at his hands, her eyes horrified.

"It wasn't supposed to happen. I was just supposed to watch the house."

She kept looking at him, shock on her face. "You were alone?"

He nodded. “I had no choice. They fired on me. They tried to get away.”

She covered her mouth with a hand, the other clutching his arm. “Are you alright?”

He nodded. “The SWAT team hadn’t arrived yet.”

She began to cry, “Andrew—”. Her hand went across her womb.

He got up, a sudden angry energy flooding. “I *know*, Madeleine.” His voice rose. “It’s not what I expected to happen either. But it did. That’s life. Don’t you know I know, damn it? I can’t control everything.”

She looked down, a quiet sobbing.

“Don’t you know that I know what it would be for Chris not to have his dad?”

She tried to stop sobbing, “I’m… sssorry, Andrew.”

After moments he calmed himself and sat back down and held her. “I’m sorry, Maddy. I know more than anyone what it would mean. I think about it every day. I love you and Chris and the baby more than anything.”

Her lips trembled. “And we love you…more than anything.”

He kissed her wet cheeks.

CHAPTER EIGHTEEN

WHEN ANDREW ARRIVED at the lake house late the next morning, Lawrence was in a chair on the verandah looking out at the water. He appeared meditative, a faraway look in his eyes. Even when Andrew announced himself, Lawrence was slow to respond. He finally got up and said, "Let's go inside."

They sat in the living-room. Andrew was the first to speak. "I've never killed anyone before. And I've never come as close to getting killed myself."

"How was Madeleine?" Lawrence said.

Andrew was struck at the leap. "She took it very hard."

"But she doesn't know anything more?"

"No, nothing, but it's not easy." A pause. "Last night was big for me."

Lawrence's voice was slow, a mix of respect and compassion. "I know, Andrew. And I know that being alone makes it so much harder. But you have to work alone, no one else. And you are the only *possible* person for this assignment."

Why was that? And why just him, alone? Was it all those reasons Lawrence had enumerated before, the special attributes and skills, the plane? Andrew sensed it was something more, something else entirely.

But he said, "And me knowing about Sylvie dying from the abortion. Am I the only one who knows?"

Lawrence's eyes moved to him. He nodded.

Andrew looked at him moments before speaking. "You of all people know that telling me laid a big responsibility on me. Even though it was long ago, there was a death. You orchestrated the abortion, a crime, and I'm an officer of the law."

Lawrence's eyes only watched him.

"And how was it that nobody pinned you for setting it up? The abortionist would have been charged, would have identified it was you to get leniency."

"You're very good, Andrew. I knew you would be." He took a deep breath. "There is more to things than I've told you. First, last night was really only…a side show."

Andrew felt himself tighten. Killing two men and almost getting killed himself was a side show?

"And your analysis is correct," Lawrence said. "There was, in fact, no abortion."

Andrew felt anger spiking. There was a big hole here. He stood up. "A side show? What's going on? And why tell me about her at all then? What has she to do with anything?"

"Everything." Lawrence looked steadily at Andrew, but spoke calmly. "You have to listen. Please, Andrew."

Andrew locked eyes with him.

"Andrew, will you listen? Please." Lawrence's hand motioned to him to sit. "Please."

Andrew could feel his heart pounding. He had to compose himself, hear Lawrence out however much he didn't want to. He sucked in a breath and sat.

"I was to take Sylvie to the abortionist a particular night. She showed up late at my place. She said she didn't want to go through with it, wanted to tell her mother. She was angry, crying, hysterical. She yelled at me, said I took advantage of her, said, 'Why did you have to do it? I trusted you.'

Lawrence became agitated at the memory. Fear and anger boiled in me. I tried to calm her. It only made her worse. She lunged suddenly, her eyes blazing, punching me hard in the face, totally unexpected. I was already so on edge… my reflexes…"

Andrew felt himself tighten.

Lawrence's hand trembled. "I hit her once, just once, with my fist, on the chin. I know it knocked her out. She fell straight back. Her head struck the brick hearth, a bone-splitting crack…"

He looked at the floor and blinked as if he saw her again. "Her eyes didn't move. Her face was serene. I knelt to her, her very pretty face, now just a child's. She wasn't angry with me anymore. She was gone, her young life over. There was nothing I could do about it, nothing…"

Andrew's insides were trembling. "No one knows of this?"

Lawrence shook his head.

Andrew got up, not looking at Lawrence. He walked to a side window and looked out as if to anchor in something *real*, something outside this room, his mind jumping. He turned to Lawrence. "What is the truth here?" His voice was sharp. "Tell me what's going on. Why I'm hearing all this."

Lawrence said quietly, "It's the only way."

"The only way *what*? *Why* did you tell me? This is *way* out of line!"

"It's the only way you might understand."

"Understand *what*? Stop talking in riddles!"

"Understand everything that's gone on in my life since then."

"Why *me*?"

"I need *you* to know this, *you*."

Andrew's voice rose in an angry surge. "This whole thing, getting me here, getting me the transfer east, was all a sham. Right? You wanted me for some other purpose. *What is going on here? Tell me.*"

Lawrence shot back with equal anger. "Do you think this is easy for me? I'm *confessing*, Andrew. I'm not going to get up and run away. You can arrest me if you want. But just listen first. Trust me a bit longer."

"*Trust you,* after you deceived me?" He looked at Lawrence with fire.

Lawrence's eyes pleaded for calm and he motioned to Andrew to sit again. Andrew took another deep breath. Yelling was of no help to either.

"I'm sorry," Lawrence said. He paused to let the waters calm. "I was so afraid. Please try to understand what I was going through, Sylvie's body lying there."

His body was shaking lightly. "What I did afterwards was so wrong. But try to understand, I was only twenty-one. All I could think to do was protect myself. I was jumpy, couldn't think straight at all. Nobody knew she was with me."

He walked the room, his nervous energy building. "Self-preservation, that was now uppermost in my mind. I tried to calm, think practically." His hands clenched. "It was just after dark. My car was in the apartment parking lot. I put the shovel in the back seat and opened the trunk. I went back in and rolled her in a sheet and carried her out cradled to my chest. I set her in the trunk, my heart pounding."

His fist rubbed at his chin. "I knew a forest not far from where I grew up, well off the old highway ten miles out of Buffalo. I was going to bury her. But…I couldn't do it. I just couldn't."

Andrew sat intensely still, watching Lawrence with full concentration, a chill taking hold.

"The only right thing I did, if you could call it that at all, was that I left her body lying in the back yard at her parents' house, left an anonymous note saying it was purely an accident, that no harm was ever intended, that she died instantly…that I was deeply sorry. Her brother found her in the morning."

Andrew stood and shouted. "Why are you confessing this? And why confess to me? Why shouldn't I turn you in right now? There's been no justice."

Lawrence was silent for long moments. His voice came, quiet. "No justice. I've been trapped in guilt, tormented for twenty-five years, my private hell. I had to speak, lock the door behind me so I couldn't run back to hiding anymore. I've locked that door now. You now know what no one else knows, what no one else has ever known. I can't go back to safety ever again."

Andrew sat silent. What had just happened?

"Do you understand, Andrew?" Lawrence's voice rose. "Yes, I am detestable. Yes, I am abhorrent. But I wanted to come clean with you. I didn't need to tell you or anyone else any of this. Or I might have just left it where I stopped the other day, Sylvie dying of a bad abortion. That would have been terrible enough on me. But I wanted to be clean with you. I had to speak."

Andrew sat trying to comprehend. He didn't shout this time. "It makes no sense at all, you and I ending right here, after you had me transferred here, brought me and my family here, telling me about my assignment, our secrecy, our special mission together." He looked questioningly at Lawrence. "Just to tell me this? End it right here? Me arrest you? And then it's over? What the hell is happening?"

"It doesn't make sense. I don't want you to arrest me yet. I'm completely in your hands now, Andrew. But you also need me out a while longer. And I trust you."

"Trust me? What does that mean? And I need you out for what? What's my next step in your plan? You must have a plan."

"I only wanted two things from you. First, to hear my confession. You are someone who knows what suffering long and alone is, Andrew, as I have, too. I only hope you'll have patience with me—not pity, not forgiveness, not understanding—but patience. I will turn myself in, but not yet. That's where I need your patience. What I did was so long ago, a lifetime ago, and I was never a suspect. I could have stayed completely in the clear forever. But…I can't live with it any longer. Please be patient with me."

"You have some plan. You must."

"I've made myself vulnerable to you in the hope that you would trust me now… at a deeper level. I've just put everything on the line."

What was he really saying? But what Andrew did register was that Lawrence's life for the past twenty-five years just shattered. And his future, what was there now for him?

"The second thing that I want from you," Lawrence said, "is to find The Watcher."

"Why are you talking about The Watcher? How does that matter?"

"I have good reason to believe that The Watcher ...is the man who killed your father."

Andrew was stunned. He stared at Lawrence. "How...what do you mean?"

"I know things that nobody else does. But I needed help, your help, the one person who has more reason than anyone to want to find The Watcher."

Andrew was still taken aback. "You're convinced you know who killed my father?"

"I wouldn't have told you all that I've just told you unless I was. I may be wrong, but I've just placed my bet on it—everything I have."

"Your plan in arranging my transfer, this was always the real purpose."

"I told you when we first met here that finding The Watcher was one goal. But, yes, you're right, it was my real purpose. I want it to be your *only* goal. Find the man who killed your father. That's why I wanted *you*."

"But still—."

"This is the most delicate operation I've ever undertaken, and it must remain between me and one agent. It's the only way it will work."

"All the secrecy...does Washington know?"

"About you, yes. But they think you're part of the conventional investigation into The Watcher. But what we will do is off-record, unauthorized, because we will not always operate to Bureau protocol. I want no paper, no reports, no one second guessing me. If it's the difference between following the rules and not finding him, or breaking the rules and finding him, I choose the latter. I considered the question—who but you would be willing to do this? Who but you would bend things to breaking to find your father's killer? I take full responsibility to the Bureau for what I'm asking of you. As far as you know, you're only following my directives, following orders, nothing more. We didn't have this… other conversation."

Andrew was silent, thinking.

"I don't want any leak," Lawrence said. "If what I know gets out to The Watcher, he'll be gone, underground, never found. We'll have lost this chance."

Andrew considered what this might mean for him, finding the evil man who killed his father, who shattered his young life, who haunted him for twenty years. He looked at Lawrence and spoke quietly. "Sylvie's death, you've confessed to me. No running anymore. I understand that part as much as anyone can who has just heard it. But you've tied that with wanting me to find The Watcher. Why is it tied with that? Why is it critical for *you* to find The Watcher, and now?"

"I admired your father. He got no justice. I saw you as a young boy, felt your struggle, saw how your grandpa was. It was heart-breaking for me, Andrew. You got no justice."

"But my father…it wasn't your fault they didn't find his killer."

Lawrence went deadly silent. He slowly crossed the room twice, his face ashen, defeated. "Guilt, Andrew. Sylvie, I failed her in not confessing to my crime twenty-five years ago. It would be no redemption now, but I want to do something to make amends in some way before I face my colleagues, and the Courts. I've worked long for justice, but I've failed it fundamentally in my own life.

I hoped that finding and bringing The Watcher to justice would offer some amends to me as well…for what I did. I might find a peace that I've never had since I was twenty-one. And it would bring to a close something for you."

As heartfelt as the answer appeared, Andrew felt it was off. He observed Lawrence without speaking, feeling far from certain about the truth and wholeness of what Lawrence was saying, still troubled and wondering why solving the case of The Watcher had the potency, the symbolic potency, Lawrence claimed it held for him.

But what Lawrence was offering him at this moment was so enticing. He would let Lawrence lead, see what he could learn, see what came of it, until he had reason to do otherwise.

"Feelings are running high in me," Andrew finally said. "But I'll hear you out. You said you're convinced The Watcher killed my father."

Lawrence nodded. "But even more," and his eyes focused sharply on Andrew, "…I believe I know who he is."

Andrew felt sudden energy, his body rigid, his voice tense. "Who?"

CHAPTER NINETEEN

"SALVATORE VELEZ," LAWRENCE said.

Andrew stared at him. "Salvatore Velez," Andrew said like it had a mystical quality, reverberating deep inside him, the man in the black hood all those years ago, two holes for the eyes. The man had a name, a name he knew he had never heard before. "Who is he?"

"A very clever criminal. He headed an organization in Buffalo—bank jobs, jewelry stores, Wells Fargo heists, fencing operations, and importantly, extortion. But there was eventually so much heat on him he couldn't operate, and he couldn't run forever. But he was clever. He died in a high-speed police chase in 1955 in the Catskill Mountains, his car slipping out on a turn, tumbling over a cliff, exploding in a fireball in a ravine below. All the occupants were incinerated. But the bodies couldn't be identified with absolute positivity."

Andrew watched Lawrence carefully. "You mean you believe… he only staged his death?"

"Yes. Once 'dead' he could alter his appearance, take on a new identity, fabricate a past, no one looking for him."

This seemed to be a leap of speculation and Andrew wondered how sound it was. But Lawrence was pinning a lot on it and he was no fool. "The man at my house, shorter than average. Does that fit Velez?"

"Yes, he is very likely shorter than average. I'll have something on that to show you later. Another key point about him—he was notorious for his use of insiders, corrupt police, always had ears on the inside."

"Like The Watcher," Andrew said.

Lawrence nodded. "Velez's name was well known in law enforcement in several States because he could outfox authorities."

Andrew's thinking suddenly shifted, beginning to see the possible shape of things from twenty years ago, an opening in a cold file. "Did that pickpocket, Macky, know Velez?"

"My belief—yes, probably even once worked for him. Your father ran a rap sheet on Macky that night. Macky had operated in Buffalo for many years, years when Velez was active there. Macky was considered one of the best pickpockets there was. He could slip a key from a security guard, a warehouseman, that kind of thing, a talent very useful to a criminal organization. But Macky was on the run, wanted in New York State, which explained why he was working his trade so far away, in Philadelphia."

"You think Macky saw Velez at the gala, recognized who he was."

"Yes. Velez would never expect to be recognized by anyone then. It was six years since his 'death'. He presumably had a new look, a new persona, and was well away from Buffalo, an unknown. But I think Macky saw through it. Pickpockets are observant. They have to be in their trade. It would explain why Macky was killed, and so urgently, unplanned, on a public street."

Connections quickly ran in Andrew's head. "Macky, a harmless nobody. His killing wasn't by some punk to settle some score, not a sudden killing like that, like you say. There was some huge reason. And the man who came to my house was no punk, and he had huge reason to come, had to have."

He looked at Lawrence. "You believe Macky told my dad that Velez was alive."

"Yes. And I'm convinced that Velez suspected that that was the case. The officers at the scene said that as your dad tried to get Macky to talk, he lowered his ear to him, and your dad at one point looked suddenly 'puzzled'. They thought something was up. They must have talked about it to others."

"And it got leaked to Velez, through an insider informant. That would explain the lengths Velez went to…to keep it quiet."

Lawrence saw emotion filling Andrew, Andrew drawing inside himself. For the first time in his life, he had an explanation for his father's death—an evil man had wanted to keep his real identity hidden. At any price.

Lawrence watched Andrew, believing he was likely reshuffling his life, the 'what ifs'. What if Macky had already been dead when his father arrived, just a minute later? Words would not have passed between them. His father would be alive.

After long moments Andrew looked at Lawrence. "My dad's report, you said it didn't say that Macky talked. But it also didn't say that *nothing* was said, which is better practice."

"Yes. Saves ambiguity."

"My father would know that."

"Yes."

"Are you confident he would have known Velez's name, and how he worked?"

"Yes."

"And you think he would have been *that* concerned about insider informants in *that* case that he would omit putting in the report what Macky said?"

"He would know there was a real risk of a mole, or, importantly, that there soon would be. Velez would want to monitor the progress of the investigation into Macky's murder because it would really be monitoring the risk to himself."

Andrew sat thinking. "My dad would keep it quiet until he could organize some plan, keep that plan itself quiet, then hunt Velez without him knowing that anyone knew he was even alive."

"That's what I think. And there's more. As I told you, I was a brand new police officer in Buffalo in '54. Velez was still operating there then, a name well known to us. One of his 'signatures' was that people who apparently got in his way 'disappeared', just as Senator Booth described about The Watcher. Not left where they were killed. Instead, never found—not in a river, a lake, a dumpster, nowhere. Less evidence."

Andrew said almost to himself. "The hooded man took my father away… in the trunk. And Macky… you said he was being dragged toward a car."

He got up and walked to the window and looked out, silent for many moments. He turned to Lawrence. "But I'm puzzled. You, and the investigators twenty years ago, they knew everything you've just told me. So why didn't they solve this?"

"I told the investigator team what I'm telling you now, but

they were skeptical of my theory. Velez had been 'dead' for six years by then. But of course they checked out every man at the gala. Turned up nothing, certainly not Velez."

"Have you ever spoken with anyone about your theory since then, someone with influence?"

"No. I came to think it was probably wrong. Two years later I was also transferred from Philadelphia to Albuquerque. New challenges."

"But something changed. You said you know things that nobody else does. What's convinced you now it's him?"

"Senator Booth came to me, told me of an unknown extortion organization, many victims, many disappearances, most here in Philadelphia. His evidence opened my thinking again into what happened to Macky and your father. In digging further, I discovered there were more disappearances, more than Booth knew of. No one realized they might all be connected to one source until Booth told me his story. It hit a nerve. Then the brazen attack on the safe house, brazen like Velez."

"And it could never have been pulled off without inside information, another 'signature' of Velez."

"Yes. And something else. Booth said The Watcher is 'unknowable'. Velez always guarded his identity. He had never been arrested, never photographed. We only had a high school photograph when he was fifteen. He didn't want to ever be identifiable."

Andrew stiffened. "The hooded man at my home, hooded even in front of his own men. He didn't fear my father seeing him. He was going to kill him. But he stayed concealed the whole time."

"Exactly, Andrew. My thinking, my theory, appeared a lot less far-fetched. If Velez was alive it would explain why your dad's and Macky's cases have remained unsolved so long—that essential piece was missing in the puzzle all along. But put it in… and things fall into place."

Andrew felt caution in himself. He wouldn't swallow the theory whole. He had been too many times disappointed in hoping for answers. But still, it might be the closest he would ever get to finding the man who killed his father.

"My father's plan of twenty years ago—side-step the usual procedures to avoid tipping Velez off, close the net without him knowing anyone even knows he's alive—that's what you propose to do now."

"It's what I propose *you* do now. Pick up where your father left off."

Andrew felt a shiver.

"But I can provide more evidence than your father had because of the investigation that followed. I can narrow the work. Something had to have been overlooked. I believe Velez was at the gala, but somehow he eluded the investigation. Some piece is missing. I want you to find it."

Andrew felt oddly in two worlds—his own, and suddenly his father's, too. Did his father really know Velez was alive, know it was Velez who stood in their kitchen behind the hood, the two gunmen watching? His father had been so calm. He seemed to Andrew's memory to have shown no surprise that day, as if he *did* know who it was, and why it was. But he had told no one what he knew…for a reason.

And Lawrence had now offered that reason.

"Do you have any idea where Velez is?"

"He doesn't live by that name, of course. I checked all relevant records and data bases and vetted every Salvatore Velez living in the U.S. I knew it was a useless exercise even before I started. But based on The Watcher's activities, I think he's in Philadelphia, or somewhere near."

They were both silent.

Andrew stood up and walked to the window, the breeze rippling the water. "Is Booth's investigation, the conventional investigation into The Watcher, getting anywhere?"

Lawrence shook his head. "Nowhere. And whatever we learn, I fear he knows."

Andrew breathed deeply. Work alone. Find Velez, or at least The Watcher. He would need very good information. "I want all the files."

"I secured a copy of everything the Bureau ever had, everything the Philly PD ever had. And I recently acquired other documents on my own."

Lawrence took a palpable breath and looked a long moment at Andrew. Andrew was watching him. "I want you to know something else, Andrew, of a personal nature. Shame drove me to drug use. Although nobody knew it, ten years ago I was struggling with it. My life was a shell in so many ways—no wife, no child, no relationship, no love of any kind. I was spiraling down, consumed by ...self pity."

Andrew saw glimmers of Lawrence's past, a long struggle, the emptiness. What Lawrence had done was unforgiveable, but justice would come in its time. For the moment there was only the next step. "But something happened?"

"One day I read about you in the newspaper, the tavern fight, your incredible courage, the young boy I knew who had been through so much, but who risked all to help another. It reached a hand to me, Andrew. I was grateful."

"You sent that money."

Lawrence nodded. "The article said you wanted to pursue a career in law enforcement. I knew you would achieve whatever goals you set. I kept abreast of your progress." He paused, looking at Andrew as if he were weighing something. "You know, you don't get into the FBI with blemishes in your past. A stint in a reformatory—rejection was written all over your application."

Andrew was stunned. "You did something?"

"I knew people with influence. I went to Washington, to HQ. I made your case. An exception was made."

"What did you tell them?"

"Many things. About your father, about the impressive young man I knew you were, about your resolve, that I would…on any day…stake my life on you."

Andrew was quiet. He had ached to be accepted into the FBI. When his acceptance did come, he felt so honored, so unbelievably lucky.

They looked at each other. Andrew said, "If I don't find Velez, or The Watcher?"

Lawrence's voice was suddenly weighted. "You really mean… what about Sylvie? What about me?" He breathed deeply and a small tremor moved on his lips. "Either way I will… turn myself in."

CHAPTER TWENTY

VELEZ HURLED THE crystal goblet across the room shattering it against the stone wall. That was now two. Nix knew there would be more. He watched Velez fill a third goblet with the dark red wine.

He and Nix were in the 'stone chamber' at Velez's home, a spacious addition off the main house whose walls were made of rough cut stone, its floor black slate, its ceiling crisscrossing with timbers. The chandeliers were dimmed, a bright fire in the open stone hearth supplying the real light, casting shadows on the walls.

"We're going to look ridiculous!" His voice echoed in the cavernous room. The killing of Kennedy and Kipling had greatly disturbed him, shaking his confidence in their very well-paid network of informers. His voice boomed. "Our reputation is based on the *excellence* of our inside information, *timely* information. People pay us big because they know they can stake their *lives* on it!"

All of which Nix knew perfectly well. But Velez needed to rant and Nix accommodated.

Immediately on receiving a message by radio from an insider that morning that Kennedy and Kipling were killed the night before, Nix sought every scrap of information from all inside sources to learn what had happened.

"All the messages tell the same story," Nix said. "Nobody in the FBI or the Philadelphia P.D. knew that Kipling's and Kennedy's hideout had been located. Nobody on either force had been involved in that search."

"Then how was it discovered?"

"Lawrence made an appearance at the office late last night and said he had just received a credible tip about Kipling's location. That was the very first indication that his hideout was known."

"Lawrence alone received the tip? Him directly?" Velez said disbelieving.

"That's what he said. But here's the important point—he said he stationed one agent to watch the house while the SWAT team was prepared, and *that* agent is unknown to anyone else. That's not something we can protect against. Our insiders are helpless there."

Velez looked at his glass, swirling the wine before taking a deep drink. His voice was full and loud again. "Nevertheless, we'll be a fucking joke!" He drained the goblet then flung it with fury. He grabbed up another goblet and launched it, crystal smithereens accumulating.

"Maybe this was just a one-off," Nix said. "Lawrence got lucky, got some tip directly, and moved quickly. We didn't get notice in enough time to warn Kennedy. Just bad luck. We aren't a personal bodyguard service."

"It's not just bad luck. It's this secret help thing," Velez said.

"That made the difference here. That worries me, Lawrence doing something new, going outside the usual channels." He sank heavily into a deep dark leather chair. "He may sidestep us on some other matter, go to his secret helper again. I don't want to be outplayed again, no more surprises. I want to know *who* that helper is. I want to know what's going on." He slowly filled another goblet.

"Should we just kill Lawrence?" Nix said.

The notion stopped the goblet from reaching Velez's mouth. He thought a few moments. "Maybe one day. But until it becomes necessary I'd prefer not to bring the whole damn FBI down on us. Let's first do fact-finding as I said. If we find out who his helper is, we can soon learn what Lawrence is trying to do behind our backs."

"Behind the backs of our insiders."

"Same thing."

Nix pondered a moment. "I learned something more. Lawrence left his office at 10:30 last night, two hours before the SWAT team was to be dispatched. He said he was going home. Kipling and Kennedy were killed about 11:30. Lawrence was back at his office at midnight and called off the takedown. He already knew Kipling and Kennedy were dead. It was now only a clean-up operation. Thirty minutes isn't enough time for Lawrence to have driven from the crime scene to his office."

"Your point being…Lawrence couldn't have been there when they were killed. He had to have heard from his mystery help," Velez said, a faint smile forming. "I see where you're going. He heard by telephone, most likely at his home."

"Yes, the simplest explanation." Nix reached and tossed a small log onto the fire sending a burst of orange sparks upward.

Velez was more animated. "So we get his house telephone records. Check calls that came in last evening and find out who belongs to the number, his secret helper. Actually, let's go back a month, everything for the last month."

He leaned back in the deep chair, staring at the lively shadows dancing on the wall. Then his brow darkened, and his voice rose, "I don't want us to be outplayed again, ever."

His dark eyes searched the far stone wall. With an angry growl, he pitched the goblet.

*

Teresa Clemens, a seasoned long-time administrator at AT&T, got the call at home in the evening when she was on her second glass of sherry. It had been quite some time since she had had a 'special request,' as she called them.

Many years earlier, a very nice gentleman who said he was a private investigator had approached her and seemed to know that she was in embarrassing financial straits at the time. He had asked if she would do just a small thing for him—divulge the private phone records of a certain man believed to be having an affair. He had explained it was a difficult file because the man was being dodgy. Teresa herself had been divorced and knew the type exactly.

She had at first balked at the shameless insolence of the request. But the man then promised her so much money that her moral clarity became blurred and her trepidation was quieted. Fulfilling special requests had thereafter become an occasional occurrence.

This time the man asked her to supply information on all calls in the last month to and from the home phone of a certain Wesley Lawrence, 5 Link St., Philadelphia, who was also allegedly having an affair. She was to supply the phone numbers Lawrence called and received, the dates and times of the calls, including the names and addresses of the registered holders of those numbers.

She confirmed she could manage all that and hung up.

Now she was feeling tipsy. She enjoyed this mischievous cloak and dagger. But those men deserved it. She reached for another cigarette, poured a third sherry, and considered with delight what she would buy with the naughty lucre.

CHAPTER TWENTY ONE

WHEN ANDREW RETURNED to Lawrence's lake house the next day, he saw a stack of banker boxes in the living room.

"These contain a copy of all FBI and Philadelphia P.D. investigation materials in the two cases—Macky's and your father's," Lawrence said. "I've told you also that Velez has never been arrested, never printed, never photographed."

He laid a high-school class photo on the table, twenty young adolescents, pimply and awkward. "I cut this out of the yearbook and had it enlarged." Lawrence put his finger on one of the boys—olive skin, dark hair, dark eyes, and importantly, shorter than most of the other students.

Andrew studied the boy closely. Even at that age, fifteen, Velez looked bold.

"He never posed again," Lawrence said. "So what does he look like now? And what did he look like twenty years ago when Macky recognized him, and when he came to your house, the man under the black hood?"

Lawrence set a large yellowed newspaper clipping on the table. "This is a forensic artist's depiction of Velez age-progressed from fifteen to twenty-eight, his age at the time I was on the force in Buffalo. This is what authorities went on then. When Velez took your father, he would have been older, thirty-four. I went to a private forensic art lab a year later and showed them the high school photo. I told them he was a cousin of mine and had the lab do an age-progression to age thirty-four." He placed that portrait of Velez on the table.

Andrew noted immediately the similarities in critical features between the earlier drawing and this one from 1962. Two different forensic artists working from the same early photograph had produced amazingly similar results, a convergence that gave credence to both. The cheekbones had taken on more prominence, the face was broader and lengthened, the eyebrows were filled in, the chin was fully formed. The face had grown somewhat downward and outward. The bridge of the nose was a little higher, the cranium expanded. The eyes had narrowed, the mouth widened.

"Note the eyes," Lawrence said. "They say a person's basic look holds true throughout life, most notably in the eyes."

Andrew felt a visceral tension as he studied them, feeling the eyes that had peered at him from behind the black hood when he was seven, eyes as cold as death.

"Photographs were taken of sixty men at the party," Lawrence said, "most of them surreptitiously. I made comparisons with that last portrait. It was a great disappointment that not one man's picture squared in any probability. I knew that Velez would likely have had plastic surgery, made hair color changes, maybe added a mustache, glasses, and so forth. I accounted for that, but still nothing."

He walked to a cabinet and pulled open a drawer. "Of course, if any of them were Velez, he would have an olive complexion, something he couldn't change. And so his hair would look out of place if dyed blond or red, so even when he altered his appearance his hair was probably black, or dark brown, or maybe made graying to look older than thirty-four. His eye color would be dark brown; they hadn't invented colored contact lenses in 1961. Those are all things I looked for, but still came up empty."

His face showed deep disappointment. "I want you to know everything the investigators knew, everything I knew." He stopped a moment, introspective, like he was looking at an unfinished frustrating puzzle. "Something somewhere was overlooked. There had to be."

He reached into the drawer and took out a laminated 8x12 color drawing. He studied it a few moments, not yet showing it to Andrew. "Three weeks ago, I visited another private forensic lab and again gave them the enlarged high school photo, the only hard starting point we have. Velez is now fifty-four. Admittedly it's a difficult task to project what someone might look like at age fifty-four from a picture at age fifteen. But the science is much better now, much more reliable growth data today, allowing for better predictions of facial changes."

Lawrence set the laminated drawing on the table. Andrew looked at it with steel cold attention. If it was like Velez today, he had now developed jowls, his lips were thinner, his hairline somewhat receded. His face had grown a bit longer.

"The artist made a set of assumptions on hair color, style, and length, all favoring a narcissistic personality, reflecting the choices a man would likely make today, if he is no longer in strict hiding."

"You ran it through a photo-license check?"

"Yes. Nothing."

Andrew picked up the portrait. He took a deep breath and burned the image into his mind. This was the man he was going to find.

*

North of Philadelphia, just off 611, he pulled into a quiet motel, the Weeping Willows. He had seen it on his many trips to the aerodrome and decided it would suit. He wanted seclusion for a few days, free of all distractions, free of Madeline asking any questions. He had told her he had to be away on an investigation but would call her every day. She said she would have Nadine over for a good overnight visit, some girl time to talk about the baby.

Carrying one at a time, he toted eleven bulging banker boxes into the single-room unit. Then he rearranged the furniture. He moved the desk into the middle. He shoved the single twin tight against the wall. He moved the lamps to direct the light to the desk. He dragged the sofa-chair to one side of the desk to receive the stacks of files he wanted to keep within arm's reach.

He unpacked the boxes and arranged the materials: interviews and tapes onto a lamp table; bound summary reports onto the sofa-chair; loose documents and photographs categorized and placed in neat stacks behind the desk on the floor; detailed surveillance memos piled at the end of the bed.

He set up a coffee-maker he had just bought. The two-cup variety offered by the motel just wouldn't cut it.

He stood back and surveyed the room. The volume of paper

was staggering, thousands of pages, an initial investigation of almost 300 men, reduced in short order to 60, and ultimately a comprehensive drilling down on 15. He hoped he could sift through this mountain of paper finely enough to make it give up just one telling detail that had been overlooked.

He propped the laminated 'portrait' of Velez as he might look today on top of the television. He sat at the desk and looked around the room. There was a lot of paper, a very big haystack. He was under no illusion. Lawrence said the paper gave up nothing.

He looked at the portrait staring back at him, cold eyes taunting him. They would keep him resolute.

CHAPTER TWENTY TWO

THE YACHT, *MISS Nomer,* was under full sail under a sun-drenched sky. Velez was at the helm wearing a rakish seaman's cap working the magnificent teak and brass wheel. Nix stood nearby, his sunglasses glinting as he peered at the open water ahead.

Velez's tall girlfriend in white French bikini appeared with a silver tray bearing colorful drinks. She served one to Velez, along with a succulent kiss, then, with exquisite poise, served Nix, along with a sparkling smile. She floated away with a ballerina's grace, disappearing down a hatchway.

Nix had just made it to the dock moments before departure. At that point, Velez had been preoccupied with taking off and getting the sails up as quickly as possible. With *Miss Nomer* now on a long straight tack, Velez could be attentive to what Nix had to report. He knew Velez would not be pleased.

"We hoped to discover who Lawrence's secret outside help is.

This morning I received Lawrence's home phone records—calls in, calls out—for the last month. He's not a big talker. There were three calls to or from the office—not his secret helper there, of course. A few calls out for pizza or Chinese. But there was the one call in, right on the money, 11:40 on the night Kennedy and Kipling were killed. It came from a payphone outside a general store two miles from Kipling's house. I'm certain that's how Lawrence knew what happened because twenty minutes later he appeared at the office and terminated the takedown."

Velez was not pleased. Nix could see his tension, his arms pushing needlessly against the wheel. "A payphone. So we can't trace who called Lawrence?"

"No."

"We're absolutely no further ahead."

"Well, we know he didn't use his home phone to call *to* his secret help, at least not in the last month. But he had to be communicating somehow, secretly."

"Maybe meetings away from the office. Let's tail him when he's not at the office. See if he's doing secret meetings anywhere."

Nix nodded. "It's become more imperative now."

Velez looked at him. "What do you mean?"

"We just got a new customer—Lorenzo Marza. The job's within Lawrence's bailiwick. It's a big job, difficult too, but an opportunity to erase doubts about The Watcher's abilities."

Velez's finger tapped on the wheel with anticipation. "Good. So tell me about this Mr. Marza."

*

With infinite disdain, Lorenzo Marza considered the cheese sandwich on the dinky paper plate, one thin, dry, plastic-like slice of cheese lying on stale white bread. No butter, no lettuce, no mayonnaise. No flavor.

He thought of Parmesan tortellini casserole, garlic chicken, and a good Chardonnay. He hurled the sandwich into the prison-orange wastebasket.

Marza was the head of a wide ranging, prosperous drug organization. He was rich, very rich. He had everything—the houses you dream about in places you dream about, the fast cars, the faster women, the best restaurants, the usual baubles—everything, except, at the moment, his freedom.

He was in custody awaiting trial. For three months he had lingered in the dank, dirty, stench of a jail. Three months was a very long time for a man like Marza, a man used to the high life.

But as rich as he was, he was still in jail. You don't get bail when you're charged with double homicide and one of the victims is a five-year-old girl, and when you have serious priors and are not, in any other respect, a good citizen.

Still, he would soon be walking free. Things were underway.

Not that he wasn't guilty. Of course he was guilty. He had gunned down Ted Filion on the street with a rather loud submachine gun. Filion was a guy who needed to be dead because he threatened the smooth running of Marza's operation.

As for the five-year old kid, how was he to know some mother and her kid would be walking on the sidewalk at that late hour, or that they would turn the corner just when he was spraying bullets all over the goddam place? The kid should have been at home in bed at 10:00.

What really got to Marza was his own stupidity, that he had grabbed the machine gun from his side man in the first place. He never did his own shooting. Why, as the boss, would he ever need to pull the trigger? But he had become enraged in the moment. Filion just stood there defying him, brazen, even smiling his twitchy mouth, throwing everything back in Marza's face, not cowing to his threats. Marza had felt his mind reeling like his brain had been dunked in testosterone. So he'd made a split-second decision, if you could call it that, to kill Filion then and there. He had grabbed the Heckler and Koch 9mm machine gun from his side man and just let Filion have it, although not without some initial aiming problems.

He wasn't very adept with a machine gun, never having fired one. The kicking recoil took a little getting used to as Filion ran away. He'd managed almost two hundred feet before Marza could get the juddering, jerking barrel to stay in one spot, to get the spray off the bricks and parked cars and onto the quickly receding Filion. Where the other bullets were flying he didn't know.

He hadn't confessed, of course, and was never going to confess. If they wanted his head, they were going to have to prove he was there at the time, and that he was the one who pulled the trigger. They would have to prove every element of the offence, proof beyond a reasonable doubt.

But he was going to make sure they couldn't prove a thing. There was a lone witness, Fleming, a men's clothing wholesaler who happened to be sitting in one of the parked cars he sprayed. Neither Marza nor his side-man had noticed anybody around. The girl's mother was in so much shock she couldn't remember seeing anyone. Fleming was probably slouched down when the bullets were flying and he had given a description of what went down, later identifying Marza from photos as the killer. It was Fleming who had called the ambulance for the girl, but there wasn't much hope there, machine guns packing a wallop.

So the question was, what to do about Fleming? The prosecution's case turned on Fleming identifying him. Take that out and the case would fall like a house of cards. He didn't want Fleming flatly rubbed out because that would look obvious and serve to put the heat on him forever for another murder. What he needed was Fleming to testify in court, but have a serious case of uncertainty, back away from a positive identification of Marza. Killing Fleming would be easy, but pulling off an intimidation of Fleming that would stick and hold under the pressure of a prosecutor in a courtroom, that would be much more difficult. It would take special talent.

The problem had occupied Marza's mind for months. The police had locked-down surveillance on his people, aggressive, around-the-clock surveillance so tight they couldn't take a piss without being followed and notes taken. Make any move against Fleming and the police would be on it like a cat on a woolen ball. And Fleming was also getting around-the-clock police protection.

So, what to do about him?

Marza had put out the question and had learned through an invisible connection deep in the underworld that there was one outfit that could do it—The Watcher. Nobody knew who The Watcher was or where he was. Nobody went to The Watcher in a conventional sense. It was a one-way street. You asked, and if the thing you wanted done was something that interested him, he would let you know.

Frying in the electric chair was a fate Marza desperately wanted to avoid. So two weeks ago an advertisement seeking vintage stopwatch parts had been put in the *New York Times* on his behalf. And arrangements were made.

CHAPTER TWENTY THREE

IT WAS MIDNIGHT of the fifth long day at the motel. Andrew sipped a black coffee as he sat on the edge of the bed, his eyes bleary. It was dangerous to venture close to the bed let alone sit on its edge, the pillow and soft linens a siren's call.

He got up and walked to the middle of the room and did a few stretches. He needed to resist the bed. He had set goals for himself each day, today's unmet.

The room, once orderly, now appeared in chaos. What had been neat piles of documents were now indiscriminate masses of paper on the floor like someone had taken a push broom and spread things around to hide every inch of the carpet. No level surface area in the whole room—not on a table, not on a chair, not on a counter—was devoid of paper. Except for the bed. Or at least that part of the bed where the pillow was, plus the four feet he curled on to sleep. The rest was a sprawl of documents that spilled onto the floor.

He had recruited the walls too, affixing dozens of large, colored, squiggly charts he had devised. There were even stick figures. The walls looked a lot like the walls in Chris's kindergarten classroom, without the smiley faces.

It was Lawrence's strong theory that Macky had been at the gala just before he was killed, and that was where he saw and recognized Velez, which would mean that Velez's new identity, although probably altered after he 'died', wasn't impenetrable.

At the time of the investigation the hotel management and gala organizers compiled a complete list of the 500 guests. Although all women were questioned, they were rapidly eliminated. When investigators looked at the approximately 300 men, they were looking for three possibilities: first, Macky's actual killer, a man described by the teenagers as white, solid, and at least six feet tall; second, the hooded man who had taken Andrew's father, a man who was shorter, probably five and half feet tall, and had a lower voice; third, any man whose background or current activities even hinted at involvement in criminal enterprise.

Initially every man had to be considered a suspect. Each was back-grounded and screened. Investigators whittled the numbers down, first to eighty, then to sixty. Eventually fifteen men were elevated to possible suspect status. For two years their phones were tapped, secret cameras took pictures, and intense surveillance was conducted. All produced nothing.

Was Velez's cover that good? Or wasn't he at the gala?

Andrew was acutely aware that Lawrence, after his careful review of these same files, hadn't discovered Velez among them. Yet

Lawrence was convinced Velez was alive, and was behind his dad's murder, and Macky's.

His first goal in vetting the material was to see if he could identify Velez, whom investigators could only refer to as >the hooded man.' If he could not find Velez, he would review the material looking for Macky's killer, the tall, white, solid male. If that produced nothing, he would look for anything missed, or an erroneous conclusion made about the men who might, in a wider sense, be connected with crime, and might have figured somehow into Velez's organization.

He reviewed the pictures, comparing them with the artist's portrait as Lawrence had earlier. Many fit the parameters of height, skin tone, voice, and age, but didn't square well enough with the portrait. Andrew decided not to give the portrait as much credence as Lawrence had, although it was still highly useful. He made generous allowances for error, but held the line at skull shape. Plastic surgery didn't go *that* deep.

Of those who had any reasonable possible resemblance, Andrew drilled down, reviewing every scrap of information about them, cross checking every detail. He considered that Velez's documentation would not be a legitimate U.S. birth certificate, of course. He would either have a false U.S. birth certificate, or he might be an immigrant with false documents.

He traced every piece of evidence on the dozen or so acknowledged immigrants who broadly fit the parameters and who had arrived in the U.S. between 1951 and 1961. Many had olive skin, many were shorter, and many had lower voices as indicated in police interviews.

Still, he came up empty.

So he broadened his search. Velez might have sneaked into the

U.S. but claimed to be born here, producing a false birth certificate. He paid special attention to anyone who had a shallow history in the U.S., anyone who did not have independent confirmation of family or work connections going back enough years, given that Velez had 'died' in '55. Again, he found the investigators spared nothing to verify all documentation through cross-checks where there was any possibility that the document might be false.

For days he had reviewed the interrogatories of the investigators, the wiretap transcripts, the background checks. He had read reports, reports, and more reports. He had analyzed the careful logic used in eliminating one suspect after another.

He now eased back in the chair, stretching his arms. He was exhausted. He closed a thick report and slid it to the side of the desk. He weakly lifted a fresh report from another box and set it in front of him. He stared at the cover for a moment, yawned, and looked over at the bed like a lover.

He got up and stared out the motel room window for several minutes watching the moving white dots of light on the distant highway. He let the drape close and walked back to the desk. He poured himself a coffee from the carafe without even looking at the carafe or the cup.

He sat down again, looked at the cover of the report, opened it, and began to read.

CHAPTER TWENTY FOUR

NIX, WEARING A dark suit and carrying a black leather briefcase, the quintessential lawyer, walked through the front door of a squat, professional office building. He didn't use the elevator—too slow for him. Taking two steps at a time he climbed the three flights of stairs to the top floor. He strode a length of corridor stopping at a stout oak door that proclaimed, 'Lorne Nix, Attorney-at-Law.'

He unlocked the door and entered the outer office. It contained a reception desk and two waiting chairs, although there had never been a receptionist or secretary or even clients. He locked the door behind him. He walked past the desk and across the thick carpeting to another door, unlocked it, and entered the inner office.

Again he locked the door behind him. He bent to a mostly concealed mini alarm pad on the baseboard where a tiny red light glowed. He entered the four-digit disarming sequence. There was more plush carpet, and on two walls hung heavy Persian carpets, all suited to muffle sound. There was a large desk with a phone, a wall of recessed shelving filled with legal textbooks, and a deep leather swivel chair. Set near the window was another table, massive mahogany, on which sat a radio transmitter, a microphone, and two reel-to-reel tape recorders. On one of the walls were the stuffed heads of two real tigers, their teeth exposed in an open snarl.

He glanced at his watch, 9:50 a.m., and looked out the window, light cloud in the sky. The weather report called for good weather throughout the afternoon and evening as well, no rain. That was good.

He took off his suit jacket and threw it over the chair. He sat at the table, switched on the transmitter and turned the frequency dial. From his briefcase he withdrew a thin, three-ring black binder displaying several colored tabs.

He opened the binder and flipped to the blue tab. His finger ran down a list of hotel names. He glanced again at his watch. 9:55.

*

In an upscale high-rise condominium several miles from Nix's office, Kell sat at a table by a window with the drapes drawn. He glanced at his watch. 9:57 a.m.

A small ham radio sat on the table. He raised its antenna and switched it on. He located a certain frequency, and opened a thin, black, three-ring binder with several colored tabs, identical to Nix's.

At precisely 10:00 a.m. Nix's voice came over the radio. "Group three, frequency K. Group three, frequency K."

Kell didn't know Nix, didn't even know his name, had never seen him, knew nothing about him. He was just a voice that came over the radio and gave instructions.

Kell quickly changed the frequency to K, a coded reference to a specific frequency. During longer communications, the frequency was changed several times for enhanced security. Fifteen seconds later, Nix spoke. "Blue Martha. Blue Martha."

Kell's finger opened the blue tab. On the left side of the page was a column of twenty women's names in alphabetical order. Opposite each name, in a column on the right, was the name of a hotel and the city in which it was located. Kell drew his finger quickly down to M. 'Martha' was the Hotel Clarendon, Philadelphia.

Nix said, "14 dash 115. 14 dash 115. End transmission."

The time was always expressed in hundred hours, 14:00. The room number was always given backwards. Beside Hotel Clarendon, Kell jotted '2pm, room 511'.

Two years earlier, Kell had been offered big money for small jobs, such as delivering a parcel to a train station locker without asking questions. He felt he had been hand-selected, and he was honored. He was paid well because he was clean, meaning he had no criminal record, had never been fingerprinted, was unknown to the police, was not on anyone's radar. Clean. And smart, fit, and single. Those were The Watcher's hiring criteria, all prerequisites.

Soon he was paid bigger money for bigger tasks, such as driving a car stashed with dirty cash across a border. Then one day he came home to find a shortwave radio transmitter/receiver in his apartment. He had made the big time. He was an enforcement cell member, one of the elite members employed by The Watcher for more daring tasks, with pay commensurate to risk, very handsome pay, more than he could ever make doing anything else. He never knew what he would be called on to do, but he had never been disappointed.

Next to the money, he liked the anonymity. Cell members didn't know each other's real names. You created a name, a first name only, whatever you wanted. He had decided on Kell. It was short and different, very different from his real name, Aloysius.

Kell came to respect how precise, how thorough, the planning for the assignments was. Things always went like clockwork. No cell member ever got hurt. No cell member ever got arrested. But if you ever were, you were promised the best defense attorneys money could buy, all without cost to you. So long as you kept quiet, wads of money would be yours. And your freedom would again be secured by hook or by crook. But if you weren't quiet, you soon would be, and on a permanent basis. There was no doubting that. He had been on enough assignments already to know that The Watcher's reach was long and unerring.

*

At 1:57 p.m., Kell walked the last block to the Hotel Clarendon.

He checked automatically for any sign of a setup, any car that might be an unmarked police car, any man or woman too stationary or too observant. The police were usually better than that, of course, but not always. He knew he always ran a risk, but that's why the money was so good: higher risk, higher return.

He entered the hotel and, as per protocol, took the stairs, not the elevator—fewer eyes. Only rambunctious kids took the stairs.

He knocked the customary signal on the door of room 511. The door was opened by Leader, not only his pseudonym but also his function. Sitting close around an oak coffee table were Steve, Franks, and Smithy. Kell never saw any of them except on a job. As he often joked to himself, he didn't know them from Adam.

He took a chair. There was no talk among them, no gestures of familiarity. They were a unit but they were there to focus solely on gathering the information they needed to do the job.

Leader laid a large color picture of a man's face on the table. They all studied it. The man had a narrow face and an unconvincing smile. "His name's Fleming. He owns a small clothing wholesale outfit. He's the key witness in a murder trial that starts in three days. He needs to have a serious memory problem. But we're under strict instructions not to hurt him. Terrorize, yes. Intimidate to the core, yes. Hurt, no."

Leader slid another photo onto the table, a picture of a small gravel parking lot and the rear of a brick building with a loading dock. "He's under police protection. Two officers sit in an unmarked car in the parking lot at Fleming's clothing warehouse. By the time we get there, Fleming will be alone inside, finishing up just before closing. But the officers will still be outside."

Leader said to Kell, "You and I will be in police uniform. We'll be riding in the back of a cube van. It's been painted and stenciled to look precisely like the vans that regularly deliver there."

*

At his warehouse, Fleming glanced out the window to the gravel parking lot. He was a jittery little man. Even after three months of continuous police protection, he still habitually looked out the office window to the police car for reassurance. It was there, of course, as it always was, two policemen in the front seat, the windows down.

The trial was always on his mind and made him edgy with worry. Well why wouldn't it, for heaven's sake? He was the *principal* witness in a trial against Lorenzo Marza, a criminal gang leader.

However, at no time had there been the slightest threat. But maybe that was only because he had good police protection. Even when he went home he had an escort, and a car remained outside through the night. He was a very important man at the moment.

*

A solid-black cube van with slanted silver lettering proclaiming 'Phil's Clothiers' turned into the gravel parking lot. The two policemen turned their heads to follow it in. Phil's Clothiers' vans made appearances several times a week. The policemen sat back comfortably in their seats.

The van driver and passenger, Steve and Franks, carefully noted that the police showed little concern, one of them turning the page of a magazine. The Watcher had planned well: routine is the biggest enemy of vigilance.

The cube van reversed and backed slowly to the raised loading dock bringing the rear door of the van almost flush to the wall of the warehouse. More out of boredom, the police watched Steve exit the driver's door and scan a clipboard. Still reading, he reached around and rubbed his back and made an awkward stretch, giving a slightly pained expression. Franks exited the passenger side and took a last draw on his cigarette.

Steve looked up from the clipboard and called over to Franks just loud enough for the police to hear, "Only a small delivery. You get it? My back's really acting up."

Franks nodded, "Ya, no problem," and stubbed the cigarette into the gravel with his shoe. He walked over and Steve handed off the clipboard to him. Franks walked to the rear of the cube van, squeezed up through the tight space between the van and the wall and pulled on the van's door cord, noisily drawing it up.

He climbed in and a moment later reappeared, trundling a trolley with a rack of suits and disappeared into the warehouse.

Steve stood in the parking lot, twisting and rubbing his lower back, watching a crow squawk in a tree. He made a half wave to the police to acknowledge their presence. The one on the driver's side nodded. If anything went sideways here and the police went into action, Steve was calmed by the knowledge that Smithy, who was concealed in the van with his Uzi submachine gun, would cancel them quickly.

Inside the warehouse Franks parked the trolley and approached Fleming who Franks could see standing in his small office, its walls made of glass from the waist up. Fleming watched Franks' approach. Franks appeared frustrated, flipping through pages on his clipboard. At the open glass door to the office, Franks said, "Hi. Phil's. I'm just trying to find your paper order."

Surprised, Fleming said, "I wasn't expecting that one yet." He glanced at his watch. "You're delivering a bit late today."

"Yeah, a bit behind. Damned order forms are mixed up. Just a second," Franks said. "Let me check the paperwork with my partner."

"We can just check my paperwork. The order will be here."

"I think I better check with him. I'm new." Franks turned and walked back toward the rear of the van.

Outside in the parking lot Steve was still rubbing his back and trying some back bends. He gave it a couple of quick jerks. He saw the policemen smiling at him. Steve called out, "Can't swing a bat anymore without throwing it out. Real temperamental." Their smiles broadened. Policemen know bad backs.

Fleming was shuffling papers at his desk to find the order. Franks approached, pushing the trolley of suits right to the office door. The trolley obscured Leader and Kell, two fully uniformed policemen, who were suddenly in the office. Fleming looked up, startled.

"Is there a problem?" Fleming said?

"Just checking who this guy is," Leader said, looking suspiciously at Franks.

Kell moved closer to Fleming as if in protection.

Fleming was somewhat incredulous. "He's with Phil's. Truck just came. Trolley's right there."

From behind, Kell's hand moved quickly and slapped tightly over Fleming's mouth and held his head as Franks held his arms. Leader closed the door of the small office. Fleming's eyes were wide with fright. Leader jammed a gag into Fleming's mouth and fixed a strip of duct tape over his mouth, cheek to cheek.

A brutal jerk and Kell rammed Fleming to the floor. Leader drew a short machete from inside his uniform. Fleming shrank against the wall, his screams muffled by the gag. Leader looked at Fleming then stepped to a mannequin. With one terrible blow Leader severed the mannequin's head. It fell into Fleming's lap.

Leader said, "Mr. Marza says hello. I'm going to explain some simple facts to you, beginning with the fact that you do not have, and will never have, police protection. We will always get to you. And it doesn't stop only with you."

Five minutes later, Fleming, shaking with uncontrollable fear, peered through the window and watched the cube van pull slowly away from the parking lot. He looked at the patrol car where the two policemen continued to sit on guard duty, relaxed and unbothered.

CHAPTER TWENTY FIVE

ANDREW PORED OVER the documents for another two days and most of two nights. It was now midnight. He always noticed when it came.

He had been reading reports tonight from interviews very early on when all the people who were at the party were being questioned. Those reports yielded a monotonous litany: nobody had seen Macky at the gala; nobody had seen anything unusual occur at the gala; nobody had had any money, jewelry, or other valuables lost or taken at the gala, or at the hotel at all. Except that wallet, of course.

He was fatigued from the endless hours of concentration and the growing recognition that nothing seemed to have been overlooked, that he could shed no new light on any of it, that he had no new insights. That he had failed.

He pushed himself back from the desk and rubbed his aching eyes.

At the end of each day, when he had finally exhausted his ability to sit upright and read, when his eyes were lumps of pain, he had gotten into the routine of lying in bed and listening to the taped interviews of the dozen or so men who had most interested investigators.

He took a tape and put it on the spool and wrapped the free end around the other spool. He hit the play button and stretched out on the bed. He heard the familiar sounds of one of the detectives clearing his throat before an interview began. He thought he could hear something unusual in the background. Sobbing?

The detective said, "October 13, 1961. 6:20 PM."

It was the day his dad had been taken.

The detective continued. "Interview conducted at the home of Detective Paul Locke. Interview and statement of Andrew Locke, age seven."

Andrew sat up. He heard the sobbing growing louder as a microphone was brought closer to him, age seven.

He was unaware that any such tape existed even though he knew he had been questioned at the time.

"Andrew," the detective began in a gentle voice, as fatherly as he could be, "I understand you can tell time."

He heard his young voice breaking with a sob, "Yes, sir." Andrew had never heard his child's voice before. There had never been any family recordings.

"What time did you arrive home from school today?"

There was a delay with more sobbing.

"Here's a tissue, Andrew. I know this is difficult. You're a brave boy."

His little voice broke in, squeaking, "3:45." Andrew heard his childhood self blowing his nose.

"When did the hooded man arrive?"

Andrew sniffled. "After five minutes."

"When did the hooded man and the other two men leave the house with your father?"

"I don't know, sir. I was worried for my dad." The sobbing intensified again.

"I know, Andrew. I know." The detective's voice was consoling, although there would be no consolation. "Would it be ten minutes later? Or a lot longer, like half an hour?"

"I don't… know… for sure… I think ten." His sobbing broke up the words. He struggled to get them out evenly.

"The man with the hood, Andrew, what color was the car he drove?"

"Green."

"What color were his eyes?"

"I don't know."

"Please try, Andrew. Try to see him and remember."

"I can't. I'm sorry."

The sound of uncontrollable weeping, a cry that swelled loud. He struggled over and over through difficult breaths to say, "Please…help my…dad. Please…help."

"We're going to do everything we can, Andrew. Everything." There was a tremble in the detective's voice. He called for water. His voice quavered. "Let's break for a few minutes." Andrew heard the detective sniffling.

There was a click. The recorder had been turned off.

He realized he was shaking. He got off the bed, walked to the door and opened it, and took a deep breath of the night air. Painful memories pushed to the surface and tears came.

After a few moments he heard another click, the interview resuming. He closed the door and went back and sat on the sofa.

"Are you doing better now?" There was a long pause. "Here," the detective whispered, "hold my hand." A pause. "Is that better now?" Another pause. "Andrew, you said the man with the hood, his eyes were only up to your dad's chin. Is that right?"

"Yes."

"How do you know for certain?"

"They were talking close together." He seemed to be catching his breath, still sniffling.

"His voice, do you recall, was it high or low?"

"Low…like Mr. Sadler's."

"Who is he?"

"The principal at my school."

Andrew recalled a file that referenced Sadler was interviewed. He was a baritone in the church choir.

"Did the hooded man speak the way you and I do? Or did he have an accent? Do you know what an accent is?"

Andrew's voice had begun to tremble. "When you say words… different because you really speak German…or Spanish."

"That's right. Did he have an accent?"

"No…he talked like us."

"Did he ever take the hood off? Did you ever see his face?"

There was no answer. Maybe he was shaking his head no. The detective asked nothing more. The sobbing worked its way in again, again overwhelmed, his crying louder and louder. The words he struggled to say fell out like small puffs of air, unintelligible.

But Andrew knew what he had said all those years ago… he

had said it, prayed it, unendingly for months, years, afterward. "Please help my dad."

He didn't move. The reels turned faintly for another minute. Then the player clicked and stopped. So strange to hear his voice as a child. Far stranger still to hear the very words he had spoken at that time.

He felt his body shaking again, the vivid memory of the struggling, defeated little boy crying in a corner for his dad to come home.

He sat in the silence of the room, the sound of his desperate cries in his head. He wished he could go back to be there with him, to hold him, to offer some comfort to a small boy who felt he had no one.

He finally got up, shut off the lights and lay in bed in the darkness.

But he couldn't sleep. "Please… help… my dad."

He was so young then, his innocence ravaged. Fragments of memories floated in and out, sharp and stabbing: The hooded man standing in the living room talking, his father quiet; his father holding him for the last time, looking at him for the last time, loving, brave, preparing to die.

All the years between then and now vanished and he was seven again, the aching so suddenly intense, that aching without a cure.

After a time, the pain ebbed. His breathing calmed.

Velez had coldly taken his father, coldly murdered his father, coldly shattered his young life.

He couldn't sleep. An hour passed.

He got out of bed and snapped on the lights, an anger rising. He walked to Velez's portrait and grabbed it close. "You killed my father. Killed me. But I'll find you. Nothing, *nothing*, will stop me."

CHAPTER TWENTY SIX

MADELEINE AND CHRIS ate breakfast on the floor in the family room as Madeleine watched the morning news.

The anchorwoman announced, "The trial of Lorenzo Marza is in its third day." A picture of Marza flashed on the screen, bull necked, a smug expression. "He's charged with the murders of Ted Filion and five-year-old Samantha King." A picture flashed of a bright eyed, wide-smiling little girl with a front tooth missing.

Madeleine stopped eating. The anchorwoman had a halt in her voice, "She was walking with her mother… and was killed instantly by stray bullets. In other news…"

Madeleine shut off the TV and stared at the blank screen for a moment. She glanced over at Chris who had not seen any of it, intent only on his cereal. She reached over and gave him a hug. He giggled at her surprise squeeze, trying to balance the milky cereal on his spoon.

"Don't squeeze me, Mom. I don't want to get it on my pajamas." He pointed to his primary yellow pajamas. "My teacher said yellow is *sunshine*."

Madeleine said, "And *happiness* and *warmth*. When you were little, you couldn't say 'yellow'. You said, 'Yeyow. Yeyow'". She poked him as she said it, making him squirm.

*

The courtroom was filled with spectators and the press, the tension in the room palpable. All eyes were on the witness, Mr. Fleming, whose strain was obvious. He traced a nervous finger along the wood trim of the witness box.

The DA was on the edge of open anger. Fleming was, after all, the key witness for the State. But he was not cooperating. The DA had stood ever closer to Fleming during the questioning and was now only two feet from him.

Marza looked on calmly, his eyes never wavering from Fleming.

The DA leaned in at Fleming. "Mr. Fleming, I'll ask you again. Please look at the accused." Fleming looked to Marza, but only a moment, his eyes unsteady.

The DA said, "Tell me whether he is the man you saw brandishing a machine gun."

Fleming's eyes flickered. Marza continued to look steadily at him. There was no threat to Marza's gaze, only cold composure. Fleming's eyes darted to a young couple, the parents of the deceased young girl. They tightened their handholding and watched Fleming, their faces showing terrible strain.

He looked back at the DA, his eyes imploring him not press further. The DA folded his arms and pursed his lips and waited.

Fleming was apologetic. "I just can't be sure now."

The DA fired back, "Mr. Fleming, you're under oath!"

Fleming swallowed. "I know."

"Look at the accused, Mr. Fleming. How far away is he?"

Fleming hesitated and said uncertainly, "Thirty feet?"

The DA was exasperated. "Yes, Mr. Fleming! Yes! About as close to you as the man you saw fire the gun!"

Fleming blurted, "but it was dark, and I was badly shaken that night. I could be mistaken. I just can't be certain. You can understand."

Marza's defense counsel rose to his feet, holding both of his hands in the air and shaking his head. "Your Honor, I have been patient. I have given the DA generous latitude. But I must now vigorously object. He is cross examining, even *badgering*, his own witness, at a point of critical testimony!"

The judge nodded and looked at the DA. He had crossed an inviolable line. Sheer desperation had driven him there.

The judge looked at Fleming. "Would it help if I gave you a few minutes to compose yourself?"

"No thank you, Your Honor. I identified the man who I thought might be the man. I assumed there would be other evidence that might point the same way, or to correct me if I was wrong. Now that I see him in person…"

The judge sat back with an air of significant concern.

Fleming sputtered, "It was d-dark. The police shoved picture after picture at me. I felt pressured."

The judge took a long breath and looked grimly at both attorneys. "Counsel, there will be a short recess. Please come to my chambers."

In the judge's chambers, the DA exploded in the defense attorney's face. "Marza got to him! Didn't he?"

The defense attorney held up his hand as if this was nonsense. "Witnesses can be fickle. You know that. They don't have to be in thumbscrews to correct their testimony."

"Knock it off!" The DA hit his fist on the table "Marza touched him, dammit!"

Marza's attorney yelled back. "How could he? He was in jail! His organization was under lockdown surveillance the whole damn time. Fleming was under extreme police pressure to nail somebody that night. A little girl, dead. There was blood in the air! We've seen it again and again!"

In the courtroom the murmuring spectators went silent when the attorneys returned. Marza's attorney leaned back in his seat and took what seemed to the spectators to be a satisfying deep breath.

The judge entered and climbed the two steps to the bench and took his seat. His gaze swept slowly across the room. It stopped at Marza. Without hurry, the judge opened the hardbound notebook in which he made trial notes. He removed the top from his fountain pen. He pressed the notebook open. He wrote for a few moments. Then he carefully replaced the top of his fountain pen and gently closed the notebook.

He looked again at Marza, then spoke quietly. "Mr. Marza, this case is dismissed. You are free to go."

Marza stood up, a smug smile on his face. He shook hands with his lawyer. He turned and pushed by two stolid policemen who didn't make easy way for him.

The young mother began to weep. Tears came to the young father as he tried to make his way along the bench to intercept Marza in the aisle before he passed. He almost made it. He leaned over the last two people in the row, trying to stretch out to the aisle.

With a barely controlled sob and a voice that trembled helplessly, he said, "Our daughter…"

Marza didn't acknowledge that he had heard, his smile still ripe. He pushed open the courtroom doors. Outside, at the bottom of the courthouse steps, he roughly shoved through reporters and jumped into a waiting car driven by one of his lieutenants.

As they sped off, the lieutenant said, "Isn't the law terrific?"

"Very smooth. How much did it cost me?"

"Three hundred."

"I thought it was half a million?"

The lieutenant smiled, "Three hundred. The Watcher says he hopes you're happy."

"Happy? I'll fucking say. I would've paid the half million and still been over the fucking moon. Fleming wouldn't have recognized his own mother if it wasn't convenient for me."

He eased back into the thick leather seat and watched the crowds scurrying along the sidewalks in the shopping district. "Take me to the best steak dinner in the city. And I want a couple of girls go with it."

The lieutenant smiled, then mulled aloud, "The Watcher does one hell of a job. I wonder who he is?"

Marza made a questioning gesture with his hands. "Well that's the genius of it, isn't it? Nobody knows. If we could know, then the cops could know too."

*

Lawrence heard a knock at his office door. "Come in", he called.

His assistant, Fiona Cummings, opened the door, an angry look on her face. "Marza just walked. The key witness, Fleming, couldn't identify him."

Lawrence felt like a weight had suddenly been added to his frame. He took off his reading glasses and set them on the desk. He turned in his chair and looked out the window. He spoke quietly, "We were watching Marza's men?"

"Around the clock. Those animals haven't been out of their cages."

"And Fleming was getting police protection?"

"Every minute." Cummings paced. "But somehow, *somehow*, Marza got to him. I don't know how he could've done it. It's a damn travesty. If I were that little girl's mother, I'd want to kill the slippery bastard with—"

Lawrence held up his hand. "Bring me the file, will you? Everything."

CHAPTER TWENTY SEVEN

THREE BRIGHT WHITE umbrellas shaded Velez and Nix from the late afternoon sun as they celebrated, seated at an ornate teak table at Velez's terraced slate patio near the water's edge.

Velez was jubilant as he poured the last of the Chablis into his glass. He held the empty bottle in the air to signal to the attendant by the house that he wanted another bottle. An hour earlier they heard the news that Marza had walked from the courthouse a free man.

Velez raised his glass to Nix. "To you, my friend. What a coup!" He grabbed another skewer of barbecued lamb and peppers from the silver platter. "But," he paused, "I must not forget vigilance. Where are we with our old friend Lawrence?"

It had been a week and a half since they had put a tail on Lawrence and Nix had not given him a report. "He doesn't have contact with anybody outside of the office," Nix said. "No visitors at his home. No meetings, very solitary. He has a lake house an hour and something north of the city on an isolated lake. No phone there, no neighbors, one long private lane in and out. He's been followed there on two occasions. They watch his road. Nobody but him goes in or out."

The second bottle of Chablis arrived on ice and the attendant quickly uncorked it.

"Still getting his phone records?"

Nix nodded. "Nothing new there."

"Maybe his outside help was a one-off thing, although I don't see why it would be. He hasn't solved his leak problems. Let's stay the course. I don't want to be blindsided again."

*

It was early evening and Lawrence had just arrived home from work when he got a call from his assistant, Fiona Cummings.

"You know we had Marza's people's phones tapped everywhere but got nothing from it," she said. "They were obviously instructed to stay quiet. But we know the habits of some of his people. One of his lieutenants frequents a little Portuguese restaurant and always takes a table in a certain corner."

"Yes, I recall seeing we planted a bug there in the wall a few weeks ago hoping he might come by."

"Well last night he did, with a friend who isn't on the inside about Marza. I'm going to play a part of the tape for you. It picks up with them just arriving. The lieutenant has obviously been drinking. His is the first voice, speaking to a waiter."

Lawrence heard the flecking sounds of a tape playing, then restaurant noises— murmuring conversations, cutlery against dishes. He heard an approaching voice, loud and harsh, noticeably under the influence. "Thanks, Afonso. Is he cooking *arroz de pato* tonight?"

"But yes. For you, always," the waiter said.

"Good, good." There was the sound of scraping chairs. The harsh voice was now subdued, conspiratorial. "What you said there, about the law watching us?" There was a crackling, wheezy laugh.

A new voice came on, thin, "Yeah, what's so funny about that?"

A rasping sound twice, a flint wheel on a cigarette lighter being flicked? A long pause, a metallic snap. The lighter cover closed? The harsh voice of the lieutenant, "Yeah, of course the law was watching us."

The thin voice, "Yeah, so what's the deal?"

The lieutenant said, "They watched us all day every day. Didn't see nothing because there was nothing to see."

A smoker's hacking cough and the lieutenant's voice continued. "The law watching us. We could play the watcher, too. And nobody sees nothing." A long wheezy laugh.

"You're talking in riddles."

"That's the way I like it. Okay, so enough about all that. You like duck? Get the *arroz de pato.* Comes with smoked sausage. The best, the best."

Lawrence heard a click and the tape stopped.

Cummings said, "What do you think?"

"Yes, 'play the watcher'. You said the other guy's not part of the organization?"

"No, just a friend of this lieutenant."

"So, under the influence, the lieutenant's kind of telling this other guy something, but kind of not. Would love to tell him something, but coy is the best he can do."

"Yes."

Lawrence mused, “Odd phrasing, ‘we could play the watcher, too.’ It’s like saying ‘put the watcher into play because we can’t do the job ourselves’. What else can it mean?”

“Yeah, that’s the thing.”

“It’s only conjecture that Marza somehow got to Fleming,” Lawrence said. “But if he did, how did he pull it off, and that kind of intimidation, while we had such tight surveillance?”

“It would be impossible. He had to have somebody’s help, like The Watcher.”

“But still, it doesn’t get us one inch closer to knowing who The Watcher is, if Marza even used him.”

“I know.”

“Okay, I want to pick up a typed copy of the transcript and think on this over the weekend. Can you have one ready for me if I’m there in an hour?”

“Will do.”

Twenty minutes later Lawrence left his home and drove to a payphone four blocks away. He called Andrew’s second line. As per the protocol, the phone was never to be answered. He left a message. “Andrew, we might have a break. Meet me tomorrow morning as soon as you can.”

*

When Lawrence left home and made that call from the payphone, a white Dodge Charger had followed him. It drove past him when he parked at the curb to use the payphone. The driver had observed him at the phone booth and penciled the precise time, 7:10 pm, and the street intersection of the payphone.

In the time they had been watching him, Lawrence had made only one payphone call, to order Chinese on his way home after work so it would be ready for pickup when he got there. If he wanted fast food tonight, why not call from home? the driver wondered.

The Dodge Charger then followed Lawrence down to the FBI offices. Chinese food? Maybe. Do they deliver Chinese to the FBI offices?

But twenty minutes after Lawrence entered his office, he was out again, and the Charger followed him back home. He didn't go anywhere else that night. No visitors. No Chinese.

It was not the driver's job to reach a conclusion about what he observed, just observe. He pondered, nonetheless. Making a call from a payphone four blocks from home after you just left your home, where there's a phone. Then driving directly to work where there are lots of phones.

It seemed odd, at the very least odd, but also suspicious.

CHAPTER TWENTY EIGHT

EARLY THE NEXT morning Andrew touched down on the grass runway and quickly did the one mile hike along the tractor path to the lake house, eager to learn of the possible break regarding The Watcher.

At the kitchen table, Lawrence unzipped a leather portfolio and took out an accordion file eight inches thick. "Marza," he said, and shoved the file across to Andrew.

Lawrence then slid a glossy picture across—a close-up of a sparkling-eyed child with a wide smile, a front tooth missing. Little Samantha King.

Andrew looked at it.

"A five-year-old bystander, gunned down," Lawrence said.

Andrew looked at Lawrence a moment then opened the cover of the thick file. A large picture of Marza's face looked back.

"We had him in custody, had him nailed. It went to trial but he walked. I'm reasonably certain someone got to the key witness, a guy named Fleming. It's highly unlikely Marza's people could have done it without outside help. We had them under very tight watch and Fleming had protection 24/7. His office phone and home phone were tapped. There was nothing there. No threats, no anonymous calls."

Andrew studied Marza's face.

Lawrence continued. "Nevertheless, I have reason to believe Marza had outside help, and I think it was The Watcher."

Andrew looked up quickly, expectant and eager. Lawrence produced a typed sheet—the transcription of the relevant section of the bugged Portuguese restaurant conversation. He handed it to Andrew.

Andrew pored over it for a minute.

"What do you think?" Lawrence asked.

Andrew nodded. "Yes, I see, 'play the watcher.' Sounds like somebody wanting to boast about some clever, secret goings-on. Knows he shouldn't, but as drink made its way in, a little something made its way out."

"That's my take on it, too. If Marza used The Watcher, Marza may give us something that leads us to The Watcher."

Andrew mulled. "So we don't know if Fleming was actually coerced by someone. But I'll pay him a visit and talk to him. See what he coughs up."

Lawrence nodded and got up. "Good."

A large photograph was still laying on Lawrence's side of the table, the photo upside down. Andrew's finger pointed. "Is that for me?"

Lawrence glanced to it and hesitated, reluctant. "I'd rather not. What a 9 mm machine gun does to a little girl. Same age as Chris."

They looked at one another a moment. Andrew motioned with his finger. Lawrence slid it across, still upside down.

Lawrence watched Andrew turn it over. He saw his jaw muscles clenching, his hands balling into fists. He looked like a powerful man set to explode. He looked at Lawrence a moment and took a slow deep breath and carefully slid the picture into the file.

*

Fleming worked late into the evening and decided to go to a bar before going home. He lived alone and, since the trial, felt more often like being around people and having a couple of drinks.

When he got home and entered his bedroom he was startled to see the window curtain shifting in a breeze. He always closed and locked the windows, especially lately. Had he forgotten to close it this morning?

He had just walked through the house and had heard nothing, had seen nothing out of place. He stood stock still, straining to listen. He knew he had to check the house, especially the basement, or he wouldn't be sleeping tonight.

He tiptoed from the bedroom, ears pricked, eyes darting. He moved soundlessly along the hall, through the living room into the kitchen. A door on one side led to the basement. He went to the door, held his breath, gritted his teeth, and snapped on the basement light. He listened for a few moments before starting down the stairs.

As he descended his knees felt weak. He checked every corner of the basement, even behind the furnace, *especially* behind the furnace. Then his breath eased. He must've just left the window open this morning; the night air had been warm. He clambered back up the basement stairs to the kitchen and closed the door behind him. He turned around.

Andrew was wearing a balaclava. "Long day?"

Fleming stiffened like he had been hit by a brick. He saw a fat pistol protruding from Andrew's waistband.

"Don't k-kill me!" Fleming sputtered.

Andrew led him by the arm to the bedroom. Beads of sweat formed on Fleming's forehead, his skin a distinctly unhealthy pallor.

Andrew pulled the gun from his waistband and forced Fleming to sit on the edge of the bed. Fleming stammered, "I d-d-didn't say a word to anyone. You people promised! I d-did what I was told! You saw that!"

Andrew could hardly believe his luck, an admission right out of the gate. He shoved Fleming onto his back and held one hand on his throat. "We heard some cop came around snooping, getting you to talk."

"No! No one came!" Fleming's voice was tremulous. "I swear it! Honest! I haven't said one word to anyone. Not one word!"

"Not good enough! I've got to know the truth or I've been told to end it."

"I didn't say a word. No one came. No one. I wouldn't say a word anyway."

"And why not?"

"Because even the police can't protect me. You guys are too big. You have friends in the police." He was sobbing now, tears smearing his cheeks. "I'm more afraid of you than the cops," he gurgled.

He was struggling to breathe. Andrew lowered his face close. "I've got to be sure!" he said, his knee leaning on Fleming's chest. "Maybe I can believe you, maybe not. I want to hear you tell it again. What if the cops ask?"

"I wouldn't tell them anything. I promise. Nothing."

Andrew's knee pressed and he lowered the gun to Fleming's eyes. "Because what's going to happen if you do?"

Fleming was crying hard. Andrew's eyes narrowed but he only whispered. "I said, what's going to happen if you do?"

Fleming tried looking away from Andrew.

Andrew screamed in Fleming's face. "Tell me!"

Fleming raised an arm as if you were being hit. He stuttered, "I g-g-get it. And my niece, too."

Andrew was now furious inside. He was going to make Marza pay. Whether Marza had used The Watcher or not he had still thwarted justice completely. He would make Marza confess, whatever it took to make him confess. Damn the consequences. And it just might include Marza giving up something about The Watcher if Andrew pressed him hard enough.

He lowered himself close to Fleming's face again. "This was a little tune-up. Don't ever give me reason to come back. Now forget I was here."

He walked to the bedroom door and looked back. Fleming was watching him, terrified, his arm raised to his face. Andrew found himself thinking, yes, Fleming lied under oath and that had saved Marza, at least until now. But there was also his niece. So give the guy something.

"You passed. I believe you."

He heard Fleming still mumbling "thank you" as he closed the back door.

*

Nix received a radio message from Leader. Lawrence had gone to the lake house in the morning and the tail watched the lane from the highway. Nobody else in or out all day. The tail had checked once near the cottage and saw Lawrence on the veranda alone just staring at the lake.

Nix wondered about Lawrence. He certainly prized his solitude.

Nix was now more impatient to hear back from Teresa at AT&T to tell him who it was that Lawrence had called last night from that payphone booth at 7:10 PM.

CHAPTER TWENTY NINE

DAWN HAD JUST broken when Andrew's biplane lifted off the grass runway into a pale sky. In twenty minutes he was banking gently at two thousand feet over Sand Hurst Woods Golf Club.

The fairways were empty but he could see greens' keepers moving hoses and equipment near the clubhouse, preparing for the day's work.

He had reviewed and eliminated all realistic possibilities of getting himself safely to Marza, except one. The FBI file detailed Marza's routines, including his beloved golf. There he was methodical, more planned stroke by stroke than he was in murder. And more predictable.

Andrew swung the plane sharply to the east, momentarily blinded by the sun's low glare, then dropped to fifteen hundred feet. He slowed and checked his controls and looked down at the wide-open fairways sliding by, their boundaries delineated by rows of trees. These would not offer him the cover he needed.

An expansive and densely treed area appeared on his right. He banked steeply bringing the ground into full view and made a slow circle. He studied the terrain, observing the layout of three fairways directly below him, noting the generous stretches of woods that bound them.

What caught his attention was a narrow river near the sixth tee, dropping through a steep gorge creating a cascade. Woods encircled the tee area. A squat bunker-like white cement building which he knew to be a washroom was set fifty yards back from the tee. A walking path led through the thick woods from the tee to the washroom which was also surrounded on three sides by the woods. On the fourth side the river spilled noisily through the gorge.

He flew a wide circle, pressing the button on the cameras' remote, the three cameras each taking four pictures a second. He climbed another five hundred feet and surveyed all the approaches to the sixth tee.

He flew back over the clubhouse where he saw the first golfers stretching and practice-swinging. He climbed higher still until the entire course was in view. He wheeled slowly, refining the elements of the plan he was hatching.

*

Two mornings later, he sat having coffee on the patio of the golf course clubhouse. He had been there the day before and had done an entire dry run to confirm Marza's routine, particularly between the fifth and sixth holes.

From behind aviator sunglasses, he watched Marza take several practice swings at the first tee. Now Marza glanced down the fairway once before addressing the ball. He swung hard and watched it slice badly into the rough. Agitated, with hands on hips, he stomped once.

He was accompanied by a bodyguard who doubled as a caddy, a hulking figure who Andrew knew concealed a semiautomatic pistol that could rip out a twelve bullet clip in two seconds. The bodyguard, standing silently to the side, reached out to accept the club that Marza threw with an angry toss. He marched aggressively off the tee in the direction of his ball uttering an array of profanities. The bodyguard quickly shouldered the heavy bag and followed.

Andrew looked at his watch and calculated. The group ahead of Marza was a capable twosome. They had a good ten minute start so would not hold up Marza's progress. He would be at the fifth tee in forty-five minutes. Behind Marza was a foursome, two women, two men, all in their 70s, with body profiles indicating they favored the 19th hole. By the fifth tee, that group would be at least fifteen minutes behind Marza, affording Andrew all the time he needed.

*

Marza was not having a good day.

It had started first thing with his empty-headed girlfriend throwing a deranged tantrum over nothing. And now, after only four holes, he was eight fucking over.

He and his bodyguard walked a steep rise on the fifth fairway, Marza muttering curses and slapping the head of his three iron on the ground. The bodyguard, bearing the golf bag, ran ahead to locate the ball and improve its lie before Marza arrived.

When Marza got close, puffing with the climb, the bodyguard pointed to the ball, a hundred and twenty yards to the green. Marza took a practice swing with his eight-iron. He glanced to the green and looked down at the ball and concentrated. He swung and watched his ball loft weakly, land, and dribble to a stop forty yards short of the green. He stared for many moments. He thought of his stupid girlfriend. Through gritted teeth he made a vicious swing with the eight-iron, burying the club's head in the soft turf.

*

After Marza had teed off at the first tee, Andrew did a little practice putting, then packed up. Soon he parked on a neglected gravel road that ran parallel to the eighth hole, thick woods bordering the road. From the trunk he removed a golf-cart and oversized golf bag.

He had taken an old set of golf clubs and hack-sawed through each shaft two feet from the club head. Fastened and protruding from the golf bag, the shortened shafts and club heads gave every appearance of a normal set of clubs. In the body of the bag, in place of the discarded lengths of club shaft and handles, he had hidden Kevlar body armor, an extra-large nylon jacket and pants, a black wig, a baseball cap, a rifle with silencer, and an extra small .32 caliber pistol.

He lifted the bag and cart over a sagging split rail fence at the side of the road and carried it over high grass and through the thick cedar woods and stubby underbrush which provided good cover. He exited onto the doglegged eighth fairway pulling the cart and clutching an apparently found ball. A teenaged greens' keeper was turning a tight bumpy circle in a riding mower, concentrating on not spilling his drink. He took no notice of Andrew.

Pulling the cart, Andrew made his way unseen to the woods by the sixth tee. He deposited the cart well back into the woods.

Crouched and hidden with good vantage of the fifth green and sixth tee some fifty yards away, he waited until the twosome teed off the sixth. He saw Marza preparing to pitch onto the fifth green from forty yards.

He quickly put on the body armor, slipped on the bulky nylon pants and jacket over the armor, and fitted the long-haired wig and baseball cap. He appeared overweight, slow, and unkempt. He pocketed the short, snub-nosed pistol. He walked around to the side door of the bunker-like concrete washroom building but didn't enter, instead hurrying a hundred feet straight into the woods to a spot not visible from the washroom door area. There he deposited the silenced rifle in tall grass beside a single birch tree. Then he returned to the washroom.

*

Marza habitually used the washroom after the fifth tee. The bodyguard, always with the golf bag, habitually stayed outside taking his leak at the noisy gorge precipice two hundred feet away, a little time alone while he waited for Marza to finish up in the washroom.

The door to the washroom was on the opposite side of the building from the gorge. There were no windows. Inside the men's there was one urinal, one toilet cubicle, one sink with one tap.

Marza entered the washroom and walked to the urinal. He was aware of someone in the cubicle, apparently finishing up. There was a flush.

He finished at the urinal and walked to the sink and turned on the tap. The door to the cubicle opened and he glanced in the mirror above the sink and saw a bulky, long-haired man wearing a baseball cap, his eyes down. Marza looked back to his hands.

He suddenly felt his throat gripped from behind as his face was pushed forcefully into the mirror, his body pinned firmly against the sink. His face was pressed so squarely into the mirror that his mouth was mashed half shut. "…out..your..ucking mind? Wha… doing?" He struggled but realized he was wholly overpowered.

Andrew locked an even better grip on Marza's throat and put the snub-nosed revolver against Marza's head and said, "Don't yell or you're dead."

In the mirror, Andrew could see Marza's eyes blazing with hatred as they stared back at him. He was aware that neither of Marza's hands went into a pocket for any gun.

Andrew pressed the gun more, Marza watching the gun in the mirror. Andrew wanted him to see the little snub-nosed gun to make him draw the conclusion that that was all he had.

He jerked Marza's head over, just past the mirror. He slammed his face into the rough concrete wall then brought his head back and pressed Marza's face into the mirror again. He leaned in close and whispered, "I don't want you. I want The Watcher."

Marza's eyes were springing tears with the pain. "Who…uck.. are you?"

Andrew said into his ear, "I know you touched Fleming. You used The Watcher. Tell me who he is, how I contact him. Nobody will know. And you don't get hurt."

"Wha…alking…about?" He tried to pull his face back from the mirror. "You think… can just…"

"Yes, I do. Just like you do." Andrew drove Marza's face into the mirror so hard it cracked the glass. Blood spurted from his nose, smearing red all over the mirror. Andrew forced Marza's unwilling head back in place against the mirror.

Andrew pressed the gun into Marza's cheek, distorting the face more. "Tell me! And make it the truth. Or I won't be this polite next time."

Marza's eyes were flicking around trying to contrive something or maybe just stalling, hoping his bodyguard would come in. But what Andrew registered most was that Marza wasn't denying that he had touched Fleming or had used The Watcher. He would be showing far more surprise, confounded at the mention of The Watcher if it were untrue. Instead, Andrew saw a guilty mind trying to figure a play.

He pounded Marza's face again into the mirror, the crack widening. He groaned in pain. His lip was split, a front tooth now crooked and bleeding.

Andrew gritted at Marza's ear. "Your goon can't help you. *Tell me*!"

Marza hesitated. Andrew pulled Marza's head ready to smash his face into the concrete beside the mirror. Marza blurted through a twisted mouth. "I don't oh who.. is. Reewy!"

He was breathing hard, pain stabbing him. Andrew eased off slightly so Marza could speak. He knew he would talk to make this stop but he wasn't sure he would get truth.

In short pained bursts Marza said, "I don't know… who he is. You put an ad… *The New York Times*….old stopwatch parts. He gets in touch. Nobody knows who he is."

Andrew leaned in. "When did you put the ad in?"

"First week of July."

"If it's not there, I'll kill you. You won't be able to stop me."

"It's there."

It seemed likely to be the truth. It would be hard for Marza to be that creative at the best of times let alone when his face was being minced into hamburger by a wild man pressing a gun to his head. But still, the apparent truth had come out too easily.

But Andrew knew why. Marza had no intention of letting him walk away from this. Divulging the truth to Andrew about how to contact The Watcher was one thing. But Andrew had obtained more, a confession of extortion of Fleming, and that he had used The Watcher to do so.

Marza's eyes watched as Andrew waved the little gun, the apparent sum of Andrew's firepower. "Don't walk out that door for another fifteen seconds or you're dead."

He threw Marza down into a corner and ran out of the washroom. He hurried into the woods unobserved by the bodyguard who was walking towards the building from the other side. Andrew grabbed up the hidden rifle and continued deeper into the woods, and not quietly.

As he climbed a treed slope unseen in the thick undergrowth, he heard Marza yelling at the bodyguard, "Come on! He didn't look like he could move fast."

The bodyguard and Marza raced into the woods and began to climb the slope, the bodyguard gripping a high-powered silenced semiautomatic pistol. Marza was right behind him clutching a similar gun produced from the golf bag.

For Andrew, this was now a simple case of self-defense. They had drawn weapons. The bodyguard would soon overtake him. Just as planned.

Andrew took up a position. He saw them below on the slope, saw that the thick-leafed branches obscured their view, saw their arms swatting at branches. He lost sight of them for twenty seconds, but the snapping twigs and crunching of leaves told him exactly where they were, clumsy pursuers in the wild, more accustomed to back alleys in the city.

He heard Marza again, quieter now. "Don't slow. He's only got a fucking cap gun."

From behind the concealment of a tree, Andrew saw the bodyguard break into view, his eyes keenly scanning for any sign of Andrew, his ears pricked for the slightest sound, his face like an angry bulldog.

The bodyguard was in full forward stride, Marza close behind, when the sun broke free of cloud and the bodyguard caught a glimpse of sunlight reflecting off metal. He hesitated.

The thwack as the bullet pierced the bodyguard's forehead was as quiet as the slap of a hand. His head lifted and he fell backward ramrod straight.

Marza stopped, his eyes wild, trying to find his aim.

But too late. Thwack. Then again, thwack. As deadly as before.

Andrew watched him fall. The first was for Fleming, the witness who feared for his niece. The second was for little Samantha King who was just walking late one night with her mother.

CHAPTER THIRTY

AT A PUBLIC library, Andrew scoured the want ads of back issues of *The New York Times* for the first week of July. In the Wednesday edition he found it: 'Seeking vintage stopwatch parts.' A phone number was included. It was all just as Marza had said.

Andrew considered the next step. Should he place an ad and provide a contact number? But what number? The Watcher would most certainly investigate before making contact. Whatever cover Lawrence and Andrew could create would have to be perfectly above suspicion.

From a payphone he called Lawrence and brought him up to date about Marza's 'confession' and the unavoidable rough play that followed. Lawrence was happy. But the newspaper ad posed issues.

"Too extreme a risk for you to go into that contact process unless we can make it airtight," Lawrence said. "I don't know how good The Watcher's eyes and ears are, how far the reach. If he got even a whiff of us, things would fast get dangerous as hell. We have to be ahead of him, not behind him. I need some time to think through this, not rush it. And you've had a few tough days, Andrew. Why don't you go home. I'll be in contact."

Andrew realized he was exhausted, that he had no fresh ideas. And going home sounded good.

*

Madeleine was at the kitchen sink wearing an apron and peeling carrots. Chopped onions were heaped on the cutting board.

"Hi," she said, still peeling, wanting to finish.

He sat at the table, tired. A loose contraption of wire clothes hangers hung at the base of the low kitchen window that looked onto the backyard.

"What is that?" he said.

"A trap Chris made. When any bad guys try to climb in through the window, those hooks will pull their pants down. And then, you see, their *underwear* will be showing."

He looked at the twisty contraption, the projecting hooks. "And what bad guys are those?"

"Oh, you know, the usual."

She was finished now, wiping her hands on the apron. She turned and looked at Andrew. Her cheery smile shrank. "Bad day at the office?" she asked gently.

He nodded. "You might say."

Her voice was sympathetic. "Those bad guys just never go away."

He tapped a finger lightly on the table. "Some do, with a little urging."

She sat down across the table. "You're far away, Andrew. Why not tell me what's on your mind?"

He looked at her with a tired smile. “I was just thinking how wonderful it would be to feel your skin touching mine.”

“Yeah?” She folded her arms. “That can be arranged. Now tell me what you’re really thinking.”

He sat forward, leaning on the table, folding his hands. “A lot’s going on. I can’t talk about it.”

“You really look terrible, you know. You really need a holiday.”

He gave a halfhearted nod.

“I’m serious, Andrew. You need a little holiday. *We* need a holiday, you and me, alone. We haven’t gotten away alone in ages.”

“A little holiday would be nice.”

“Good. I’m a bit ahead of you. Nadine already said she could stay here with Chris. She would arrange a few days off. Apparently she’s not indispensable to the survival of the Pizza Palace.”

He looked at her. “A few days?”

“From Friday night to Tuesday night. Four days. Canoe camping like we used to. Do a couple of two day loops. We could leave Friday at supper. For that night, as a start to the holiday, there’s a little Inn up that way that I’ve heard is kind of romantic.”

“You mean this Friday?”

“Yes. It’s only Monday. What do you say? I’m sure Lawrence owes it to you.”

He tried to think about it, but felt so tired.

“Andrew, you’re hitting the wall. You look exhausted. We need this. Let’s take a few days together. Just us. You don’t think I feel the stress you’re under, but I do. I want to give you room for that. But we need this too, private time together. It’s been a long time.”

*

Andrew’s father asked, “Where do the bodies go?”

"What bodies? No bodies, no crime," the hooded man snorted a laugh.

He was a child again, sweating and chasing the car. He was so close to the trunk. "Dad, don't go."

From inside the trunk his father called him. "Where are you, Andrew?"

He kept pace with the car. "I'm here, dad. I'm coming. I won't let them do it."

His father called out, "Where do the bodies go?"

"I don't know, dad. I just don't know."

"I looked for you there, Andrew. I waited. I didn't see you. I waited a very long time."

"I'm so sorry I didn't find you."

The car flew into the dark woods. The hooded man suddenly appeared sitting on a tree branch. "Where do the bodies go, Andrew?" he said, mocking his father's words. Behind the hood shook a bitter laugh.

"Dad!" he screamed.

A flash of white light.

"Andrew, Andrew." Madeline's voice broke in.

His eyes squinted. She had turned on her reading light.

He felt his sweat under the covers. She was stroking his forehead. "You were tossing and making sounds again. What was it?"

He looked at her, his heart still racing. He slowly eased out of bed. "Can you kill that light?"

She snapped the light off. He went to the window, opened it and sucked in the cool air.

"That hasn't happened for a long while," she said.

He looked at the trees moving gently to a breeze. "I've got to tell you something." She sat upright, an anxious look on her face. "This top-secret assignment—I'm investigating my father's killer."

"My heavens. Why didn't you tell me?"

"You shouldn't know anything about it."

"But why *you* of all people? Your own father."

"I can't tell you anything more. I needed to tell you because it has stirred up things."

He looked at her. He could see her distress well enough by the light from the street. "I shouldn't have told you."

"No, no. I'm glad you told me. But… just so strange, your own father. Are you alright with it?"

"It's been a little rough. But I have to be the one."

She watched him at the window.

"They believe the man who took my father has taken several other men. It's the way he works. They just disappear."

"Do you have any idea who it is?"

"I can't tell you anything more."

"But—"

"Anything."

After a moment she said, "I'm glad you told me, Andrew," but her voice was uncertain.

CHAPTER THIRTY ONE

THE WHITE PORSCHE 911 pulled to the curb at the front entrance of the Museum of Art. Velez came down the last few steps and got in. Nix drove to a park very close by and pulled over under a quiet row of tall shading elms away from all people.

Velez was distraught. "What's this on the news I'm hearing about Marza and his bodyguard being killed?"

"By an unknown shooter when they were golfing," Nix said. "The odd thing is it seems they were pursuing the shooter into the woods. And Marza's face was beaten up, too, sometime before he was shot."

"You're saying the shooter roughed up Marza, then tried to get away?" Velez said, mystified.

"Yes, unless it was a trap, maybe two guys, one of them waiting."

"Anyone being fingered for it?"

"Nobody has any idea. Marza had enemies, wasn't exactly loved by everyone."

"But it's still odd. If it was a planned hit on Marza, it was a very odd plan. Or something went very wrong with it. Why rough him up? Why not just shoot him?"

"The thing is, whoever did it is a sharpshooter. Both men took it in the head from a rifle at a distance."

Velez looked worried, and perplexed. "First it was Kennedy and Kipling, now Marza. Our customers getting knocked off like some cause and effect thing. Hire The Watcher and you soon get snuffed. Not great for business."

"I just can't see a connection. It was Lawrence's outside help who killed Kennedy and Kipling when they were trying to get away. That's legitimate. But that can't be who killed Marza. The law just doesn't do what was done to Marza."

"You told me the guy who killed Kennedy and Kipling was a damn good shooter, too."

"But I can't see it being the same guy."

"Well I don't like that there's even a possible connection, our customers eating lead like that."

"I have some news that could move us forward, maybe clear this up. I learned who Lawrence called from a payphone four nights ago."

Velez looked eager.

"The number's unlisted, registered to a Madeleine Nelson. It rings at a house on Morley Street, an upscale neighborhood. I had the title checked out. The home's owned by a cardiologist, Dr. Curran."

"Lawrence has heart trouble?" Velez said.

"Don't know. But if he was calling his doctor, why at home?"

"Maybe he's a friend."

"Why call from a payphone? Why secretive?"

"Maybe he wasn't calling the doctor," Velez said. "Maybe the Madeleine woman is the doctor's wife. Maybe Lawrence has another kind of heart trouble. He calls from a payphone so the doctor can't figure who was calling."

"Lawrence doesn't seem the type, more a solitary man."

"Or maybe the doctor just owns the house but doesn't live there. It's just an investment, rents it out."

"Possible. But I'm on it. I'll get answers."

*

That evening Andrew was alone, driving, taking a series of quiet residential streets to avoid construction and congested traffic in downtown Philadelphia. Darkness had fallen and a light rain patted the windshield, the wipers gently sweeping it away.

He thought back to yesterday. He felt little about having killed Marza and his bodyguard. Marza had killed a man in cold blood, and a little girl. They had pursued Andrew to kill *him*. What little he now felt could not be called remorse.

What he regretted was not getting better information from Marza about The Watcher. What he got only showed how exceedingly careful The Watcher was. If you made contact, it could still remain impossible to know who he was, but you would have exposed yourself to him, and if he sniffed out who you really were, you could find yourself dead, and very fast.

He suddenly became aware of where he was—on the same quiet tree-lined street and in the very block where Macky had been shot and died, where he had told his father the startling truth that had killed his father, and gutted his own young life.

On an impulse he pulled over and parked. He shut the engine off and sat for several minutes, the windows up, allowing his mind to settle. No one was on the street. No cars passed. Rain pattered on the windshield and a light wind lifted the leaves in the splendid oak trees.

Something had compelled Macky to leave the ballroom after only maybe ten minutes. The ballroom was a ten-minute walk to this spot. Macky had been on foot, no car, and it was determined he hadn't used a taxi. He had been overtaken and killed. He had detected danger in that ballroom, but what was it precisely? Lawrence was convinced it was Velez. But no Velez appeared anywhere in the investigation. The files, top to bottom, produced no Velez.

The rain eased, and Andrew felt the need to walk. He would do the reverse of the walk Macky had done that night. He would go to the hotel.

He had gone there once before when Lawrence first told him about his father's case. The night he had gone, he knew there was a large function on in the ballroom, a dance. He had insinuated himself into the crowd, just as Macky must have done. He had breathed in its atmosphere, played out scenarios, hoping that something in the experience of actually being there might spark a useful new thought, a new angle. He had considered where else in the hotel Macky might have tried to ply his trade that night, and so he walked the halls, the washrooms, the lobby, all hoping an insight would occur. He had only drawn a blank.

Now, after nine minutes and six blocks of fast strides, he entered the hotel, crossed the lobby, and followed the corridors to the ballroom. The door was unlocked and the room was empty.

He took a seat in the silence and contemplated the grand

room, its tapestries, its vaulted ceiling. He imagined the party that night twenty years ago—the music, the pageantry of five hundred elegantly dressed people. He thought of Macky weaving invisibly through the crowd, his fingers humming.

At the far end of the room a door opened. Two men entered, talking, intent upon each other. They didn't notice him. One appeared to be a prospective customer, the other a hotel representative.

"Who do we coordinate with?"

"The manager or me."

"The night of the awards, will there be a hotel representative in this room?"

"For something this size, a staff supervisor will be present at all times."

The customer was eyeing the richly dramatic swirls in the plastered ceiling. "It's a beautiful room."

"The hotel was fully renovated when the owner bought in '58. But the ballroom and the lobby were new additions, finished in October, '61, twenty years now."

"A lot of money."

"Yes."

"Is it locally owned?"

"No. A foreign outfit, private, but who it is, I couldn't tell you."

"Maybe oil money?"

"No, Swiss, I'm told. Maybe chocolate money." They both laughed.

It struck Andrew like a thunderbolt.

It suddenly made so much sense.

He got up. The hotel representative noticed him. "Can I help you?"

“Just admiring the architecture,” Andrew said, and strode from the room.

He quickly found a payphone and called Lawrence at home. Andrew’s voice was excited, hurried. “I have a theory that can explain things. Velez *was* at the gala, *but not as a guest.* That’s why investigators didn’t know he was there because he wasn’t on the list, so was never questioned, never vetted.”

“But why was he there?”

“Observing the party, enjoying the night, because *he owns it, owns the hotel.* No one knew who Velez was. They would assume he was just another guest. *But he wasn’t on the guest list!*”

There was silence several moments. “How did you figure that?”

“I just learned tonight the hotel was bought in ‘58 by some private Swiss outfit. Now, hear me out. I know it’s speculation, but this makes sense of what happened.”

“I’m listening. Slow it down.”

“Okay, so in ‘55 Velez ‘dies’, like you said. He disappears for a couple of years during which time he gets some plastic surgery in some discrete and renowned clinic, like the ones they have in Switzerland. His money is in some tax haven, like Switzerland. But he wants to live back here because this is what he knows. He wants to get his money back here, too. But how does he do that legitimately? What better way than to buy a property, a big income-producing property like a hotel. He buys it in ’58, not in his own name, of course, but in the name of some Swiss company. You know the Swiss have tight privacy laws. Hard to ever know who is really behind it. And with that company he could pour dirty cash into the hotel from his ongoing criminal operations, laundering his own money.”

“Yes, I follow, but—.”

"In the original investigation, investigators would not have thought there was anything suspicious about the hotel being owned by a Swiss company. The Swiss are nice people; they make chocolate. It's only because of your theory about Velez being alive that it raises the possibility."

Lawrence saw the theory had logical direction to it. "I get it, but it's a very thin proposition without more evidence."

Andrew was really revved now. "Sure. And here's the evidence. The ballroom had just been completed in October of '61. The gala was in October so it would have been one of the ballroom's first major functions, maybe the first. Velez, if he's the owner, would have natural reasons for wanting to drop in that night and watch the operation, without, of course, anybody knowing who he was, a kind of eavesdropper. He's just there, nobody taking attendance. I mean, Macky got in. Nobody knows who Velez is. Nobody asks questions. No one there could possibly know all of the other five hundred people."

"I agree it's likely nobody would know who he was back then." Lawrence seemed to be gaining enthusiasm. "No reason to ever announce himself as the owner, the man behind the Swiss company. Maybe he even took a room as a guest at his own hotel, in whatever his new name is."

"Remember also, if it was Velez who wore that black hood at my house, he had to be around Philadelphia at that time because he was at my house the next afternoon."

"Yes, a good piece of speculation, Andrew, but still speculation. You *may* be onto something. See who's registered as the owner of the hotel. Check at the office of the Recorder of Deeds. Then dig in from there."

CHAPTER THIRTY TWO

THE OFFICE OF the Recorder of Deeds was a buzzing hive of mysterious activity. At the front desk he was told he would need to hire a title searcher. A young woman, Nancy, was available.

Using the Hotel Continental's street address, she obtained the legal description of the property. From that, she was able to check the property's legal registrations including ownership.

"Okay, so the deed was registered in 1958," she said. "That transferred ownership of the hotel to a Swiss numbered company operating as 'Moniker Holdings'. And Moniker still owns it." She made a photocopy of the deed and gave it to him.

He had a few questions on his mind. "So…Moniker would have needed a lawyer, right?"

"Oh, yes. That's him right there," she said, pointing to the name on the deed, 'Lorne Nix, Attorney'. It showed a Philadelphia address. She added, "He would have been the one who filed the deed."

"Okay. I'm wondering also whether Moniker got a bank loan. Is there something anywhere that would tell you that?"

"Sure," she said. "If they got a bank loan that was secured by a mortgage, it would show up here."

After searching a minute, she said. "There was a mortgage registered, but not from a bank. It was a loan from a private company, a private lender. In fact, there were two mortgages registered, both with the same private lender company. Did you want a copy of those?"

"Yes."

She copied them and showed them to him. "The first mortgage was registered in 1958 at the same time the deed to Moniker was registered. Presumably that mortgage was for the money Moniker needed to borrow to buy the hotel. The second mortgage was registered in 1960."

Andrew figured the second mortgage loan was Moniker needing to borrow more money for the major additions that were completed in 1961—the ballroom and lobby.

"It's the same lender both times, a private company?" Andrew asked again.

"Yes."

"Is there anything unusual about a mortgage being with a private lender company instead of with a bank?"

"Not at all, see it all the time. Not everybody can get a mortgage with a bank. Banks have tighter lending rules. So you have to borrow from a private lender, usually paying a higher interest rate. The risk is greater, so the rate's greater, kind of thing."

Andrew considered that, so far, there was nothing that was a clear red flag. Moniker could still be a legitimate foreign company owned by a law-abiding Swiss who just wanted to own a hotel in Philadelphia. Nothing sinister in that.

"Where can I find out who's behind Moniker, and this other lender company?"

"At the Bureau of Corporations. They have the records."

*

Through radio messaging, Nix had instructed Leader to find out about a Madeleine Nelson at a certain address on Morley Street. Leader had briefed Kell, saying, "A phone rings at a house owned by a Dr. Curran, a cardiologist, on Morley Street. The phone's unlisted, registered to a Madeleine Nelson. She might be the wife, might be a girlfriend, maybe a daughter. Find out what you can about the doctor and about this Madeleine."

For two hours Kell had been on the streets of the doctor's neighborhood, alternating between driving and walking, making sure he wasn't noticed as anyone unusual. It was now the fourth time he passed the doctor's house, this time driving. There was still no car in the driveway. Maybe it was in the garage. Either way, there was no getting a license plate to run by The Watcher's insider at the Department of Motor Vehicles. Maybe it would belong to a Madeleine Nelson. Other vital information on her would then be revealed too.

He had seen some gardening tools lying at the edge of a flower garden like someone had been at work. He had hoped someone would reappear, but no luck.

He decided he would go to Dr. Curran's office at the address Leader had provided and work the little scenario Leader had devised. He entered the tasteful low-rise glassy building situated by an equally tasteful treed green park. Three cardiologists were listed on the gleaming outer glass door of what appeared to be a large suite of offices.

He showed himself at reception where a young receptionist smiled pleasantly at him.

He smiled back. "Hello there. I'm here on behalf of my mother, wondering if Dr. Curran is taking new patients? My mother heard good reports from a woman in her card group."

"Well, no, I'm sorry, but he's not taking new patients right now. He's actually away for an extended time, on vacation."

That was unexpected information, the doctor being away, but a Madeleine, or someone else, getting phone calls at the house.

Kell showed sincere disappointment. "Oh, that's too bad… for my mother. She was so hoping—"

She cut in. "The other doctors are covering for him, though. Perhaps—."

"No, I don't think so. My mother was quite specific. When is he back?"

"Not for several months. Six or seven actually."

"Wow, sounds like a wonderful vacation." Then who is this Madeleine? How best to put the question. "Must be traveling the world. His wife and kids, too?"

"No, he's unmarried. But I could take your mother's name."

So Madeleine Nelson wasn't his wife, maybe his girlfriend, but not with him, which would be odd. "Thank you, but I'll have to report back to my mother, see what she says about waiting that long until he's back. Her friend didn't mention Dr. Curran was gone."

"Well, he's only been gone a few weeks now."

"Oh, okay. Well, thanks again. I'll maybe get back to you."

He made contact with Leader who considered the new information. "Use the parcel delivery routine," Leader said.

*

An hour later, after collecting a wrapped parcel that he had been told to pick up at a picture-framing shop, Kell drove to Dr. Curran's house. He was happily surprised to see a very attractive twenty-something in shorts and a light top with long chestnut hair watering the flowers with a watering can.

He parked along the street just a bit further on. Better than a mere delivery, this now allowed a few pictures, a bonus. He snapped several of her.

Kell heard her calling to someone in the house, "Chris?"

He waited. The door opened and a young boy came out carrying a baseball glove and ball. The young woman and boy began playing catch. He watched for another couple of minutes, taking three more pictures and thinking through his questions. With the doctor away, was she a renter? Maybe a relative who was house-sitting? He would have to be careful how he did this.

In his car trunk was a wrapped and secured framed painting, an expensive limited print of one of the Masters, he was told, not that he knew anything about Masters or art at all.

*

Madeleine saw a nice-looking, well-dressed younger man get out of a car just down the street. He had a clipboard in his hand and seemed to be checking something on it, writing a note with a pen. As she played catch with Chris, she noticed the man open the trunk and take out a wrapped flat parcel.

She saw him glance in their direction and he walked across the street and into their driveway. He waved.

"Hi there," Kell said. "I'm delivering this package to a Dr. Curran. Is this the right address?"

"Yes," Madeleine said. "But he's not in."

"Oh. Do you know when he will be in?"

"Well, not for quite some time actually. He's away."

"Are you Mrs. Curran?" He was smiling pleasantly.

"No."

Madeleine saw that he was puzzled.

"Oh. Do you know how long he'll be away?"

"Well, actually a few months or so."

Now he seemed slightly distressed.

"Oh, that's a problem. You see, he ordered this painting and it was slow in coming, just arrived, but I'm sure he still wants it. But we can't hold it for long. I'm not sure what to do now."

She felt for his dilemma and also wanted to do the right thing by Dr. Curran. "Well, I wish I could reach him to ask, but that's difficult…where he is."

"Are you a relative? Maybe you could sign for it."

"Not a relative. But…was he expecting this to be delivered?"

"Oh, yes. He's been waiting quite a while. It came to us from Europe. We tried to keep him posted, but you know how it is. Unfortunately, we'd have to send it back. He'd be charged shipping and cancellation costs."

"I'd feel awful if he was expecting it…"

"Yes. You're just house-sitting or something?"

"That sort of thing."

"Are you going to be here until he gets back? So you could be sure he gets it?"

"Yes, for sure. I'm sure he would trust us. You can trust us. Why don't I just sign for it?"

"I'd need some particulars. Rules, you know. A full name and signature would do it. I already know where you live," he laughed.

He handed her the clipboard. She read the company name at the top of the paper: 'BALZAC OBJECTS D'ART (NEW YORK)'. She saw a line for a signature.

"Yes, just there, your signature," Kell pointed. "And then please print your full name there. And a phone number right there beside in case anything comes up."

As she signed and printed, she heard him say to Chris, "I saw you're a very good catcher for your age. How old are you?"

"Five."

"Do you like your new house?"

"I like the one in Minnie more."

"Minnie?"

"Minneapolis," Madeleine explained with a smile and handed the clip board back. "There you go."

He took it and looked at it. "So…it's… Madeleine. And is that… 'Locke'?"

"Yes."

He paused a moment looking up at her. "Okay, well here you go," he said smiling and handed over the parcel. "Thank you for your help with this."

"Sure, happy to help."

CHAPTER THIRTY THREE

AT THE BUREAU of Corporations, Andrew learned that the Swiss company, Moniker, had been incorporated in 1957, and that the sole director and president was listed as Albert Baumgartner, with an address in Zurich, Switzerland.

If his theory was correct, Andrew figured Baumgartner would actually be Velez, or a front man for Velez. He was willing to bet big that Baumgartner, whoever he was, would be a highly elusive man, impossible to find.

He asked the very accommodating clerk who was assisting him, “Moniker being a foreign company, I’m wondering is there something to say who filed this paperwork here?”

The young man shuffled through a few pages. “A local attorney, Lorne Nix. Filed in 1957.”

The same lawyer who, a year later, did the legal work for

Moniker to acquire ownership of the hotel, Andrew considered. Nix was shaping up to be Moniker's very trusted lawyer in the U.S.

As if in absolute confirmation of Andrew's thinking, the clerk pointed out that Moniker had also given a 'power of attorney' to Lorne Nix, authorizing Nix to sign legal documents on behalf of Moniker. That would be very convenient, a buffer, serving to remove Moniker at least one big step away from snooping eyes. All questions would stop at the door of an attorney who could remain uninformative, claiming attorney-client privilege.

But then the clerk, a chatty fellow, said that giving power of attorney to a lawyer in the U.S. was a common step taken by a foreign company with business affairs here.

Andrew felt the letdown, accepting that so far nothing pointed to a nefarious situation, not even a questionable situation.

Next he asked to view the details of the private lender company that had made the loans to Moniker to buy the hotel, and again later to finance the ballroom and lobby. He found the company was made up of three Philadelphia businessmen and had been incorporated thirty years earlier, in 1951. That immediately told Andrew that it was not connected to Velez. It reached back too far, well before he was even operating here. On the other hand that made sense because if Moniker was actually Velez, a legitimate lender would help to deflect suspicion from Moniker. It would serve as another buffer.

But Andrew worried. Maybe he was just rationalizing here, self-deluding, allowing his thinking to grasp in any hopeful direction instead of looking at the plain evidence without bias.

The clerk said, "As far as getting other information on Moniker, you might also want to check at the Philadelphia Licenses and Inspections Office. They might have something useful for you."

Andrew took him up on it. That office did have something on Moniker.

Through Nix, Moniker had given authorizations to a local firm of certified public accountants to deal with all licenses and inspections needed for the hotel's operations. More broadly, Andrew realized, that's how the hotel could run its operations without hotel management ever meeting Velez or even knowing who Velez was. Their contact, as well as who they reported to, would only be the accountants. And *their* contact would only be Nix. The hotel owner could remain a very absent owner, a very unknown person.

But again Andrew felt creeping self doubt. There was still nothing unambiguous here. This could be the way legitimate foreign owners managed their business affairs, removed from all the operational headaches. Was Moniker actually owned by a real Baumgartner, not Velez? In a brief fit of frustration he pictured a real Baumgartner in his mind, sitting in a luxurious chalet on some splendorous mountain in faraway Switzerland enjoying alpenhorn recordings.

He left the Licenses Office and called Lawrence and filled him in on everything, including the names of the three businessmen.

"I recognize the name of one of them," Lawrence said. "Max Hardy, a wealthy Rotarian, does a lot of community works. He's as straight as an arrow. Not likely going to touch anything even slightly shady let alone a Velez, at least not knowingly. But I'll run a check on him and the other two."

"I haven't come across any real red flags anywhere. Nothing to sink my teeth into," Andrew said. "If I don't first make the assumption that Moniker is Velez, there isn't anything that would in itself tip me off to believe anything was unusual."

"Andrew, your theory was inspired. Really. Trust your instincts.

Velez's hand is never going to be obvious. He's too smart for that, so keep digging."

Andrew was grateful for the pep talk. "Thank you." He paused. "I've been wondering, though, thinking about everyone who could know, or have known, who's behind Moniker. I'm certainly wondering about the attorney, Nix. There's an obvious close relationship there. If Moniker is Velez, the attorney is either being played by Velez, or they're in it together. At the very least, the attorney had to have regular contact with someone to do the legal work setting up Moniker, and then doing the paperwork for the purchase of the hotel. And he's the contact for the accountants who run the hotel operation. I'm not saying he would necessarily know if anything was dirty, only maybe. But he also has power of attorney for Moniker so presumably has regular communications even now."

"Well if he *is* crooked and connected with Velez, you don't want to go up and ask him."

"But he would have records."

"But he would very much mind if you took a look at them."

"After hours, of course."

"That's very dangerous if there's anything dirty there and he's part of it."

"That's why it would be after hours. He'll never know."

"Well—."

"But I was also wondering how a foreign company like Moniker would have gotten financing from private local businessmen here? What's the process?"

Lawrence thought a moment. "They could contact a mortgage broker here and ask about borrowing private money." Lawrence paused further, considering where Andrew was going with it.

"You're thinking the local broker here might have known a lot more about Moniker?"

"Yes, likely more than the lenders would. You would think he would have to. There should be records, like who came forward from Moniker."

"Maybe the attorney. Or maybe their accountants here who have agent authority, like you found out."

"Right," Andrew paused, "but still, wouldn't Moniker have to show their income picture, their assets, their credit history, things like that, just like if you're buying a house and need a mortgage. They were buying a whole hotel and they didn't even live in this country. They've got to make the private lenders happy, feel secure and sure they're going to get paid back."

Lawrence liked it. "That's good, Andrew, very good, safer than checking out that attorney, Nix, just yet. I'm going to put a call into someone who will speak to Hardy for me to say he only wants to know if Hardy can recommend a good mortgage broker, find out who he's used over the years, see what we get."

"And then we hope the records of that deal are still in existence."

"Yeah, let's hope."

"But," Andrew said, "that attorney. I want just a quick look for now, see who he is. See if anything raises the hairs on my neck."

*

Andrew had Nix's office address from the paperwork at the Bureau of Corporations. As he climbed the four flights of stairs in the four-storey professional building in downtown Philadelphia, he considered what his ruse would be to appear like a potential client.

He decided he would ask for a quote to have Nix incorporate a private business for him…a stock-car race-track club that Andrew had up and running already. And business was… roaring.

He walked the corridor until he came to an imposing oak door with a brass plaque that read, 'Lorne Nix, Attorney at Law.' He tried the door but it was locked. At 2:20 p.m. He thought that was odd unless the whole office had taken a late lunch. Or it was closed for summer vacation.

He left the building and found a payphone. In the phone book he found an office number for 'Lorne Nix, Attorney', and called it. After only two rings an answering machine kicked in. A man's voice said, "This is the office of attorney Lorne Nix. Please leave your name, number, and a brief message. Thank you."

Andrew didn't leave a message. Instead, he looked up the number for the Pennsylvania Bar Association. He knew that some limited information about individual lawyers was available to the public through the state bar associations. He called and was put through to a woman who confirmed that Lorne Nix was indeed an attorney in good standing. He appeared to have an impeccable record.

Andrew felt the wind leaving his sail. But he pushed on. "What is his area of practice?"

"Corporate law."

"And how long has he been licensed to practice?"

Andrew could hear her flipping pages. "Licensed to practice law in Pennsylvania since…1957."

It struck him that Nix had been licensed for only a year before he was involved in the hotel acquisition, and less than a year before filing the corporate paperwork on Moniker at the Bureau of Corporations. "Do you mean he is, or was, licensed to practice somewhere else?"

"I see he's a member of both the Pennsylvania bar and the New York bar."

"Do you know when he was licensed in New York?"

"You'd have to check with the New York Bar Association."

Andrew had already looked for a home address for Nix in the telephone book but found none. "Would you know his home address?"

"That's not information I'm free to divulge."

"Okay. Thank you."

From the New York Bar Association, he learned that Nix had been licensed since1953. "Does he have an office in New York State?" Andrew asked.

"I only see a Philadelphia address." She recited the office address he already knew.

"Oh, I see. But I suppose he had an office in New York State somewhere before he was licensed in Pennsylvania," Andrew said.

"The records show…Buffalo."

Andrew was stunned. Buffalo was where Velez had operated back then, until he 'died' in '55. What were the chances that a lawyer licensed to practice law in New York State would be practicing in Buffalo? Based on population, it would be about…one in fifty!

He thanked her for her time, his hand shaking as he hung up the receiver.

He called Lawrence, his excitement barely controlled. "From '53 to '57, Moniker's attorney, Nix, practiced in, get this, Buffalo! Then he became licensed to practice in Pennsylvania in '57, setting up an office in Philadelphia. Remember I learned that he's the one who filed the Moniker corporate documents at the Bureau of Corporations here in '57. The hotel was bought in '58. He hasn't maintained an office anywhere in New York State since then. Coincidence or what?"

"*Very* significant, Andrew. *Very.*"

"I'm going to check his office again. If no one's there, I'm going in tonight."

"Not so hasty. If he is dirty and connected with Velez and you step on one tripwire, this could all be over. That kind of thing has to be better prepared, much better prepared."

Lawrence's voice eased, "I have a safer first step, the mortgage angle you asked about. The mortgage broker who Hardy has always used is Glen Forsythe of Forsythe Mortgages. It's likely his office was the broker involved in financing Moniker's purchase of the hotel. There may be useful records there, telling us something more about Moniker as you said earlier. For the moment that's safer than going straight to the lawyer now that you know that about him. You just can't expose yourself directly to Velez or you're dead. The more we can learn just circling the suspect first, the better our chances of success, of surviving."

"Okay. Tonight it's mortgage man, Forsythe," Andrew said. "I'll call you tomorrow. We'll talk about attorney Nix then."

*

In the study at his penthouse, Nix reviewed the pictures Kell had taken of Madeleine Nelson aka Madeleine Locke. She was beautiful, a warm smiling face, an athletic form. He looked at the other pictures where she was in the act of throwing a ball to a young boy wearing a catcher's mitt in the front yard of an upscale home. He knew the boy's name was Chris, age five.

For a second time he listened to a recorded message from Leader which relayed all that Kell had learned about her and Dr. Curran.

Within the last month the doctor had left for an extended vacation. Madeleine, who signed Madeleine Locke, but had an unlisted phone number in the name of Madeleine Nelson, was house-sitting, or maybe renting, but appeared to have no other relationship with the doctor. It was reasonable to assume she had moved within the last month, and from Minneapolis, based on what Chris had said. Kell had done well, had been suitably discrete, not pushing for information about Madeleine's employment, if any, which could have triggered suspicion. Nor had Kell asked anything about a husband, although she wore an obvious wedding ring, or any question to Chris about his dad. Again, it could have appeared too inquisitive, particularly to someone who might have reason to hold her cards close.

Knowing that Dr. Curran was away ruled out the possibility that Lawrence's phone call had been intended for the doctor. So the connection wasn't between Lawrence and the doctor, but purely between Lawrence and the new house-sitter, Madeleine, or someone else there, but not the doctor. The phone number she had written down on the form Kell had given her was not the unlisted number. So Madeleine had two phone lines.

Why? And why the unlisted number? And why in another surname, maybe Madeleine's maiden name? Why secretive? Why would Lawrence have called that number and why from a phone booth when he was so close to his own home?

It spoke of a high possibility of a connection between Lawrence and his secret helper. But he didn't think it would be Madeleine herself. Surely she wasn't the person Lawrence placed near Kennedy and Kipling's hideout alone that night and who then took them out so skillfully when they tried to get away. And more assuredly, she surely wasn't the one who beat up Marza and then blew him away, along with his gunman, in extraordinary fashion, that is, if that job was indeed done by Lawrence's helper.

It would make sense that if Lawrence wanted to have a secret agent working for him who insiders at the Philadelphia FBI offices wouldn't know of, he would bring in an agent from elsewhere. Minneapolis? He decided he would have an insider run a silent check on the names of FBI agents in Minneapolis, looking for any Nelson or Locke.

Who had put that wedding ring on Madeleine's finger? That's what he wanted to know. That was very probably where the danger lay.

CHAPTER THIRTY FOUR

AFTER TELLING LAWRENCE he was going to uncover what records he could at the mortgage broker's office, Andrew went directly home.

"I'm going to be away for a couple of days on surveillance," he told Madeleine.

"Is everything okay?" she asked, anxious.

"Everything's fine, making progress, feeling good."

He began to gather some clothes from his closet.

"You'll still be here by Friday afternoon to pack for the canoe trip?" she asked.

"Of course." He went to her and held her. "I'm really looking forward to that, Maddy. Really. Lawrence just gave me some things to look into. They're urgent."

They looked a moment at each other and kissed. He pressed her tightly to him.

"You're okay?" she said.

"I'm okay."

At the front door as he was leaving she said, "On Friday, Nadine will be here by 4:00. We should really get away by 5:00. Then four days together."

He drove directly to mortgage broker Forsythe's office. He wanted to case the place to see what he would need to get in later tonight.

On a side street off Manayunk Avenue, he pulled up to what had once been a grand colonial home that now served as Forsythe's offices, and had for 35 years. Andrew wanted just a few minutes inside to get the lay out and to see what he could learn.

He parked around back in the small paved lot. He saw there was a back-door entrance, an old door, probably used by staff. He walked around to the front, noting as he entered the building that there was no alarm system. He didn't bother to check the lock mechanism on the front door because he would go in the back way tonight, far less conspicuous.

The receptionist was on the phone so he took a seat in the waiting area. He already knew from Lawrence that Forsythe would not be in today, a Tuesday. Forsythe golfed Tuesdays and Thursdays. A couple of hungry young associates handled most of the business day-to-day anyway.

As he waited, he noted the windows to see what could be seen from where. He noted also the hallway leading to a room which would somehow connect to that back entrance. A secretary in high heels came from another room into the reception room and opened a deep drawer in a tall metal filing cabinet behind the receptionist. There were several cabinets. The drawers were alphabetically marked. The secretary ran her polished fingernail along the tops of index cards. He hoped their file card system would be obvious and tell him something about their archiving system.

The secretary drew out an index card and left the room reading the card as she walked, high heels tapping on the hard wooden floor, down the hall and through a doorway into another room. He heard a door squeak from somewhere at the back of those rooms. He heard her high heels start to negotiate down hard wooden steps.

The receptionist hung up the phone and looked at Andrew. "May I help you?"

"Yes, I would like to speak to Mr. Forsythe if he's available."

"He's away today. But Ms. Jones or Mr. Baker would be happy to help."

"I would prefer to see Mr. Forsythe. Can I get an appointment for next week?"

She took his name, Andrew Coulter. She checked the schedule and jotted the date and time on a card and handed it to him.

He heard the high heels mounting the wooden steps and the same door squeak again. He paused, appearing to check the time on the business card. "That looks good."

The secretary with the index card appeared, coming down the hall with a fat file. She looked peeved, dusting off her forearm, then checking for a broken fingernail.

Just as Andrew was leaving, closing the front door behind him, he heard her say with disgust to the receptionist, "What a hell hole down there."

Now he knew where old files were archived.

*

Just before 2:00 a.m., he left the Weeping Willows Motel and drove back into Philadelphia. He parked two streets over from Forsythe's office, walked to the office and went around to the building's unlit back door. The door was old and had only a handle lock. Training his penlight, he worked the lock-pick at it. In under a minute he was in without causing any damage.

He banged into a rolling chair as he entered and knocked over a coat rack before his eyes adjusted. The place was a rabbit warren. He was in a small room that connected to a back hallway and then through another room and then another hallway to the reception room with the filing cabinet with those index cards.

The penlight beam found the front of the filing cabinet. He looked at the alphabet notations on each drawer. He opened the drawer marked >K to N'. Flipping through the index cards he slowed at Monahan, Monger, Mongrain. Then ...there it was! Moniker Inc! It was like magic. He could have gotten down on his knees and thanked the office manager for her excellent organization.

The door to the basement was ajar and squeaked when he opened it further. He began down the wooden stairs, closing the door behind him. Walking by the building earlier, he had seen that the basement windows had been fully covered in plywood from the inside for security. So he knew he could use the basement light and not be seen from outside. He snapped it on.

He could only agree with the secretary—'what a hell hole.'

The basement had a stone foundation and a very low and dangerously sagging ceiling. Two dangling bare light bulbs did their best to penetrate the darkness but mostly failed. Here and there cedar posts had been jammed vertically to prop up the floor like a last ditch stand against a cave-in catastrophe. Every inch of the basement was honeycombed with ancient wooden shelving that bowed under the strain of overflowing banker boxes. A gray dust layered every flat surface including the banker boxes. Cobwebs laced the entire ceiling and ventured downward like hammocks. He pitied the secretaries.

The year of the filing of every box was announced in magic marker on its side. He found a short row of boxes of '1980', a few of '1979', around the corner, '1978', and so on. He soon discovered the pattern in the system. He hoped the files would reach back to the 1950s.

He found two banker boxes marked '1958', the year Moniker had borrowed the money to buy the hotel. The files appeared to be in alphabetical order. He quickly flipped through the labels looking for "Moniker." He found nothing. He tried "Hotel Continental." Nothing. He tried just "Continental." Nothing.

He knew there had been that second mortgage in 1960, presumably for the money required for the hotel's expansion which included the ballroom and lobby. He found the 1960 boxes and scanned through the 'M's and saw a thick and tattered brown accordion file with a half-torn label—'Moniker Holdings.'

With excitement he took it from the banker box and immediately saw that, buried inside, was a separate file from 1958. It would take considerable time to review it all. He decided to take it with him. Nobody would miss it, even for years. He carried it up the stairs, snapped off the almost useless light, and left by the back door.

He arrived back at the motel at 3:30 a.m., put on the coffee and began to read.

The oldest notes showed that Forsythe had been approached by a new local lawyer, Lorne Nix. Well, well, thought Andrew. The notes said Nix was looking for substantial private money for his Swiss client who wanted to acquire a substantial property in Philadelphia. One note had the words, "possibly Hotel Continental" scratched in the margin.

It was evident from notes that Forsythe was in regular communication with Hardy to determine whether Hardy's group was interested in funding such a loan. Based on log notes, there had been several meetings with Nix over a month period.

The theme that emerged from 'memos to file' was that Hardy's group had concerns about lending to a foreign owner. They were concerned that Moniker couldn't provide any credit history. That was because, it became clear, the company had no credit history; it had been incorporated less than a year and had never borrowed money. Secondly, the owner of Moniker, Albert Baumgartner, who was maybe Velez, who lived in Zurich, Switzerland, would not give a personal guarantee. Thirdly, Hardy didn't want to ever have to chase a Swiss company to Switzerland to get paid if Moniker defaulted on the loan. Based on the notes, the parties appeared to have reached an impasse for about another month.

Then, out of the blue, Moniker disclosed that it owned real estate, 500 acres of pristine forest in Franklin County in central Pennsylvania bordering the Appalachians. Moniker had bought it outright, a cash sale, only six months before for its "resort development potential." To make the hotel loan happen, Moniker offered to allow a mortgage to be registered also against the 500 acres as collateral security. This would allow Hardy's group to seize it also if Moniker ever defaulted in payments on the hotel mortgage.

It seemed this broke the impasse and it was cigars all around.

But Andrew wondered why Moniker hadn't offered that property as collateral before, like when the impasse first occurred. Why the reluctance? Was it something more than just not wanting to put up more security?

He sat back, fatigued. He looked at the window, the sun just coming up. Apart from a two-hour nap before midnight he had not slept. He closed the curtains tightly and stretched out on the bed in his clothes.

His mind cycled through the basic facts. Nix was licensed to practice law in Pennsylvania in 1957. He moved his offices to Philadelphia in 1957. Moniker bought the 500 acres in 1957, and Andrew saw from a copy of the deed in the file that Moniker had used Nix as the attorney for that purchase. Then Moniker bought the Hotel in 1958, using Nix again.

Nix, a young lawyer from Buffalo, moves to Philadelphia. How did he come to represent a moneyed Swiss company so quickly? Or did it really point to a relationship that existed *before* he moved to Philadelphia, a relationship in Buffalo?

Andrew had been struck by something else—the complete absence of any mention of a meeting with Baumgartner in person. If Baumgartner was really Velez, that would certainly explain that.

It wouldn't arise in the mind of others that there might be something unusual in a Swiss company owning 500 acres of pristine land near the Appalachians for future development potential. And there might not be. But, he thought…500 acres…absolute privacy, absolute secrecy. Where do the bodies go? Maybe that was a stretch, a wild connection.

But still…with a chill he found himself wondering if he had stumbled on the place where his father had been taken twenty years ago…that car roaring away with his father in the trunk… and he a trembling little boy kneeling in the gravel, so very alone.

CHAPTER THIRTY FIVE

HE WOKE AND checked his watch. 10:30. He had slept four and a half hours.

He felt his mind was slow. Today's Thursday, he said to himself as a kind of orientation. And tomorrow evening, Friday, Maddy and I take a little holiday. But today, he wanted to know about that 500 acres.

He put the coffee on and while waiting for it called the operator and got the number for the Recorder of Deeds office in Chambersburg which handled Franklin County, just at the edge of the Appalachians. He phoned and got the number of a title searcher there, Cindy.

He called and told her he had a copy of an old deed and mortgage for a 500 acre parcel of property in that County. "It was bought in 1957 by a Swiss numbered company operating as

Moniker Holdings," he said. "I want to update things. Don't know what's happened as far as ownership since then."

"Sure, no problem" she said. "Just read me the legal description on the Deed and I can check what registrations have taken place since then."

He read it to her and she said, "I'll get right back shortly."

He was sipping his second coffee twenty minutes later when she called him. "I checked the title for you. Moniker Holdings doesn't own that property anymore. They sold it in 1962 to something called 'Pleasant Hunt Camp'."

Andrew's heart sank. He had thought he might have discovered a key piece, like where Velez took his victims. It had been a long shot, if Moniker Holdings was Velez.

So," he said with reluctance, "Moniker sold it just five years after they bought it?"

"Yes."

"Was attorney Lorne Nix involved in the sale?"

"Let me see here. Yes, his name shows as acting for Moniker. Another attorney acted for the buyer, the Camp."

The sale sounded legitimate. Andrew felt his disappointment begin to eat at him. "Okay," he said slowly.

He was just about to thank her and hang up when something struck him. The mortgage broker's notes said Moniker had bought the acreage for its 'resort development potential.' So why sell it only a few years later to a hunt camp, not exactly the highest and best use of 500 acres that had 'resort development potential'.

"Hey," he said, "did the Hunt Camp sell it to someone else later, like a developer?"

"No. The Hunt Camp still owns it."

"You mean the whole thing, the whole 500 acres?"

"Yes, whole thing."

So it had never been developed, not even a part of it.

"Well, did the Hunt Camp pay a lot more for it than when Moniker bought it?"

"Let's see. Well…looks about…maybe 20 percent more, or so. And that's five years later, so kind of a normal increase I guess."

A thought was in his mind. Maybe it had only been a paper sale, to break the connection between the property and Moniker, and hence between the property and Velez, if Moniker was Velez. Not many investigators today looking into Moniker would think to dig into a mortgage broker's personal notes from twenty-five years ago and so would never know Moniker owned that property at any time. So if Moniker really was Velez, no one would know that he owned it today. So no one would have any reason to ever be looking at that property with any suspicion.

He cautioned himself. It was thin speculation, hinged on hunches, hanging from guesswork.

"If I was there by 1:30, can you have a copy of that deed from Moniker to the Hunt Camp for me?"

"Sure can."

"And could someone then tell me where exactly that property is?"

"I can, sure."

What he needed to do was get a good look at that property. And when it was 500 private acres you were checking out, nothing was better than a low flyover.

*

The information Nix had been waiting for came in just after lunch on Thursday over the radio. A silent check had been run on FBI agents in Minneapolis. And Bingo!

There was indeed an FBI agent named Locke, Andrew Locke, four years of service, born Philadelphia. But he had been transferred from the Minneapolis field office almost a month ago on a classified assignment, location undisclosed.

In Minneapolis he had performed normal investigative duties as well as flying air surveillance. He was also a SWAT trained sniper.

An odd mix of talents, Nix thought. A lone agent, Lawrence's undisclosed helper, had taken out Kennedy and Kipling with a sniper's accuracy.

If maintaining secrecy or anonymity was paramount, putting a phone in the wife's maiden name for a covert communication link with Lawrence would be a reasonable precaution.

And then there was the 'born in Philadelphia'. What turned over and over in his mind was the name Locke. Prominent in his memory was detective Paul Locke from all those years ago, here in Philadelphia.

Locke was, however, a common surname, hundreds in the phone book. Why would there be a connection of any kind anyway? There probably wasn't.

But to satisfy a niggling curiosity he went to a drawer and shuffled down through papers to a yellowed collection of old newspaper clippings. He spread them out looking for one in particular—the lengthy article in an October 1961 issue of the *Philadelphia Post* of the abduction of Detective Paul Locke. He found it, the article led by a large picture of Detective Paul Locke.

His eyes drew down the article quickly, slowed, then stopped. He read carefully.

That little boy, the son, was named Andrew.

Curious indeed. But Andrew was also a common name.

The article said Andrew Locke was seven. That was twenty years ago, so *that* Andrew Locke would now be twenty-seven, about the age of Madeleine, the wife. She had been here less than a month, which fit with the timing on the scene of some unknown outside agent. Lawrence was concerned about insider leaks after Senator Booth's killing. Bring in an unknown agent to skirt insider knowledge and help him discover who The Watcher was.

All very reasonable.

But was this Andrew Locke actually *that* Andrew Locke, Paul Locke's son? What a remarkable coincidence that would be, startling, really. Would it be simple coincidence? How could it not be? What else could be going on? What else could Lawrence know?

Velez would be back tonight and they would talk.

The real point was that he was certain he had found Lawrence's helper, an Andrew Locke, so the first step of the mission was accomplished. Again they were on top, knew what Lawrence was up to and could control how things played out. That was the natural order.

But if things ever got threatening, they could quickly make Locke and Lawrence disappear.

*

Just before 1:00 p.m., Andrew touched down at the small municipal airport in Chambersburg, just beyond famous Gettysburg, 150 miles west of Philadelphia. When he reported in at the airport, he learned that a thunderstorm system was moving in quicker than expected from the west, over the Appalachians. A staff person said, "If you want to return to Philly today, you've got two hours at most to get in the air and out of here. It won't clear again until late tomorrow morning."

He took a taxi to the Recorder of Deeds office where he met the title searcher, Cindy. She gave him a copy of the deed to the 500 acres and showed him on a large wall map its precise location. He jotted down the coordinates, north-west of Chambersburg ten minutes' flying time. He hoped the bad weather would hold off.

She pointed out on the Deed that the Hunt Camp's address was "c/o Max Staweki, PO Box 1385, Chambersburg, Penn."

He got directions to the post office. When he got there an obliging postal clerk informed him that there was no PO Box number 1385. "Mistake there somewhere. I've been here 32 years. There's never been box numbers higher than 1000."

Well, a bogus address, Andrew thought.

"Do you receive mail for a Max Staweki?" he said.

"Can't say I've ever heard that name." He opened the local phone book and flipped to the 'S's. "And there's no such name in here."

When Andrew left the post office, he could see dark cloud formations building to the west. His time was getting tight.

If the property was undeveloped, he thought, there would be no mail like utility bills being sent to that PO Box address. But there would be property tax bills. If the mailing address for the Hunt Camp was bogus, what about the tax bills? Somebody had to be paying them.

He got directions to the tax office. He went in and showed the clerk the deed and said he was Max Staweki. "I've been having trouble with the mail lately. Was afraid I might have missed getting a tax bill."

The woman looked up the records for the property. Still reading the record she said, "You appear to be all paid up." She was reading something else now, a note stapled on the file. Still reading it she said, "Looks like you call in twice a year and get the amount owing and mail us cash."

"Right," Andrew said, thinking, yes, that would make sense if you wanted to avoid being traceable.

She read further and frowned. "The bills we send always come back." She looked at him, eyebrows pinched, then glanced back to the record. "We have PO Box 1385, here in town. A problem there? Can you give us another address?"

So, no corrected address had ever been provided. "No, I'll speak to the post office about it," he answered casually.

"I definitely would," she said.

From the runway at the Chambersburg airport, he saw a brilliant flash of lightning and black clouds building to the west. No time to fly over the 500-acre hunt camp today. He would come back and scout it when the weather system cleared tomorrow late morning. He increased the throttle and the biplane raced along the tarmac and he lifted off. Reluctantly, he pointed east in the direction of home.

*

Late that afternoon, Andrew again checked Nix's office. Still no one was there, the door locked.

He called Lawrence. He wasn't at the office, but he reached him at home and filled him in on what he had learned from Forsythe's files. "That 500 acre property really intrigues me. What would a Swiss company want with that?" Andrew said.

"You said the file described it as resort potential. Doesn't seem unusual that Swiss money would invest in that kind of thing."

"Yes, but Moniker sold it only a few years later, and not for resort development. It's a hunt camp, and the camp still owns the property. So it was never developed, not any part of it. It's just birds, not condominiums."

"Moniker might have stretched the truth about the property's development potential to get the hotel loan. Businessmen have been known to exaggerate."

"Sure, but why buy it in the first place? And something else smells. The address for the hunt camp is a PO Box that doesn't exist. If I wanted to continue to have a property available to me for whatever uses, but didn't want anyone to know I owned it or had any connection with it, I could paper sell it to a fake party. I maintain control without anyone knowing I still own it. I also use a bogus mailing address."

Lawrence seemed unimpressed. "Mailing addresses get screwed up all the time. But here's the thing. If it was important to Moniker to only paper sell the property to hide from ownership all those years ago, why didn't Moniker do the same thing with the hotel? Moniker still owns it in that name."

That hadn't occurred to Andrew. Damn, he needed more sleep. But then a notion came to him. "There's a difference. The hotel carries on legitimate business. Nobody but you and I have any reason to suspect it. But the acreage, well, if a body turned up there, the police are going to go to the registered owner."

Lawrence was quiet several moments. "Okay, I see your point. It would take authorities a while to learn the Hunt Club is a fake, then trace it back to Moniker, and that would lead them to a dead end in Switzerland. *If* Moniker is really Velez."

"Yes, that's my thinking. So listen, I'm doing a flyover of the acreage tomorrow. See what's there. But for now, tonight, I'm going into Nix's office."

"But Andrew…"

"I understand your concern," Andrew interjected. "But it's the next natural step. I've got to know. I don't know what else to do."

Lawrence heard the force in Andrew's voice, the resolve. But if Nix was in fact dirty, things could get very dangerous. But Andrew was determined, and really, what better next step was there? It was still less dangerous than trying to contact The Watcher directly through the *New York Times*.

"Okay," Lawrence said. "But watch every damn step."

CHAPTER THIRTY SIX

IT WAS AFTER seven that evening when Velez walked into Nix's penthouse. "I'm starving," Velez said.

"I have some news," Nix said.

Velez looked at him, impatient for dinner. "Well?"

"Lawrence's helper. I'm quite certain I've found who it is. His name's Andrew Locke. He may even be Paul Locke's son."

He had Velez's full attention. "Detective Paul Locke's son?" Velez said.

'Maybe."

Velez stared unbelieving for long seconds. "That little kid?" He was staggered and his voice boomed.

"Same name as the kid, same age, born Philadelphia. He's an FBI agent, recently transferred here from Minneapolis on confidential assignment. Did routine investigations there. Also a crack shot. And he flew air surveillance. And his wife's that Madeleine woman, the unlisted number that Lawrence called."

"That little kid?" Velez repeated, still astonished. He ignored Nix's motion to take a seat in the living room. His eyes darted about as he struggled to comprehend. "Something's rotten here."

Nix tried to soothe him. "If that's who he is, I really don't think his being here is more than coincidence, small world stuff."

"Small world? It's fucking *claustrophobic*."

Velez pondered several moments. "Prudence dictates we assume *this* Andrew Locke *is* the son of Paul Locke. If he isn't, fine. But let's err on the side of caution. The question then is, why did our old friend Lawrence select *him* for this peculiar top-secret assignment? Locke can't be all that experienced at that age, not that long in the field."

"Yes. But he's from Philadelphia, knows the area."

"I don't think that would be a critical factor. His sniper skills, though, they certainly came in handy with Kennedy and Kipling," Velez said.

"Maybe with Marza, too, although I'm still not convinced the secret helper did Marza. Seems too radical for an agent to do that. And did Lawrence really expect his secret helper would have to use those sniper skills? It's an investigation, not a stake-out."

"But the fact that it's maybe him who used those skills twice says Lawrence's expectations were accurate," Velez said, "those skills highly relevant."

Velez was pensive, concentrating. "Let me walk through my thinking, a chain of connections. So, because of how we took out Booth, Lawrence knows he has an internal leak problem, or it's in the Philly PD. He doesn't know which, or both. He brings in an unknown outside agent, Andrew Locke. Somehow Lawrence learns where Kipling and Kennedy were hiding out—maybe Andrew's air surveillance skills somehow. Then he posts Andrew to watch the hideout while Lawrence gets a conventional take-down operation in motion. But Kennedy gets word from you, and he and Kipling try to escape and Andrew blows them away. He was hoping the SWAT team could have taken them alive, or at least one of them, to find out how they communicate with The Watcher. Lawrence knows perfectly well Kennedy got tipped off to the take-down, the leak again."

"But he's no further ahead. No closer to knowing who we are."

"Maybe. Then with Marza, Lawrence suspects that that prime witness at the trial was touched, intimidated, threatened, and he sets Andrew on a mission to meet directly with Marza to find out who it was who helped him out, thinking it was maybe The Watcher who helped him out. If the answer is yes, then find out how to communicate with The Watcher. That would explain why Marza was beaten up, a little questioning going on there. Then Andrew kills him and the bodyguard during a pursuit."

"If that's true, then we need to stop using the New York Times. Or we use another phrasing."

"Yes, like right away. And if there's anyone trying to make contact with us that way right now, we tread very carefully because it could be Lawrence. But anyway, shut it down."

"I will."

"If I'm correct in thinking Andrew did Marza, then this Andrew is willing to do very extreme things. He's got some headstrong motivation. That concerns me."

Nix poured wine and Velez drank it in silence. The wine had a calming effect. "I need to think some more on this," he said. "We want to watch this situation *very* closely."

Nix nodded. "At the moment we have no operations in Philadelphia that involve our insiders anyway, so no current exposure. Lawrence and Andrew don't really have anything to work with."

He handed Velez a picture. "That's the wife, Madeleine, the one with the unlisted number."

Velez took his time. "Nice looker. Where's Andrew?"

"Don't know. I had someone watching the house from late afternoon yesterday until two in the morning today. Nobody came or went. He's not staying there it seems."

Velez slowly rotated the wine in his glass, watching it as he spoke slowly. "If it's the kid, we killed his father. The kid is now FBI, a killer agent on a highly secret mission here. And he reports only to our old friend Lawrence."

He looked at Nix, sullen. "I've survived because I trust hunches. And I'm having hunches right now. Doesn't it look like more than a small world thing to you?"

"They don't know a thing. After all this time, twenty years, how could they?"

"I've got to think about it. But I'm beginning to wonder about Lawrence…all these years…maybe the strain of conscience too much…" His voice trailed off.

Nix walked to Velez and clapped outstretched hands on his shoulders. "Relax, will you? Let's enjoy dinner. I have everything in hand."

*

An hour after midnight Andrew slipped on thin gloves and picked the lock on Nix's office door. He let himself in and closed the door behind him. From the slit of streetlight, he could see the curtains were closed so he switched on the lights.

He was in a single room with plush carpeting, a secretarial desk and two waiting chairs. A door to an inner office was closed. On the secretarial desk sat an electric typewriter, a phone, a business card holder with cards.

He went to the desk. The drawers were unlocked. The desk revealed no personal items belonging to the secretary, just standard office supplies. Things seemed exceedingly tidy for a working secretary's desk. Andrew had expected to find personal items—maybe some women's shoes tucked under the desk or a sweater hanging on a rack like at Forsythe's office. There was none of that. There was no personal address book. There was no client file index. How did they keep track of clients? The garbage can was empty, too.

There was only one filing cabinet in this outer office. It was also locked. On top of it, fully visible, lay a thick sheaf of twenty-dollar bills. Before tackling the cabinet, Andrew wanted to see the inner office. He found the door into it was locked. Strange, he thought, an inner office locked.

The door wasn't difficult to pick and he was quickly in. He flicked on the lights. There was more plush carpet, a large desk with a phone, and a wall of recessed shelving filled with legal textbooks. Expensive Persian carpets hung on two walls. Startlingly, on another wall were the mounted stuffed heads of two tigers—big heads, mouths open, fangs bared, their eyes threateningly on Andrew.

An odd feature in an odd law office.

Close to a window on a large table were radio equipment and microphone and two reel-to-reel tape recorders. Maybe a hobbyist? He expected to see paper littering Nix's desk, but there was just a commercial lease document and a small stack of invoices for rent and utilities and sundries.

The desk drawers were locked and he picked them. They, too, revealed no personal phone book or client lists. Whoever worked here was careful not to leave anything confidential around.

The place didn't give the appearance of a busy law office at all, unless they had thoroughly tidied up and put everything away for the holidays, if that was even the explanation for them being away lately.

There were two filing cabinets in the inner office, again both locked. He cracked the locks and opened the drawers. A search of the file folders showed Nix had only a few clients, international corporations that seemed to have interests in a lot of places. It was clear Nix was the quarterback for their activity. There was voluminous correspondence with accountants both in Philadelphia and abroad, but far too much reading for Andrew to delve into right now in here.

What he was really looking for was correspondence with Moniker, but he couldn't find any at all. Zero. His reluctant impression was that the office was sterile, probably devoid of anything useful to him.

After forty minutes he locked everything back up again and left. He had a few ideas about what his next steps should be. He should start watching this office next week and keep it up until someone, hopefully Nix, showed up, then follow him home. Then he would stake out the home.

If he ever hit a total dead end, he could also just fly to Zurich, track down Baumgartner and compare him to Velez's portrait to see if he was one and the same. But then, if Baumgartner was actually Velez, it was very likely he wasn't going to be in Switzerland anyway. There would be just an empty office there. But that, too, would be telling.

The immediate plan was to fly to Chambersburg tomorrow and have a look at the 500 acres. Why would a Swiss company want 500 acres fit only for a hunt camp?

As he drove to the motel he kept wondering where *exactly* the truth was in all this. But he couldn't focus, just kept yawning, exhausted after another middle-of-the-night outing.

CHAPTER THIRTY SEVEN

ANDREW SLEPT UNTIL 10:00 and felt refreshed for the first time in days. The storm system was clearing. He got out to his aerodrome and took off in his plane at 11:30.

After flying an hour in a baby blue sky, he passed Chambersburg. Ten minutes more and he slowed and descended to a thousand feet and began a sweep over the 500 acre Hunt Club property.

The acreage was mixed, some mature forest, but mostly low scrub, dwarf trees, wild grasses. But what struck Andrew were the large expanses of marsh, swamp and bog. Those would surely prevent any practical realistic resort development. Pheasant, yes, vacationers, no.

He saw some low buildings and banked slowly, leveling off low at 500 feet to get a closer look. A largish cabin was set a quarter mile back from a neglected gravel road. A long, winding, quarter-mile grass lane connected the cabin to the road. A two-storey barn stood about 200 feet from the cabin. There was no sign of life anywhere, but it also wasn't pheasant season, if that counted for anything.

A kind of gatehouse stood beside the grass lane near the road at the front, but would not be visible from the road because of woods. What looked like newer fencing made of wire with black steel rod posts ran the length of the property across the front. There was also a sturdy gate across the lane at the entrance to the road. Clearly they didn't want trespassers.

He circled again, staying very low, pressing the cameras' remote, taking dozens of pictures of the cabin, barn and immediate surroundings. It looked like about five acres around the cabin and barn may have once grudgingly supported mixed farming but was now only wild grass and some thin trees.

He really wanted to get into that cabin. There might be something there that could tell him who used it, who really owned it, give him a toe-hold on some useful information.

But there was nowhere to land, and with his time and fuel limited he would have to come back another day. As he banked and turned away from the buildings, he almost missed seeing a trail winding its way back from behind the cabin into the woods and grassland, meandering past wide, expansive marsh and swamp and bog, and carrying on about a mile to the rear of the property. The trail ended just short of what looked to be a little-used dirt road that bordered the acreage at the rear.

He considered that if Velez needed to dispose of bodies over years, this would be the perfect place, a remote, no-snoopy-neighbor-for-miles expanse of land. With its extensive swamp and bog, organic matter would quickly decompose. Bare bones would sink in ooze to unknown bottoms. There would be nobody around to witness the disposal of a body, no bloated corpses floating to the surface in some public lake, no shallow grave uncovered by animals and discovered by hikers. And no cementing required.

It was a place where Velez could also hide himself, and who would ever think to look for him here?

He flew back to the Chambersburg airport. When he was refueling, he asked about a landing spot closer to the location of the Hunt Club. One of the older fellows who flew a Tiger Moth overheard his question and said, "There's a disused section of old highway about a half mile west of Rona's Corners. The new highway bypassed that section years ago. I've landed on it a few times. Some weeds coming through the asphalt but it's level and firm. Your biplane can handle that better than my old bird anyway."

Andrew had seen Rona's Corners on the map. By his reckoning it would be a two mile walk to the Hunt Club acreage from there. But he had no time today.

When he landed back at his own aerodrome, he called Lawrence from a payphone. Lawrence wasn't at the office. Again Andrew reached him at home. "I flew over the 500-acre camp property. It's half swamp and bog. Some of it's good, but it never had resort potential."

Lawrence sounded tired. "But it does sound like bird hunting terrain."

"For sure. But why would Moniker have ever bought it in the first place?"

Lawrence's voice was weak. "If Moniker is Velez, then buying it was to launder some dirty money early on. And then he sold it because he didn't need it anymore because he had the hotel for that."

"I agree with that. If Moniker is Velez, he may not have any connection to the acreage now."

But still, Andrew thought, there's that bogus postal address that didn't exist and had never been corrected by the hunt camp owner. But he decided Lawrence wasn't in a frame of mind to profitably continue the discussion. "Hey, I wanted to remind you that Maddy and I are away canoeing for four days, starting tonight. I'll call you when I'm back."

Lawrence's energy rallied. "I remember. You've been working hard. Enjoy yourselves."

He wondered why Lawrence was so tired. "You sound down. Are you okay?"

There was silence for moments. "Not sleeping well. Things catching up with me."

Andrew thought of the depression, maybe drugs again, and of what Lawrence was preparing to face if Andrew found Velez, or even if he didn't. Was he cracking?

"Are you going to the lake house on the weekend?" Andrew said.

"I don't know. I'll see."

As Andrew drove home he felt a rising sense of urgency, a growing obsession about getting into that cabin. If Moniker was legitimate, why had it bought that land when it was clear that it had no resort potential? If Moniker was actually Velez, and it was just to launder money as Lawrence suggested, why that land, way out there? Why not something with real capital growth potential? That land was, as they say, for the birds.

Would there be something in that cabin, Andrew thought, something that would lead him to one real person, just *one* real person, and maybe from there to some real answers?

*

He arrived home at 4:30. Madeleine was in the garage with her younger sister, Nadine. It was easy to see they were sisters. In fact, they looked almost like twins, the same attractive features and physique, the same long chestnut hair.

Andrew gave her a big hug and thanked her for babysitting Chris for the next four days.

Nadine was enthusiastic. "I'm *really* looking forward to it! Chris and I are going to have a blast!"

Madeleine's excitement was also obvious. "Everything's packed and ready to be loaded into the car, Andrew—the food, the tent, the sleeping bags, the air mattresses, the cooking gear, your clothes, your hatchet. Test me if you want."

"Matches," Andrew said.

"Oh shoot!" she laughed, putting her hand to her mouth. Then she gushed, "Just kidding." She tapped her front pocket. "They're right in here, smarty pants."

*

Nix went to his office at 4:45 to pick up a file to work from home as he most often did. He passed through the outer office and unlocked the door to the inner office. He went in and bent to a small keypad just above the baseboard and entered a 4-digit code.

He almost missed noticing that the tiny red light was flashing. His mind was habituated to no longer noticing the light at all. It had given off only a tiny dull red glow for years and years. If anyone entered that inner room but didn't key in the correct code within fifteen seconds, the light would flash on and off instead of glowing, and a concealed camera would silently begin to take pictures. He had never wanted an alarm, per se, as his goal wasn't to scare an intruder away, but more importantly, to know *who* it was.

He stopped himself and looked at the light carefully. It was actually flashing! *Damn! Someone had broken in!* It wasn't that he kept anything incriminating here, or had valuables here. It was more importantly *why* was someone here?

He saw nothing disturbed anywhere. He checked the outer room and saw that the bait of the sheaf of twenty dollar bills was still there. So theft wasn't the motive; so that was bad news. So what was the motive? And who was it?

He reached up with both hands and carefully lifted off one of the mounted tiger heads from the wall. He unhooked a wire running to a camera inside the head. The wire fed back behind the drywall down to the keypad at the baseboard which activated the camera to take pictures at five second intervals if the code wasn't entered correctly, or at all. The camera's lens, hidden at the back of the mouth, had an excellent vantage of the entire room. Nix tested the set- up twice a year.

He took the roll of film out of the camera and left the office. At the photo shop he paid for the one hour developing. Less than an hour later he was handed a thick package of photos. He hurried back to his car and ripped open the package.

The photos showed a man in his late twenties. He was handsome, his face somewhat familiar. Where had he seen that face before? Nix felt his heart racing. Naturally, because of all the talk last night, he thought of Andrew Locke. But he had no picture of Locke, just the damn wife. He hoped it wasn't Locke, just some nosy snoop. There were more than sixty photos and they showed the man looking *carefully* through the desk and the filing cabinets. He was far more attentive than a simple snoop.

But *why* was that face familiar? As he drove, it finally came to him. A chill shot through and he began to shake. He pulled over at a payphone booth and called Velez immediately. "My office was broken into. Meet me at my place right away."

He drove fast, distracted, and angry, his fist repeatedly slamming the steering wheel as other cars blared at his erratic driving. That picture of Detective Paul Locke in the newspaper clipping he had looked at yesterday. That was fucking it! The kid looked *exactly* like his father.

What the hell was going on?

*

A knock at his penthouse door and Nix let Velez in.

"It was him, Andrew Locke," Nix said.

Velez was surprisingly calm. "I think they call this a seismic shift," he said.

He stood at the impressive window in Nix's penthouse staring out at the Philadelphia skyline, smoking a cigarette, quietly thinking.

Nix didn't interfere. It was no longer a small-world thing. He had been complacent. He had been wrong. He would defer.

"The first question is how did he get onto you?" Velez said. "The second question is what's an FBI agent doing investigating his own father's disappearance? Surely that's against Bureau protocol. It tells me it's completely off the record."

Nix was startled at the leap. "His father's disappearance? Why do you think he's investigating his father's disappearance from twenty years ago and not Senator Booth's murder?"

"A hunch. No one could connect you to Booth. We've been too careful. But twenty years ago, things were messy. You killed Macky. Something we don't know about has come up. Andrew Locke is now here on an extraordinarily secretive assignment reporting only to our friend Lawrence. Locke has found you. Too many planets are aligning, tic tack toe."

Nix wasn't going to question Velez's hunches anymore anytime soon.

Velez continued, "But whatever case Andrew Locke's investigating doesn't change what we have to do. He's investigating *you* and that's all we need to know. It's not for dodging taxes. We have to go with worse case scenario—he wants you, and maybe me, for murder, in the plural. We need to stop him dead in his tracks."

He stubbed his cigarette in the ashtray, lit another one, and stared out the window. After a few moments, he said, "I think something else is happening here the possibility of which hasn't occurred to you. There are just too many coincidences, too many unusual strings that don't tie together. Let me toss out a thought. When we took Detective Locke we asked him if he had told anyone what he knew. He said 'no.' We beat him. He still said 'no.' So I believed him."

He took a seat on the couch and a long drag on the cigarette. He continued, slowly, "I knew why Detective Locke hadn't told anyone right off the bat what pickpocket Macky said. Locke was keeping it quiet, cooking up something on the side to get around any possible insider leaks. But he would have to tell someone eventually…to be able to find me and take me down. I was willing to continue to believe he hadn't told anyone because nothing ever came out after. No one was looking for me, no one saying I was alive. But…"

He drew on his cigarette more. "Lawrence was the local FBI's liaison person to the Philadelphia Police Department back then, wasn't he? What if Locke had lied to us? What if he *had* talked, talked to …Lawrence, told him what Macky said, but Lawrence didn't say anything to anybody because…well, it's obvious why he wouldn't, isn't it? Obvious to us, anyway."

Velez smiled and looked at Nix.

"I see your point," Nix said with admiration. "That's a real possibility."

Velez stubbed out his half-finished cigarette. "Detective Locke's disappearance and Macky's murder never get solved. Lawrence carries a burden a very long time. He wants to unburden—find me, kill me, so no one ever knows what he really did. But he can't do it alone. He sees a possibility recently, brings in the kid, who is highly motivated. And Lawrence has enough seniority to sidestep FBI protocol, keep the whole thing secret."

He turned to look at Nix and half smiled. "Sound crazy?"

Nix shrugged. "Maybe a few holes, but I think there's something to it. Still doesn't explain how Locke is onto me. The point is he is onto me. And Lawrence knows whatever Locke knows."

Velez nodded. "You know what's beautiful here? All this secrecy they've got going is perfect for us. Not a peep about this side-investigation anywhere in his office. I think nobody knows what's really going on but those two. They're tighter than a vacuum pack. We don't have to take on the whole FBI. We just make those two disappear and the law won't even know what happened and why. Nobody even knows about us because Lawrence wants it that way."

"Andrew Locke's a very dangerous man when he wants to be," Nix said. "And we don't even know where he is right now. Seems he's not staying at home."

"There's a way to find him and make him helpless. Make him sing like a bird." He picked up the picture of Madeleine and eyed it carefully.

Nix was already nodding. "Yes, that could work."

CHAPTER THIRTY EIGHT

THEY WERE SPENDING the first night, Friday night, at The Lakeside Inn. It was completely charming, their room romantic. When they went to dinner, there was white linen on each table, candles glowing softly, the food divine.

But Madeleine was sad. Although Andrew had tried—held her hand, smiled at her—she knew he was preoccupied. His mind just couldn't settle and she knew it. She desperately wanted them to have fun together, just the two of them, not them *and* this investigation that was sucking the life out of her husband.

It was late evening and they were sitting beside the lake on a dock, alone in the dark, quiet, looking at the stars. They hadn't spoken for five whole minutes. She knew his mind was turning something over and over.

She looked from the stars down to the dark water. "Andrew,"

she said gently, "you've been somewhere else since we arrived. Is there anything I can do?"

He was slow to answer. "I'm sorry, Maddy. I'm not much company, am I?"

She didn't say anything.

"I wish I could explain everything", he said. "I want this to be over."

She took his hand. "I know I have only some idea what you're going through. It must bring up so much for you."

He didn't answer.

She said, "I just hoped we could have some time together."

He looked down at the dark water that was reflecting the moon like a black mirror. "I know. It's just…there's a piece in the puzzle I hoped to get to today, a look inside a remote cabin, a stone unturned. I thought I could then let things go for a few days. But I didn't manage to get to it. I was short of time, just a little time."

She perked a bit. "Do you mean if you took some time tomorrow, you could do it?"

He was surprised at the offer. "Maddy, I don't want to spoil things."

She pressed. "No, listen, I'd really like to salvage this holiday. If that would make the difference for you, let's do it. Maybe I'll take a walk, maybe go to that knit shop we saw and look for some new baby stuff. You could be back by when?"

His mind raced through some time calculations: Get to the aerodrome, fly to the property, check out the cabin, fly back, drive here. "If I get away *really* early, which I would, I could be back here by 2:00."

"That would be fine," she said.

"So…we would canoe for three days, not four."

"I'm good with that. If we get to the canoe outfitters before three and then to the launch site by four, we could put in and do a three-day loop."

The original plan was first to do a two-day loop, Saturday and Sunday, returning to the launch site Sunday late afternoon to call Nadine from the payphone there to check on things at home. Then do another two-day loop.

"We'll call Nadine tomorrow instead of Sunday, just before we launch. Let her know our change of plans," she said.

He nodded.

"So, you do what you have to do. Then we give it another try tomorrow afternoon. Just us. Do we have a deal?"

He stretched over and kissed her. "We have a deal."

*

Earlier that evening, just after 7:30, Leader did a drive-by of the Locke house. There was no car in the driveway but a young woman and boy were sitting on the front porch eating ice cream. Leader glanced at one of the pictures of Madeleine and Chris that Kell had taken a couple of days before. He looked up again at the young woman and boy on the porch—yes, as to be expected, of course, Madeleine and Chris.

He reported what he had seen and added that there was still no evidence that Andrew was home, which was just as Velez expected. Where was Andrew, and what the hell was he up to precisely? That was the question that burned at Velez.

He quickly gave the green light to the team to continue as planned.

Three hours later, at 10:30 p.m., Leader entered a payphone booth and dialed the number that Madeleine had written as her home phone number on the form Kell had her sign. Leader had to confirm that Andrew was still not at home so that the plan would go forward as arranged.

*

Nadine was curled on the couch. The Friday night 'fright' movie was on television, an old horror flick, Dracula and the Curse of something or other. She was glued to it, her eyes duly frightened, her mouth half open.

The sudden ring of the phone jolted her. "Geez," she blurted with alarm. She jumped up and grabbed the phone in the next room. "Hello?"

"Hi, would Andrew be in?" Leader said.

"No, he isn't," Nadine said, stretching the telephone cord around the corner so she could see the television.

"Any idea when he will be in?" Leader said.

"He's away. Who's calling?"

"Joe Decker. I'm a friend of Andrew's."

Darn. She was missing a really good part. "Oh, well, he and Madeleine are away canoeing."

There was a pause, Leader's voice surprised, uncertain. "You're not Madeleine?"

"No. I'm Madeleine's sister."

"Oh. Well, I'll get back to him next week then. Sorry to bother you."

"Okay, sure."

*

At Nix's penthouse, Nix and Velez listened to the details from Leader, a very unexpected change of affairs. After a few minutes' deliberation, Velez said to Nix, "We've got momentum. I don't want to lose time or control here. So what we do is just take the boy. The sister stays put. We use her to inform Andrew."

*

One of the things Madeleine loved about their rental house was the treed backyard that backed onto a spacious and forested green belt. The moon was weak tonight, but still enough light for the trees to cast long shadows.

At 11:20, new shadows appeared, moving stealthily toward the back of the house. Eyes saw that lights were still on in the living room. A closer look made out the television was on, too.

A ladder was run silently up to a second-floor bedroom window. Kell climbed it and with a thick box cutter cut the bug screen along the bottom and both sides of the window.

As he passed his leg through the opening, his pant cuff hooked onto something as he brought his leg down in the room. He brought his other leg in and saw he had caught on some wire clothes hanger contraption. He unhooked it and slid it over to the side.

He opened the bedroom door a little and poked his head into the hall and listened. He heard only the television downstairs—loud talking, creepy movie music, a short bloodcurdling scream, more chilling sound effects.

He went to the bed and leaned over Chris who was breathing evenly and very deeply. He slipped a loose black hood over the boy's head. If he half woke it would be dark and he wouldn't see he was in the arms of a stranger.

He lifted Chris and walked gently to the window, passing the limp body smoothly through to Smithy who was standing at the top of the ladder. Smithy descended the ladder silently with no disturbance to Chris. Then Kell passed through the window and was quickly down.

Moments later the moving shadows disappeared into the green belt.

Five minutes later, the phone jolted Nadine off the couch again. But this time she remained jolted.

CHAPTER THIRTY NINE

ANDREW WAS UP and quietly gone from the Lakeside Inn at 5:30 a.m., Madeleine not even moving in her sleep.

His aerodrome was just over an hour away. When he arrived, he topped-up the plane's fuel tank and filled the supplementary tank. Although the night had been cloudy with more reports of heavy periods of rain to the west around Chambersburg after midnight, current reports said the morning sky there was clearing nicely. He was in the air by 7:30.

Just after 9:00, he flew past Chambersburg, the sky now clear, the ceiling high. In minutes more, he was over Rona's Corners which was nothing more than an intersection of two roads, each of the four corners boasting commerce—a general store, a gas station, a lumber store, a bakery.

He flew on and quickly saw the disused stretch of the old highway that had been bypassed by the new highway. Three hundred yards of it ran straight and level. He circled it once to satisfy himself that a safe landing could be made. As the older pilot had described, there was some cracking in the asphalt, but no gaps or lifting, and no tall trees on the approach.

But rather than land right away, he decided to take an extra couple of minutes in the air to fly to the Hunt Club acreage to determine the best route on foot to approach the property from the back road. He quickly saw the property coming up and estimated that the walking distance was two miles. That would put him at the rear of the 500 acres. From there he could take the trail he had seen which meandered through the property almost a mile to the cabin.

He began a slow bank to turn back, allowing himself to go out wide enough in the turn to just see the cabin in the distance. But...he thought he glimpsed something more there. He leveled and turned, pointing toward the cabin, maintaining an altitude of 1500 feet.

Was it a car at the cabin? He soon saw clearly that it was. It wasn't pheasant season; it wasn't any bird-hunting time. But it was Saturday. Maybe it was just some innocent weekend goings-on.

He hadn't considered the possibility of people being there today. He couldn't risk exposing himself, couldn't go marching up to the cabin now without preparation. He had only his Smith and Wesson 459 pistol and could too easily be outmatched if there were many men there, especially if they happened to be The Watcher's men.

He dropped to 1,000 feet, and as he got closer he could see the car was brown, a newer Ford LTD. It was parked by the barn on a small rise. It would help immensely to know whose car that was.

He needed to get a good clear picture of the license plate. He could phone it in to Lawrence and they could learn the plate's owner.

But he couldn't let anyone down there suspect anything.

*

Alone in a small room in the cabin, Chris was whispering, imagining talking to his Mom.

They are bad guys.

I told them I want to go home.

They told me to stop crying.

It's a little room with boards on the floor.

They told me to lie on the towel.

I was afraid to go to the bathroom.

The tall one took me to the outhouse.

He was mad.

He said I was walking too slow.

He pushed me to go faster.

I fell into a puddle.

My pajama top got soaked.

He said I just slipped.

Now I just have a towel.

I get cold.

They don't like me.

I want to go home.

*

The two men playing cards at a table in the cabin looked at each other when they heard the approaching drone of a plane. The tall thin one jumped up quickly, going toward the door.

The stocky one barked, "Stay inside."

The tall one looked out the window. "He's not flying regular. Some stunt guy. Now he's fucking upside down."

The stocky one got up. They were together at the window,

necks craning. The engine was loud as the biplane flew over. "Not the law anyway," said the stocky one. "They don't do that shit. That's a barnstormer type plane. Will you look at that? Loop the loop."

"Yeah, you'd have to be loopy to do that stuff. Get yourself killed."

"You couldn't pay me enough to get up in one of those. I'm not living to die young."

The tall one said, "Look, he's coming back, swooping down real low now, to barnstorm the barn. That's what he's doing here."

The bawling of the engine swept in like a wave, the engine-note then rising as the biplane climbed and snap-rolled before flying off.

Once the plane was gone and it was all quiet again, they heard the whimpering in the back room. The stocky one said, "Go tell that kid to shut up. I'm not going to sit here for days and listen to that shit."

*

Andrew had done the virtual air show not only to deflect suspicion and to orient the plane for a low photographing angle. He also wanted to see if he could draw faces out of the cabin, get pictures. But there were no takers, no one coming out to give a friendly wave, and that was unusual, because everyone wants to see a crazy flyer. So either no one was there at that moment, maybe out hiking, or they had reason to stay hidden. If someone had actually come out and watched him innocently and waved, it would have removed some of Andrew's suspicion. But nobody came out. So there was some reason for suspicion.

He flew directly back to Chambersburg, refueled, and then flew back to his own aerodrome north of Philadelphia. From there he drove to a commercial photo shop and gave them the rolls of film he took both today and yesterday. He was keen to see if the license plate showed clearly.

In forty minutes he had the photos and flipped through them until he came to the series he had taken with the slow swooping pass. The car had been parked on a short rise so the rear was somewhat more elevated and at a better angle to see the plate from above. He had gotten a clear shot as he passed it low.

The coloring of the plate was Pennsylvania, but the numbers were too small, indiscernible. He went back into the shop and had them do an enlargement of the best three pictures.

The results were better. '3V90' were the first four characters. That was four out of six. There would be a limited number of possible letter-number combinations for the last two characters. But, of course, the possibilities were narrowed further because he had a picture of the car. Its make, model, year, and color would allow Lawrence to eliminate other cars and make a match.

He phoned Lawrence at home. There was no answer. Lawrence had said he might go to the lake house this weekend, but there was no phone there. So he left the details on the home phone answering-machine and said he would call back later in the afternoon from the canoe launch site.

He was greatly heartened. The license plate, this one further piece of evidence, just might pry open the lid of his investigation and point to a real person, just one real person, connected in some way to Velez.

CHAPTER FORTY

AT 4:00 IN the afternoon, Andrew and Madeleine pulled into the canoe launch parking lot, the rented canoe strapped to the top of their car. The lot was graveled and big enough for thirty cars. The dock was fifty yards from the parking lot at the end of a gentle-sloped path down through trees.

The day was sparkling. Andrew had told her he had made progress this morning and was happy with it and now was relishing the quiet beauty of these lakes with her, just the two of them, campfires, starry nights. But he first wanted to make a quick call to Lawrence to see that he got the morning message about the license plate, if he was even home.

A dozen cars were parked but there were no people around other than an older couple who were getting close to launch, the husband and their canoe already down at the dock. The wife was getting a final few things from their car.

"Okay, Andrew, why don't you make your call while I un-strap the canoe and get the packs out. I want to re-pack some of my stuff. You might as well call Nadine right away, too. When you get her, just give me a shout and we can both talk to Chris."

The phone booth on a cement pad was on the opposite side of the parking lot and a short way into a grassed picnic area. Andrew called Lawrence. It rang and rang, still no answer. He didn't leave a message this time. He was probably at the lake house, and that was a good sign in its own way. The license tracing could wait until Lawrence got back home and heard Andrew's message.

He looked over and saw Madeleine in busy conversation with the other wife, leaning over a map spread out on the other couple's car trunk. Madeleine seemed to be giving some helpful directions, maybe where portages were.

Nadine was expecting their call tomorrow, not today, and Andrew wondered if she would be in. He dialed, and as he waited he saw Madeleine and the other wife laughing. She was in such good spirits. He was so thankful things were working out.

The phone rang several times before Nadine picked up. Andrew had expected her quick, cheery, energetic "Hello". Instead her voice was nervous, drained, afraid. "Hello."

"Nadine. It's Andrew. Are you alright?"

A long pause. Andrew realized she was choking up, sobbing. "Nadine. It's Andrew. What's going on?" His only thought was that Chris had been hurt. Nadine was swallowing as if she couldn't speak. "Nadine, please!"

"Andrew, someone… kidnapped Chris."

The words were incomprehensible to him. They repeated in his head, falling one at a time like blocks of stone. SOMEONE KIDNAPPED CHRIS.

His brain jolted, racing, the meaning sinking in. "When?"

"Last night. Late. I got a phone call." Her crying lessened as she fought to gain control to help Andrew understand. "I didn't see them. They must have used a ladder to get into his bedroom."

"Did they say who they are?"

"No. And I saw no one. Chris was just gone."

His mind saw Velez. But how could Velez have known? He had the slimmest hope it was not Velez, someone just random, for money. It was a rich-looking neighborhood.

Nadine was talking. "I got a phone call telling me not to speak to police, or we won't ever see Chris again. They said you, Andrew… you must come forward."

The terrifying truth was unfolding, what he feared the most. It *was* Velez. Where had he made a mistake? How did they know?

And now Chris, little Chris. Andrew's heart felt like it would burst.

They wanted him in exchange for Chris. Of course he would do that.

"Did you speak to anyone about this?" he said.

"No. They said if I did, they would learn of it. They're going to call again. I'm to tell them where you are."

"What exactly did you tell them?"

"That you and Madeleine were away canoeing, wilderness camping, out of contact. But that you would be calling tomorrow afternoon to check in with me. They want to know where you are."

Andrew swung to look around the parking lot, worried they might already be seen. There was nobody else but the older couple. He kept his voice low. "Did you tell them where we are?"

"No, I couldn't remember the name. They told me I better remember. What do I do when they call?"

"Nadine, we haven't talked. *We haven't talked. Alright?* I need some time. You haven't yet told them where we are?"

"No. I had to tell them what kind of car you drive. A blue Olds 88."

Andrew's mind raced. He saw one chance in this.

"That's okay, Nadine. That's okay. Now listen, I want you to tell them exactly where we are, White's Access on Rempel Lake. It's a canoe launch parking lot. Tell them you remembered, or that you found a note Madeleine left for you. Tell them that's where we're parked. Tell them! So they know you're cooperating."

She was sobbing again. "Andrew…I'm … falling apart…"

"Nadine, listen, they'll come here and check it for themselves. They'll know you're cooperating. *Just don't tell them we talked.*"

Her voice was so weak. "I keep thinking maybe I could have…"

"Nadine, there's *nothing* you could have done. *Nothing.* Please calm yourself. We need your help now."

"I don't know that I can hang on."

"You've got to hang on for Chris. Be strong for Chris."

"I will."

"I'll call you back. *But we didn't talk just now!*

"I understand."

He hung up the phone. He could feel his body convulsing with pain and fear and hate, every muscle taut, his mind wild. He fought to check his base instincts, go to that other place in his mind where he could seal himself from this emotional onslaught, where he was not a cornered animal of simple, brute, enraged fear.

He had kept his back to the parking lot during the conversation. He glanced and saw Madeleine still talking. He picked up the phone again and put it to his ear to appear he was still talking while he considered what to do. He breathed deeply, slowly, sucking in the air, holding it in, then releasing it slowly, the sniper's exercise. His hands were balled into tight fists, and he forced himself to uncurl them.

His mind kept racing.

How had Velez found out? Was it the break-in at Nix's office? Lawrence had warned him about that.

Chris was all that mattered now. Andrew's heart was pounding like a jackhammer. He had one day before Velez expected him to learn of the kidnapping. Lawrence was probably at the lake house because he hadn't answered Andrew's calls. Lawrence had no phone there, so Andrew had to go there.

But if they knew about Andrew, did they know about Lawrence too? He had to consider they did. Until he knew otherwise, he had to assume they knew Lawrence was involved. Would they know where his lake house was? Had they taken him already?

Another thing, as he had said to Nadine, Velez would send men to this canoe launch to check that his car was still here to confirm that Nadine hadn't talked. They would also be here tomorrow afternoon waiting for his and Madeleine's return.

If he did it right, he would have one day. One day to find Chris before they knew he knew anything. If he did it right.

He glanced down towards the dock. The husband had fully loaded the canoe and was sitting in it, ready to shove off, just waiting for his wife who was still at their car.

He turned his back to them, the phone receiver still at his ear as his mind raced through possibilities. He needed to get to Lawrence right away, get back to the aerodrome and fly to the lake house. If Lawrence was there and safe, at least they could work together. Lawrence could phone some agents at home from a payphone, concocting some story about why he needed them. That would avoid a leak. Lawrence could devise a strategy, something better than Andrew could ever come up with at this moment with his mind spinning like a top.

He was suddenly aware of gravel crunching. Madeleine was coming, only ten yards away. "Yes, okay," he said casually into the dead phone and hung up.

"Hey, what are you doing?" Madeleine objected. She looked perplexed and put out. "You were talking to Nadine. I heard you say her name. Why'd you hang up?"

"She had to grab something on the stove. Chris is at a friend's. She wasn't expecting our call today."

"Yeah, but she could move the pot or whatever off the stove and talk to me. Gee, Andrew." Her tone suggested he was a dunce. "I want to call her back."

"She said to give her fifteen minutes."

Madeleine's face relaxed. "Oh. Okay. So we can get the gear loaded into the canoe first and then I'll call."

"Sure."

She studied him a moment. "You seem a little tense. We have a deal, remember?"

She brought her face close to his and said playfully, "Hey, handsome, shake it loose, will you? We both deserve a nice break."

As they walked to the car, she said, "The canoe's all unstrapped, so you can take it off."

He made a quick survey of the other cars in the parking area. He saw the woman looking toward her husband hoping to get his attention. She walked halfway to the launch and called to him. "Greg!" She dangled a set of car keys in her hand. He signaled her to come to him.

City people don't appreciate how well their voices travel in the wilderness. Or they're still conditioned to the highway din. Or they're older, like this couple. The husband reached into a vest pocket. He lowered his voice to what he thought was now private conversation. "Lock up with this set. Leave your set in the car, in the tissue box in the back seat."

The woman went back to their car.

Madeleine was digging out packs and other bags from the trunk and setting them on the gravel. Andrew spent two minutes rooting in the glove box, killing time, watching the woman at her car. She finally got out, locked up, and hurried toward the dock.

Andrew got out and said to Madeleine, "Did you tell her we're going north?"

"Yeah."

He hoisted the canoe off the roof and onto his shoulders and carried it down the path to the dock. The older couple shoved off and were paddling away.

The woman turned and waved to Andrew. "Have a wonderful time."

Andrew returned the wave.

The couple was heading south to the first portage, half a mile across the lake, so wouldn't be expecting Andrew and Madeleine to follow, believing them to be going north. His immediate concern was someone else pulling into the parking area in the next five minutes.

Madeleine turned and saw Andrew just standing there at the dock. She figured he was enjoying the view and the quiet, finally beginning to relax. She watched for a few moments, happy, and went back to finishing up sorting the pack pockets.

Andrew waited a full two minutes to be sure the other couple wouldn't see anything. Then he lifted the canoe and carried it fifty steps into the woods and placed it well out of sight.

Madeleine was looking toward the dock when he came out of the woods. She didn't see their canoe anywhere. She called out, flabbergasted, raising her arms high. "What did you do with the canoe?"

He didn't answer, striding quickly up the path from the dock and across the parking area. He had already spotted the large rock he needed. He walked over and picked it up in both hands and walked to the other couple's car, Madeleine's eyes following him.

"What are you doing?" she said.

The look on his face made her extremely nervous. Something was seriously wrong here.

"Andrew?" She swallowed hard and stared.

He stood by the driver's door a moment, testing the heft of the rock in his right hand.

Then he leaned back and heaved it against the window. The window shattered through.

Madeleine dropped the pack she was holding.

He reached through the broken window and lifted the lock button. He opened the door and got in. He reached into the back seat and grabbed the tissue box and retrieved the keys. He turned on the ignition. He got out, leaving the engine running.

He finally looked at Madeleine. His expression was diamond hard. She knew Andrew well. Nothing she could say was going to change whatever was going on. Not one iota. She was terrified and couldn't speak.

"Madeleine," he said firmly but calmly. "We need to load our stuff into this car and get out of here. *Now*."

"Andrew... please...," her voice pleaded. She kept wondering why this other car and not their own?

"Time's short. I'll explain." He grabbed up three packs at once. "Get in the car."

CHAPTER FORTY ONE

THEY PULLED AWAY from the parking lot out onto the dusty gravel road heavily treed on both sides. Madeleine was watching him, her face warring with fright but edged with anger.

"I need to find a place hidden to pull over," he said. "We can't be seen."

He passed a short lane that took a jog out of sight. He stopped, backed up, and drove in. He shut off the engine. Madeleine was sitting sideways in the seat staring at him.

"It's Chris," he finally said.

Her eyes widened. She grabbed at him. "*What? Tell me.*"

"He's been kidnapped."

Her mouth opened but nothing came out. Her eyes darted back and forth across his face, uncomprehending.

"He was taken by the man who took my father. I got too close to him."

She screamed, "*What have you done?*" Her body convulsed with rage. She hit at him. He let her swing, but blocked the hits. "*What have you done*?"

He had to let her get it out. She wouldn't be able to listen or understand until she was done.

"*My baby! Where is he? Tell me,"* she screamed into his face. She tried to strike him again but he finally grabbed her hands.

"They *won't* harm Chris, Madeleine. They *won't* harm him," he repeated, although he didn't know that with Velez.

She was overcome, an emotional tidal wave crashing. She wailed loudly. "No! No! No!" She hit at the dashboard with her fist.

As her flailing weakened her energy turned inward, wreaking havoc. She cried uncontrollably. He held her a minute. Her sobbing slowed. "Where is he?"

"I don't know."

"What do they want?"

"They want me, only me, in exchange."

She looked at him, her breathing erratic. He knew she was beginning to register things now, survival instincts kicking in. She was starting to think clearly.

"We have a chance," he said. "They don't know I know about Chris. Nadine told them we weren't calling in until tomorrow afternoon. They think we won't know anything for another day. It's a chance to devise a plan."

"We need the police," her words stumbled out.

"No. We can't do that. They said that if anyone goes to the police, we never see Chris again. They have insiders, informers. They could find out. We can't go to anybody, except Lawrence. He can call some off-duty agents, pick them up from their homes without telling them what's going on. We have *one day*."

He pulled the car back out onto the road. Soon they were on the highway. Madeleine was working things through, her body squeezed tight into a rolled knot, her arms gripping her legs to her chest, swaying in pain. "What did Nadine say?" she moaned.

"She didn't see anyone. They climbed up, took Chris from his bedroom. He was sleeping."

Her eyes closed tightly, her face tortured.

"Chris will be okay, Madeleine. I'm going to make that happen for sure."

She stared straight ahead, then suddenly banged the dashboard hard with her fist again. "Sure you are." She cried out loud once, a piercing wail, like a knife.

Andrew shouted, "They're not going to hurt him, Madeleine!" He said it as much to convince himself, and to blast the world with his anger.

She didn't look at him. After a few moments, she said in a whisper, "They're going to kill you."

He didn't answer. At least she understood.

He kept grilling himself, his pain like a razor twisting in his bowels. Where had he made the mistake? Was it Nix's office? Lawrence had warned him…and now Chris...taken.

There had been no alarm at Nix's office. Was there a silent alarm? Had he been followed? Is that how they found his home? But he had gone to the motel, not home.

It didn't matter how it happened. He had blundered, fatally. And now he was tied to a stake and couldn't move. And Chris… Chris and Madeleine… would pay.

He felt his insides dissolving.

"You have to tell me everything you know," Madeleine said.

"No. If you know too much, you would have to die, too."

As they drove, he was conscious of the time, conscious of the flying time left.

He pushed words through his head and the scene formed: They came up by ladder and in through the window; Chris was sleeping in his bed; a strange man stood over him. Words. But now the words transformed into clear images imagined: a man with cold eyes, a callous mouth, a strong body, bending and picking Chris up, his thick chestnut hair, his deep breathing angel face, his limp, light limbs, his soft pajamas.

Suddenly he said urgently, "Madeleine! What pajamas was Chris wearing?"

She grabbed his arm. "The…the…the yellow ones," she stammered.

"Are you sure?"

Her words ran quickly. "Yes, I told him he could wear them while Nadine was there. What is it?"

He hit the brakes and swerved to a sliding sideways stop on the gravel shoulder. He reached into the back seat and grabbed the knapsack he always had flying. His hands were shaking. He took out the pictures he had taken earlier of the brown Ford LTD and of the cabin area.

"What kind of yellow?"

Her voice quavered, "P-Primary yellow."

This morning when he had studied the enlarged photos of the area of the Ford LTD to try to read the license plate, he had noticed a small yellow fabric something draped on a fence post nearby. Its brightness stood out against that background so had caught his eye momentarily. He remembered thinking it was probably a rag. But at that time it was inconsequential.

He flipped through the pictures he had taken today. He found one, then two, then three that captured that tight area. He studied them a moment. What had appeared like a rag hanging from a cedar fence post near the car now seemed like possibly something more.

He handed the pictures to Madeleine. Her frantic eyes devoured them, her fingers gripping the edges.

He grabbed into the knapsack for the pictures he had taken yesterday on his first flight over the buildings. The ones taken by the telephoto lens might have produced enough of a close-up.

"It's the right color," she blurted. "I think there's a sleeve. Not just a square cloth."

He could feel his heart pounding as he flicked through twenty pictures trying to find one with that same spot along the fence by the barn.

"It's a child's size," she said, "comparing it to the post size if the post is a regular size."

He found two pictures that showed that post. They weren't as close-up as the ones he had taken today, so weren't as good a resolution, but even so, they were enough. It was clear there was no yellow color on that post. It was a bare post!

"That yellow something wasn't there yesterday," he said, showing her the picture. "But the one I took this morning, it was there. It had to be put there later yesterday, or last night, or early this morning. I flew over it this morning."

Madeleine's voice broke. "Maybe…to dry…maybe it was raining."

"Yes, maybe. The weather report said it did rain there last night."

She stared at the picture of the yellow fabric. She began to cry silently.

Andrew said reluctantly, "But still…can't be sure."

He saw Madeleine's fingers rubbing the picture, her tears dripping. He wasn't sure she had heard him. She whispered, "Yellow…. is…sunshine.

*

At his aerodrome he tried calling Lawrence at home. There was still no answer.

He said to Madeleine, "He must be at the lake house. There's no phone there. It's faster if we fly." He also knew that if The Watcher was watching the road into Lawrence's lake house, it was better they fly in and be unseen.

They touched down just at 6:15 p.m. on the farmer's grass airstrip, a mile from Lawrence's.

"I'm going alone," Andrew said. "There could be someone else there. I have to be sure. Safer you stay here. And it's faster. I can run there and back."

She nodded. He knew she would be far better to rest, and she knew it, too, her exhaustion, the emotional strain, showing.

When he got near the lake house he took extreme caution, circling it at a distance to be sure no one else was there, or even watching it. But he didn't see Lawrence's car. Damn! What exactly did that mean? Did it mean he just wasn't there, as in he hadn't come at all? Or he had come but now had been taken, too? There had been no answer at his home in the city this morning or afternoon. Or had he gone into the village a few miles away for a bite to eat or to have a beer at the local watering hole. That would account for him not being at home and also not being here at the moment. But he had no way of going there to find him without a vehicle, if he were there at all. Or he might be on his way back to the city, to home, by now.

Satisfied no one was around, Andrew smashed a window at the back of the cottage and climbed in. If Lawrence was in the village and coming back, he would see a note.

He found a pen and wrote on an envelope and put it in plain sight on the corner of the kitchen table: "Saturday, 6:30 PM. Go home and check messages." He didn't leave a name. Lawrence would know.

When he got back to the airstrip he found Madeleine sitting on the grass staring off. He startled her when he ran towards her. "He wasn't there. I left a note. He might be in the village. He'll know to go home right away."

She got up, looking indecisive. "Now what?"

"We fly back to my aerodrome to refuel. My gear's there. Then I'll fly on. I want to be over the Hunt Club property before dark to see if the car is still at the cabin. If it is, then I land about two miles from the rear of that property on an unused strip of highway."

"And if the car's not at the cabin?"

"I don't know. I just think it's going to be. That's as far as I can think right now."

"Fuck," she said to the grass, her face strained.

"There's a phone at Rona's Corners nearby. I'll coordinate with Lawrence from there. When he and some agents arrive, we'll do a takedown before daybreak. The kidnappers aren't expecting anyone."

"But what if Chris isn't there?" She stared at him, her eyes on fire. Her voice went loud, accusing. "What if all this guesswork is wrong?"

"Settle down! Don't you think I'm ready to explode here, too!"

She looked away.

"It's a chance we have to take," he said. "If Chris is there, we have the advantage of surprise. If he's not, at least we haven't risked shouting out to police and having it leaked. We would also still have another twelve hours before the kidnappers expect me to know anything."

She was quieter now, but still looking away. "What if you can't reach Lawrence at all? And there's no help?"

He took her hand. "If we don't find Chris before the kidnappers know that I know, then I'm giving myself up to them as if I haven't talked to anybody, just like they want. The best I can do is bargain with them first so you and Chris will be safe."

She looked at him, fear replacing fire.

"It may be all I can do," he said.

*

At the canoe launch site, a black Mustang pulled slowly into the parking lot. Steve was driving, Kell in the passenger seat. There were no people about. Both quickly spotted Andrew's blue Olds' 88. They pulled up close and stopped.

Kell got out, his eyes casting all around the lot and he listened. The canoe rack was still on the Olds' roof. He noticed racks still on the roofs of a few other cars, too. He tested the Olds' doors, peered into the windows, walking around the car as he did. There was nothing in the car, no camping gear. Everything just the way it would be if you had left your car and gone camping.

It seemed the sister had told the truth.

The sister had also said Andrew and Madeleine would be calling her tomorrow from here. He saw the telephone booth standing on a cement pad over in the picnic area.

He walked down to the launch dock and looked out at the expanse of blue lake, quiet and peaceful.

*

Andrew and Madeleine landed back at his aerodrome. There was just less than two hours of flying time and he had to fly to Chambersburg, and then further, to get over the Hunt Camp property before dark. As he quickly refueled the plane, he watched Madeleine walk slowly back and forth across the tarmac, her head down.

In his storage compartment, he checked his M-16 assault rifle and slid it into its case along with three ammo clips. He slipped on his holstered semi-automatic Smith and Wesson 459 pistol and three clips. He buckled on a hunting knife at his waist. He grabbed up a bag that held night goggles, flashlights and a compass. His rifle had no working silencer; the quick detach suppressor had seized. He wished he had something quiet. Quiet was often so useful.

His eyes went to the corner of the compartment. There was nothing quieter—his Dad's light-weight oak crossbow, a deer-hunting crossbow, one his father had made himself. Beside it was the leather quiver holding thick-shaft arrows called bolts, each with a razor-sharp, three-inch flaring steel tip.

Seeing the crossbow bolstered him. He shouldered it and the quiver and locked the compartment.

When he got back to the plane, Madeleine was standing beside it, no longer pacing. "I'm coming with you," she said.

"Madeleine, no. It's better we're not together, for Chris. We… can't both die. And you…with the baby."

"I can't go home! I'm not going anywhere! I *have* to be with you! I have to know what's going on!"

He understood her feelings, but it was foolhardy. "Madeleine, please…"

"You think he may be there, so I'm going. *I have to know what's happening*! I'm not staying back! Nobody will know I'm there. If things look like they might go bad, I can disappear."

He barked at her. "Sure, if you're lucky enough to have a choice! What if you don't?"

"If he's not there, then no harm. If he is, I may be of some help! That's what counts now! *Don't argue with me!*"

He looked at her and saw a mother's fierce love, her absolute resolve.

An overwhelming guilt flooded him. He had succeeded in suppressing it until now so he could just think straight, keep putting one foot in front of the other. But looking into her face now, tears came to him, his innocent wife, his innocent son, paying for his *stupid, stupid failure*.

"Madeleine," he grabbed her and held her close. His voice shook with emotion. "I'm so sorry...so sorry I brought this on Chris and you. I will gladly give my life for you, for Chris. I just hope I have that chance."

She held him, crying, "I know, Andrew. I know."

CHAPTER FORTY TWO

IT WAS 9:30 and the sun had set ten minutes earlier, the sky quickly darkening. They still had a few miles to fly just to get to the landing site, a stretch of asphalt of the disused section of highway near Rona's Corners. Of course there would be no landing lights, no light of any kind but the traces of natural light offered by late dusk.

Andrew brought the biplane lower to five hundred feet and squinted at the ground at a smooth paved road to determine just exactly how well he could see to land. It was dim, time very short. The drone of the engine seemed especially loud in the darkening sky. He spoke into the headset to Madeleine. "It's too risky to fly on to the Hunt Camp to check for the car now. I've got to get us down the second I can."

He heard her 'yes'.

A minute later he saw the stretch of asphalt coming up dimly in the gloom and quickly slowed and dropped to a hundred feet, skimming the darkening tree tops. He had no time to do a fly-over check.

The plane lowered and lowered then touched, bouncing once off the asphalt before touching again, and settling and slowing and rolling to a stop. The moment it did, Andrew felt the dusky darkness envelope them.

They quickly climbed down from the plane and she slung the pack with the ammunition and night goggles onto her shoulder. She had a flashlight ready in her hand. He grabbed the rifle and crossbow and quiver. They hurried along a dark dirt road the half mile to Rona's Corners, just a quiet crossroads with two street lights and darkened buildings. Nothing was open, but there was a payphone in front of the little lumber store.

Desperate for Lawrence to be home, Andrew slipped a bunch of quarters into the phone and tried the number. He let it ring eight times.

He hung up.

Madeleine's hands were clenched. "Maybe they knew he's connected to you. Maybe they've taken him—."

He cut her off. "It makes no difference to what I have to do right now. I have to see if that car's still there."

"Even if it's there, we don't know if Chris is there. Or was ever there."

"No, we don't."

"What do we do if—?"

"But if it is there," he said, slinging the crossbow and quiver back over his shoulder, the rifle already in one hand. He began to walk. "It's over two miles there, over two miles back," he said. "If the car's there, I intend to come back here to try Lawrence once more."

"I'm coming. If the car's there, I can stay hidden somewhere."

They walked quickly away from the two streetlights, soon in darkness but for uneven moonlight between floating clouds. After walking a mile they came to the dirt road Andrew had seen from the plane yesterday.

"About a mile down this road there's a trail that comes out at the rear of the 500 acre property. The path meanders almost a mile through the property, by swamp and through woods. Leads all the way to the cabin."

Walking fifteen minutes, they found the opening to the trail. The moonlight offered more light now.

It took them almost twenty minutes to walk the whole of the trail, through woods, by expansive swamp, through low grassy lands, but the trail held clear. They arrived at thick bush cover and stopped. They were at the edge of the large grassy clearing of four or five acres, some stubbly shrubs and trees between them and the cabin and barn, two hundred yards away.

Andrew saw the car. "It's still there!" he whispered, the Ford LTD lit dimly by moonlight. There were no lights on in the cabin, no sound, no activity. He squinted through the night vision goggles, closely examining the tops of all the posts in the area where he had seen the yellow fabric. It was no longer there, all the posts empty.

"The yellow fabric, it's gone."

Someone was surely inside the cabin.

He desperately wanted to go in but he knew it would be reckless. Even though it was only 10:30, the lights were out inside which was smart after dark. He couldn't see in to see how many there were, and where they were. But they would hear him. They would see him as well as he would see them. They had the advantage of cover, could easily outgun him. It would be reckless to ever go in.

"I'm going back to make one more call. Then I'll be back." He paused, looking at her. "Over four miles return." He said it as a question.

She nodded. She was already exhausted. "I want to stay here."

He knew she was thinking of Chris. If he was here, she wanted to be here. He took the black Smith and Wesson pistol from his holster and put it into her hand. She looked at him. He showed her the safety, the on, the off. "Keep the safety on. If you have to take it off, never put your finger on the trigger until you're ready to fire. Don't give yourself away by shooting early. Don't use it until you really have to."

He hugged her then was quickly gone, back onto the trail on the way to the telephone booth back at Rona's corners.

*

Velez and Nix were at Nix's penthouse. It was 11:20, Velez looking impatient as he looked out the grand window at the twinkling night lights across Philadelphia.

He and Nix had been considering Andrew for the last hour, trying to figure how he had ever come to latch onto Nix. Some superb detective work for sure. "Probably takes after his father," Nix offered at one point.

But as much as they admired him, they were sorely put out that they themselves could not connect the dots that he had. What even were the dots? That would be a good starting point.

Regardless, they were confident they now had the upper hand. The boy, Chris, was perfect leverage, safely tucked away, and Andrew and the wife were out canoeing for now and doing no damage to them. When he and she came back to the launch site tomorrow they would be overwhelmed, swarmed by a bunch of friendly canoe camper guys unloading packs from their vehicles.

With all that well in hand, it left only Lawrence to deal with. But where was Lawrence?

Velez had dispatched eyes to watch Lawrence's house in the city and to watch the lake house road and to take a look as well at the lake house itself. But the reports were that he wasn't there and didn't appear to be at home. Two phone calls had been made to his home this afternoon by one of the cell group who was hoping to sell him some duct-cleaning. But there had been no answer and he had not been seen there all day.

At eight o'clock that evening a further update to Nix reported no changes—no lights on in the house. No movement observed anywhere.

"He has to show some time. It's not like he has friends anywhere."

Velez wanted to have a meeting with Lawrence to learn all he could about Andrew before Andrew was seized tomorrow. Better to get all he could first from Lawrence about this investigation and who all was involved. Lawrence would buckle under the right persuasion, and Velez knew the right persuasion. Then he would cross-reference what he learned from Lawrence with what he learned from Andrew who would talk freely and generously to save his son.

*

Was it real, or a dream, or a drug-induced phantasmagoria?

An orchestra tuning up? Damn, that was it. It was an orchestra tuning up in his house, at this hour! And what hour was it? Well, it was dark. And how did they get in, he wondered? And so many of them. Better not start on any kettle drums. Damn, that would hurt. He would have something to say about this when he got up and waved his pistol.

At home in a dark bedroom upstairs, Lawrence felt himself surfacing as the orchestra kept tuning, louder and louder. He opened his eyes and his head hurt.

Not an orchestra. It was the phone ringing. And ringing and ringing.

From early morning he had been wired on white magic, chasing it with straight bourbon. He had fallen asleep sometime, maybe in the morning, maybe in the afternoon. Who knew?

The phone—ring, ring, ring. Shut the fuck up, damned thing.

Just pick it up and it will stop ringing. Then just say, "NO!"

He reached an arm way over from the bed to the night table and struggled to lift the receiver. "Hello," the word slithered out.

"Wes, you're there! It's Andrew! You were out."

"No…sleeping." His voice was weak.

"They know about me. They've taken Chris."

Lawrence's mind strained to comprehend. "What…what…?" His words were slow and lacked energy. He tried to sit up in bed.

"It's Velez. He kidnapped Chris. He's onto me. But I might know where they have him. You've got to—"

"Just…just…just a second, Andrew. I'm waking up here. Let me turn on a light." His hand reached to a lamp on the night-table and snapped on the light. He glanced at his watch. 11:30.

"The Watcher kidnapped Chris last night," Andrew said. "They're holding him until I give myself up to them."

Lawrence was sitting up now, shaking his head. "Say that again?"

"The Watcher, it's Velez, he kidnapped Chris last night,"

Andrew shouted. "They're holding him until I give myself up to them."

"What the hell? How did they know?"

"They don't know I know any of this. Madeleine's sister was babysitting at our house. They're not expecting me to call her until tomorrow late afternoon. I think I know where they've got Chris. They don't know I know. They're not expecting me to call home until tomorrow late afternoon."

Lawrence struggled out of bed and stood, one hand holding his head, still getting his bearings.

"I may know where they have him," Andrew hurried on. "That 500-acre hunt camp I told you about near Chambersburg. I saw some things in a flyover today. I left you a message this morning. Madeleine is with me. They said if I went to the police, Chris is dead. I need you. Grab a few agents right from their homes so no leaks."

"How the hell did they know about you?"

"I don't know. But that's not important now."

"You said you left me a message?"

"Yes, with a license plate number and a car description, parked at the hunt camp, to trace the plate."

As Lawrence became more awake and clear-headed, he grew more worried with the news, more shaken. "But how did Velez know?" he said, insistent.

"I don't know how!" Andrew yelled, angry at the question being repeated. "But it doesn't matter now!"

"It wasn't supposed to happen this way," Lawrence said, angry now himself, "him knowing us before we know him. That wasn't the plan."

"What the hell's wrong with you?" Andrew screamed. "Yes, I

fucked up somewhere, yes! But what's that matter now? They've got Chris! That's all that matters! Get on the same page here!"

Lawrence went quiet.

Andrew calmed himself, breathing deeply. "I'm sorry. But I need your help, I really need you. We have a chance here. But we don't have much time."

"I understand," but his voice suggested something else, something entering his mind beyond Andrew's problem.

"Grab a few agents right from their homes," Andrew said again, "so no leaks, not telling them specifics yet. You've got to get here. We've got to do the takedown at first light."

"I understand," but his voice lacked energy, resolve.

"I'm calling from a telephone booth in Rona's Corners, just west of Chambersburg. There's just one telephone booth here. I've drawn a map that shows where to meet us at 5:00 a.m., a place where a dirt road meets a trail. I'm putting the map in the phone book here at page 100. I need you, Wes."

Lawrence's hand was shaking. He reached for a pen and a small spiral notebook and began making notes. "Okay, I'm writing. Go over all those details again for me, slowly."

*

The two men Leader had posted to watch Lawrence's house each had a car. They made sure only one car was visible on the street at any time. They had taken turns on this very dark night walking past the house, or being nearby but away from the lone street light, or sitting in their car down the street but in view of his driveway and house. There were no passersby now that it was almost 11:30.

One car pulled away from the curb and left the street as the other car parked close by Lawrence's house. The driver of the car who just parked stretched himself a moment and glanced at the house, still dark, no one there all boring day.

He reached his hand into the back seat for his second sandwich bag and thermos. He unscrewed the lid and poured coffee into a Styrofoam cup. He sat back to relax, bringing the cup to his lips. He stopped abruptly, his eyes staring, then blinking, and looking again.

There was a light, unmistakably a light, an upstairs room, probably a bedroom, the curtain not fully drawn. There had been no light on before at all. He was certain of that, dead certain. It must have just come on, and not a timer, too late in the evening for that, 11:35, way, way after dark. And only one room. And that room upstairs. You don't do that on a timer—only one room, and upstairs. No, Lawrence was there, probably all damn day, damn it.

He grabbed the radio and radioed to Leader who told him to standby.

Two minutes later, Leader gave him instructions. "You're to pick the lock at the back door of his house now. Then both of you scram."

*

Lawrence finished the call with Andrew and hung up.

Sitting on the edge of the bed his hands jittered as he read some of the notes he had just made in the notebook: 'Velez may have Chris at cabin; grab some agents, map at page 100 phone book, phone booth Rona's Corners; 5:00 a.m meet, do takedown.' He made a further note: 'Listen message machine'. And a further note: 'Maddy with Andrew.'

But Lawrence was badly shaken. Was this takedown idea going to work? Just exactly what did Velez know? This was not supposed to go at all like this. Andrew had really fumbled somewhere, disturbed some strand of Velez's web. He had warned Andrew about that, damn it. Velez was never supposed to get even a whiff of this investigation. Now Velez had taken an extreme step and gained the upper hand. Things were really falling apart.

He needed some pills to clear his head to think through this fucking mess. This wasn't how it was supposed to go!

But first he needed to get under the shower and wake up. He walked into the washroom and cranked the shower high.

*

As Lawrence stepped carefully from the shower he was met by a long-barreled silenced pistol.

"Mr. Lawrence, I presume," Nix said. He motioned with the gun toward the bedroom.

Velez was sitting on the edge of the bed reading the spiral notebook when Lawrence, wearing a towel, and Nix came into the room. Velez looked up. "Well, Mr. Lawrence, it's been quite some time, hasn't it? It doesn't look like life's been altogether good to you either. You look like shit." He waved the notebook. "Making some notes here I see, very disturbing ones."

Velez got up from the bed. "I'm going to go downstairs and listen to that recorded telephone message from Andrew while you put on some pants. You won't need more."

Minutes later in the living room, Nix shoved Lawrence down into a wooden chair. He strapped Lawrence's neck tightly to the chair with a leather belt then bound his feet and lashed his hands behind him.

Velez sat in a chair opposite. "I've just listened to Andrew's message from earlier today about a certain hunt camp and a car license. And there's the matter of your notes tonight about grabbing a few agents for a little surprise takedown, and Andrew's map, where to meet at 5:00. He's already there, and with Madeleine. All a shock to me, I can tell you, a real departure from what I thought was going on, Andrew and lovely Madeleine paddling on some lake."

Velez got up. "I don't want this meeting to be difficult. There's no need for you to suffer. No one will ever know what happened here. So let's start with FBI agent Andrew Locke. He has to go, too, of course, a clever snoop. The real question is who else has to go? That's what it's come down to, and you're going to decide."

He took a photograph from his pocket and showed it to Lawrence whose eyes glanced at the image. "See little Chris? And the burly man with the gun? Chris doesn't like his new babysitter. But don't look forlorn. I don't kill children. The question is what do I do with Madeleine?"

Lawrence's eyes flicked. "She knows nothing," he said. "Andrew has always made that clear."

"I'll consider that a possibility. Now, as Nix and I have much to do over the next hours, I want answers clear and full and quick. First, how did you get onto Nix?"

Lawrence's eyes moved to Nix, then back to Velez, but he said nothing.

Velez drew a long steel needle, like a knitting needle, from inside his jacket and set it on a reading table beside him with a theatrical flourish. "If I have to resort to primitive means, I assure you, you will talk. You can't help him now. But you can help Madeleine."

Lawrence looked from the steel needle to Velez. His eyes dropped, his voice coming slowly. "Andrew considered the ownership of the hotel might be a factor…the Swiss company, maybe a cover. It would explain you being there that night twenty years ago…the new ballroom…Macky seeing you. But you were never questioned…not on any list."

Velez looked to Nix, a wary concern showing, but also respect for a clever insight.

Lawrence continued, "Andrew learned that Nix did the company's legal work…checked out his law practice history…a Buffalo connection…thought it was worth investigating."

"Maybe stakeout his law office," Velez nodded. "Follow Nix around a bit. See where he goes. I see it." He looked to Nix. "Lucky thing you weren't around when he was snooping. You've got to make some changes there."

He looked back to Lawrence. "What about the hunt camp?"

"Old records from the mortgage broker when you bought the hotel. Andrew wondered about the collateral, the 500 acres… thought there was something odd there…no resort potential…no address for property taxes…wanted to look deeper."

Velez again cast a look to Nix, then back to Lawrence. "This Andrew has a long and very dangerous nose. Is he the only one who knows anything at all of this?"

Lawrence nodded weakly. "Yes."

"Nobody else at your office? No other confidante?"

"No."

"I only have to remove you and Andrew and I'm safe again. Is that correct? No lurking exceptions?"

Lawrence shook his head. "I involved no one else."

"Except Andrew?"

Lawrence's voice was quiet. "Except Andrew." He looked at Velez. "Please don't hurt Madeline, or Chris. And tell Andrew…"

Velez waited moments. "Tell him what?"

"Tell him…I'm very sorry."

"Sure, I'll pass that right along. But I want to go back to something. The way you described you and Andrew, 'he considered this, he wondered that', all like it was just sniffing around, no really solid footing. But you also said if I owned the hotel that would explain *me* being there that night twenty years ago, and would explain how it was that Macky saw *me*."

Velez picked up the needle and walked to Lawrence. "So I can only conclude from that that you already *knew* I was alive. I think Andrew's hunch about the Swiss company covering for me would only ever have happened if you made him believe I was alive in the first place. And that's what you fed him, isn't it? That I was alive. I want to know how you *knew* I was alive. I have a theory, but I want to hear it from you. And once you tell me, I'll relieve you of all your fears, all your hurts, all your guilt. A little drug I have will put you to sleep. You won't be waking up, of course, but your suffering will be over."

*

Lawrence was still conscious when Velez rolled him over to expose the artery in his neck. He jabbed a medical needle in deep and pushed the plunger, injecting the lethal dose.

Minutes later they dragged him out through the back door. Nix walked half way around the block, retrieving their car. He drove backwards into Lawrence's driveway and parked at the dark end by a hedge. They lifted his body into the trunk and quietly closed the lid.

"Locke will sit tight waiting for Lawrence to bring the cavalry. He won't make any move on his own before daylight," Nix said. "I'll get the men into place."

Velez nodded. "He was so damn close, the clever fellow. I look forward to meeting him."

CHAPTER FORTY THREE

AFTER SPEAKING WITH Lawrence from the payphone, Andrew made the long trek along the two roads and the mile trail through the Hunt Club property. There was now an unobstructed three-quarter moon and the night air was warm. It was almost 1:00 am when he arrived back to where he had left Madeleine.

But he didn't see her. She wasn't there. But with the cabin so close, he couldn't shout out her name. He felt his heart racing, his eyes wild, looking everywhere.

She stepped from hiding, the black Smith and Wesson pistol pointed. "I wasn't sure it was you," she said.

He hugged her a moment. "Well done, Maddy. I reached Lawrence. He's bringing help."

She grabbed his arm. "What did he say?"

"He'll be at the road at the back at 5:00. He'll have help."

Her eyes showed huge relief.

"Any change here?" he said, looking toward the cabin.

"No. Quiet."

"All we can do now is wait."

They crouched in their earlier position, a protected view a hundred yards to the rear of the cabin and barn.

Was Chris in there? Was anyone there? he thought.

Madeleine looked exhausted. "Rest," he said. "Sleep if you can."

She lay on the ground beside him. He stroked her hair. After a long while she drifted into a fitful sleep, her body curled, her knees tucked up.

He felt his own exhaustion weighing and it made him impatient and edgy. He began to fear they were wasting valuable time. Maybe Chris wasn't there. Maybe there was NOTHING useful here at all, a wild goose chase. He again considered rushing the inside of the cabin himself, with Madeleine remaining outside with the pistol.

He shook his head. Come on, think straight. Rushing the cabin would be foolhardy. He had no idea who was in there, how many were in there, what the configuration of the rooms was, whether he would be risking Chris too much. A rescue works when there are sufficient numbers, well armed, well trained, who can instantly overwhelm any resistance. Andrew alone was not overwhelming. But help was coming. He had to remain patient.

The night became very long, one heart beat at a time.

*

He was nodding off when he heard it, a faint sound, a car coming slowly into the property, traveling the quarter mile grassy lane that came in from the road at the front. The sound was getting louder.

He glanced at his watch. 4:30. Damn, he must have fallen asleep. He put on the night finder goggles.

Shortly he saw headlights slowly approaching, washing the grasses with light. He picked up the M16, his movement waking Madeleine with a startle. She sat up and watched the car.

It stopped near the cabin but the engine stayed running and the driver stayed put. Even with the goggles, Andrew couldn't see the driver well for the car lights, or see if anyone else was in there. After a moment the passenger door opened and a man got out, a rifle in hand, a real rifle, an automatic rifle, Andrew saw, not a bird gun. He walked to the cabin with a flashlight and knocked on the door. "Leader here," he said at the door, his words carrying in the night quiet.

Shortly the door opened an inch, then quickly wider. Leader went inside and the door closed. Andrew expected to see a light come on, a lantern maybe. But the windows stayed black except for some dim shafts from the flashlight as the beams bounced off walls.

With all that he had seen, and with the car coming at this hour, he was growing in confidence that he had discovered something very important about this cabin. But still the questions remained: Was Chris there? Had he ever been there? Or had he been there, but had been moved?

After a few minutes the front door opened and Andrew saw Leader make a circular movement with the flashlight, a signal, then he went back into the cabin. The car did a slow U-turn in the yard and rolled away down the lane, leaving the property.

Still no lights came on in the cabin, only the beam of a flashlight every so often. They were extremely cautious, making it impossible to get any view inside to see numbers or position. To rush into a building with not a single light on inside would be suicide. They knew what they were doing.

He had noted earlier there were no telephone lines to the cabin. The men had to come in person to communicate anything. But there was more than the mere passing of information here. The man, Leader, had stayed behind, reinforcing whoever else was there.

And maybe something new was afoot. Were they now going to move Chris, if he was there? The other car had left, but there was still the Ford.

Why had they come today? Why at this hour? Something very time sensitive, something very important.

Things were much worse now. He knew Madeleine knew it, too. But she just whispered, "It's getting closer to 5:00. I'll go and meet Lawrence."

*

Wearing the night vision goggles, she made her way along the meandering mile path that would take her to the dirt road at the back of the property. She would guide Lawrence and the agents back.

In her fatigue and growing fear, the night sounds of cicada and tree frogs were oppressive, carrying notes of unknown threat as she hurried along the narrow trail, leafed branches sweeping at her face. At some times the swamp and bog closed the path so tightly she felt water on her feet. Once, one foot was sucked into something like quick-sand and she fell sideways.

But she traveled quickly for fifteen minutes. Now she was on higher ground in an area of thick razor grasses that grabbed at her legs. A stand of mature fir trees stood just ahead and she knew that signaled the end of the trail, the road just beyond.

She thought she heard something beyond the trees at the roadside. As she got closer she heard it was quiet voices, Lawrence and the agents already there! She felt a surge of hope—this nightmare might soon end!

She rushed now, making out the shape of a car parked to the side of the road, right where it should be. Its lights and engine were off, but she could see the dome light was on.

She wasn't as careful now, couldn't contain herself. "Hey, Lawrence!" she called, still coming through the trees. She burst from the woods by the roadside but, surprised, she saw no one. She had expected four or five agents. There was no one, and no one in the car.

A man stood up from behind the other side of the car, rifle in hand. "Madeleine?" Steve said.

She felt hope. She didn't know him but he knew her name. "Yes."

He began to walk around the car to come to her. "Glad you made it okay."

"But where's Lawrence and the others?"

Even as she said it, she knew something was off. The man's smile seemed stiff, forced. Then something else dawned—the car was exactly like the car she had just seen at the cabin.

She heard a rustle behind her and spun. Kell stepped from concealment holding a rifle.

It hit her like a slap! She knew his face! He was the man who had delivered the wrapped picture parcel to their house for Dr. Curran. This was an ambush! She turned and ran towards the woods.

Kell ran after her. With the night goggles on, she flew surefooted. She got all the way back through the stand of thick fir trees and well on into the tall razor grasses before Kell overtook her and pulled her to the ground. Her goggles flew off. He grabbed her with both hands. She kicked and punched at him. She screamed. He slapped her hard in the face.

"Shut up or I'll kill you right now!"

But she still fought ferociously, punching him. He slapped her again. She grabbed at his hair and kicked to his groin. He punched her once in the face and she fell. He bent and grabbed her up, dragging her through the razor-grass, back through the fir trees. She was disoriented from his blow and resisted only feebly. He pulled her almost to the roadside.

Steve stood beside the car thirty feet away, holding his rifle, a smile developing. "She's a little uncooperative."

"A fucking wildcat," Kell said.

Madeleine's head cleared and she kicked Kell hard and punched at his face. He ducked his head and tried to drag her more toward the car but she struggled, digging in her feet.

There was only a sudden soft 'thwick', the crossbow arrow almost silent, piercing Steve's chest to its feathers, his throat producing strangled sounds, his eyes wide, his rifle clattering to the gravel, his hands clutching weakly at his chest.

Kell tried to free himself from Madeleine's grasp to scramble to Steve's rifle but she hauled on his arm with both of hers with all her might, digging in, forcing him to drag her, slowing him.

His hand almost reached the rifle when Andrew tackled him with such force they both rolled yards from it. He pulled Kell further away while driving two punches to his face. Madeleine was quick to grab Steve's rifle and stepped back. Her whole body shook with anger, her face livid. She pointed the gun.

Andrew and Kell exchanged punches, neither making gains. Andrew saw her and yelled, "Don't! They'll hear it."

The momentary distraction allowed Kell to connect two good blows and he disengaged from Andrew, dashing toward Madeleine and the rifle, risking she wouldn't shoot.

She jumped back but his hand landed on her arm and knocked her, sending the gun down. Andrew leaped, stretching a hand, grabbing at Kell's arm, his other hand pulling his hunting knife from its sheath at his back. Kell lunged toward the fallen gun, but Andrew lunged, too, thrusting the knife with a fierce grunt, driving it into Kell's side a full eight inches to the hilt.

Kell dropped to the ground writhing, his hand trembling just above the knife's handle.

Andrew kneeled over Kell, breathing hard. "Is my son at the cabin? Tell me!"

Kell didn't answer, his eyes closing with the pain.

Andrew shouted. "Tell me!"

Kell's face only grimaced more.

"You're dying. Do one good thing for an innocent boy before you do. Tell me!"

Kell's eyes looked wildly at Andrew.

Madeleine got on her knees and leaned in close, her face alive with grief. Kell tried to fight the pain, his hands clenching. Madeleine took one of them in hers, opened it, held it in both of hers, squeezing it. He looked at her face, so close to his, her eyes on his.

"Please," she whispered, tears coming. "Please tell us."

His eyes stayed on hers while the pain made his face shiver. After moments his head nodded almost imperceptibly and his mouth whispered, "Yes."

She squeezed his hand more. "Thank you."

His eyes held on hers, flickering, pain crossing his face.

His body seemed to relax. "Yes," he whispered again, his eyes still on hers.

In a sudden moment they went lifeless.

Madeleine looked away and stood up. "He's there. Chris is there."

Andrew was still breathing heavily.

"How did you know it wasn't Lawrence here?" she said.

"I didn't know, but that car, that hour."

"Somehow we've been tricked," she said.

"They got to Lawrence. They couldn't have known about this exact meeting spot and time."

He scooped up Steve's gun, his face angry. He pulled out the ammunition clip and hurled it across the road into thick bush. "We're on our own." He flung the gun at the car.

"Lawrence isn't coming," she said mostly to herself, her voice unsteady, not wanting to believe it.

"We've got to act now before the people at the cabin think something happened here."

"But we need help. We've got to involve the police. We need help."

"That brings more risk for Chris. And it would take time. Right now they think we're going to be ambushed by these two. They think they have the upper hand because we don't know about Lawrence."

"But—"

"If they think something happened here and think we're bringing in the police, they might run, take Chris. We'd never see him again. Or he could get killed in a firefight involving the police."

She was weighing his words. All the options were horrifying.

He said, "If things don't quickly go our way, I'm giving myself up. You…you've always got to stay well hidden."

He walked to where he had dropped the crossbow and his own rifle and slung them over his shoulder. "We've got to hurry."

CHAPTER FORTY FOUR

IT WAS 5:15, the eastern sky a yellow glow before sunrise.

They crouched a hundred yards back from the cabin, hidden behind the same thick shrubs and trees from where they had watched in the night, but now surveying it all newly in the beginning light. They could perfectly see the cabin, the two-storey barn, an outhouse, and the Ford. There were only spindly trees and tall grasses between them and the buildings. No good cover.

They had little time. But Andrew still hadn't settled on a plan. "I'm wondering if they've posted anyone down the lane at the front—."

He stopped abruptly at the sound of a squeak, a door opening.

It was the man they saw last night, Leader, who had gone from the car into the cabin. He stepped from the door carrying a rifle, looking around cautiously before beginning down the long grass lane toward the front road. His head turned again and again, observing all around him as he walked.

"Maybe wondering where the others are now," she whispered.

"But not expecting them to be dead," he said coldly.

He knew from seeing it from the air that there was a small building at the front of the property beside the grass lane just before the front road, a kind of gatehouse, almost a quarter-mile away. Presumably Leader was going there. Using the binoculars, Andrew saw he also carried what looked like a walkie-talkie.

Leader was soon out of sight.

"I'm going to the barn," Andrew said. "They won't expect me there."

Madeleine picked up the black Smith and Wesson pistol lying in the grass beside her. He looked at it, so odd in her hand. "Don't give yourself away by shooting early. Don't use it unless you must," he said.

They looked at each other, eyes holding tight. He squeezed her hand.

He slung the crossbow and quiver onto his back and gripped the M16 in his hand. Flat on his stomach, he crawled forward out from the cover of the trees and shrubs.

Not even the tall grass swayed as he wormed his way through.

She remained crouched, concealed. After a minute she saw the grasses move near the rear of the barn where she knew Andrew couldn't be seen from the cabin. A moment later she saw him stand at the corner of the barn. He was still out of any sight line from the cabin.

She heard the cabin door and tensed. A stocky man emerged, a rifle in hand. His gaze swept the rear yard for several moments. She knew he was unaware of Andrew, and that Andrew was unaware of him. Andrew was looking back to her position, his eyes keening to see her. She was desperate to signal but feared the man would see any movement from her.

Andrew stepped around the side of the barn, disappearing into an open doorway on its other side. She watched the stocky man now moving quickly but guardedly in her general direction, going first behind the outhouse which was a hundred feet back from the cabin, using it as a shield as he scrutinized the yard, then moving on another hundred and fifty feet to the Ford where he crouched down behind it. She saw just his head above the car, his eyes roving back and forth across the rear yard into the woods, a cigarette now in his mouth, a tiny blue smoke. He was just two hundred feet from her. She stayed frozen.

She heard the squeak again, the cabin door pushing open slowly.

Out stepped Chris, looking around a moment, sleepy. Madeleine gave a start, not quite stifling her cry.

The stocky man knew he heard something. He spat out the cigarette, carefully raising his rifle and aiming it in Madeleine's direction, his eyes searching, not quite sure.

Chris hadn't seen or heard anything and walked the hundred feet to the outhouse, entered it and closed the door.

The stocky man was looking intensely, studying the area she was hiding in. She pressed herself lower, trembling.

The man whistled one sharp high note.

The cabin door opened again. Madeleine saw a tall man's head appear, wary. He stepped out, carrying a rifle, looking to the stocky man crouched behind the Ford. The stocky man glanced back to the tall one and touched his ear, then pointed in Madeleine's direction.

The tall man squinted at the woods a moment and squeezed himself back along the cabin wall along a wooden decking until he was out of sight lines to the rear yard. He pressed his back to the wall to be sure. He pulled a walkie-talkie from a pocket and pressed a button. He whispered, "Leader. Leader."

From an open barn window a silent arrow flew piercing the tall man's chest, the thick shaft burying inches into the cabin wall. He was pinned like an insect on a display board, the arrow so deep not even the feathers showed on his chest. The rifle and walkie-talkie dropped from his hands and his head slumped.

At the clatter of the gun hitting the wooden decking, Madeleine saw the stocky man drop to both knees, eyes nervous, his gun swiveling back towards the cabin. But from his vantage he couldn't see the tall man pinned to the wall.

Leader's voice broke on the radio lying on the ground. "What is it?"

Madeleine watched the stocky man who kept looking back to the cabin, then back in her direction, then back to the cabin.

Leader's voice came again, much louder, "Answer me!"

As in answer, the weight of the tall man finally snapped the arrow's shaft and his body fell forward stiffly in an arc, his head and shoulders coming into the stocky man's view just before thumping the ground. Startled, fearful, the stocky man dropped flat to the ground for cover, now uncertain where the enemy was.

*

Glancing from the open barn window, Andrew saw the stocky man retreating, crawling rapidly backwards through the tall grass towards the outhouse.

He had a poor angle for using the crossbow but didn't want to use the rifle unless necessary because it would inform Leader, and more importantly, anybody in the cabin with Chris, Andrew unaware Chris was now in the outhouse.

Andrew quickly climbed a stairway to a loft. He glanced out the loft window and could see the stocky man still crawling, now close to the outhouse. He took aim with the crossbow.

A barn pigeon flapped violently out of the next window and the man glanced up, saw Andrew and rolled. The arrow missed, thudding the ground beside him. The man fired two rapid shots, the bullets ripping into wood near Andrew's head. He jerked his head in and grabbed for his rifle.

Jumping up, the man continued to fire wildly at the barn window as he scrambled to the outhouse. He yanked once on the door, but Chris had locked it. He fired again at the window and jumped behind the outhouse to shield himself, knowing that Andrew would never fire through it with Chris in there.

The man yelled through the outhouse wall. "Chris, get out, quick. Come around behind. Someone's trying to kill you."

The door squeaked halfway open. Chris poked his head part way out, looking around, frightened. The man's hand and forearm snaked around the corner to grab him. Chris stared at the arm as it flailed blindly towards him.

Whack! Whack! A bullet ripped through the man's forearm. He shrieked and whipped his arm back behind the outhouse.

Andrew yelled, "Chris!"

Chris saw him and threw the door open and began to run towards the barn. Andrew trained his rifle on the side of the outhouse and fired twice for cover as Chris ran.

Andrew yelled, "Run to Mom," pointing in Madeleine's direction.

Chris looked that way. Madeleine stood up and began to run forward, fully exposed. She and Chris were three hundred feet apart, running towards each other, Madeleine's arms outstretched, one hand holding the pistol. Andrew fired more shots at the outhouse.

But the stocky man was crawling away from it, the outhouse still shielding him from Andrew's view. Now the man could see Madeleine, dashing full speed toward Chris. He kept crawling out, improving his position for a shot. He poked his head above the grass. Although one forearm was crippled and bleeding, he steadied the gun on that hand and drew a bead on the running Madeleine.

He pulled the trigger. The shot missed.

Madeleine just kept running, her face determined, her eyes fixed on Chris.

In his urgency to better his angle on the fast running Madeleine, he shoved himself quickly forward another foot across the grass. His finger almost found the trigger.

Thwack! His head snapped sideways then flopped forward, a crimson hole gaping. He had improved his position a fraction too much, just entering Andrew's sight line.

Madeleine reached Chris, the pistol dropping from her hand into the long grass as she grabbed him with both hands and dragged him to the ground. She clutched him and frantically began to crawl with him back to the cover of the woods.

Andrew saw Leader running among the trees, coming back from the gate house out front. Andrew knew his own position in the barn was given away. He bounded down the loft stairs and was leaping out through a narrow door at ground level when two bullets splintered the door frame. He ditched onto the grass and rolled. He glanced and saw Leader dodging among trees a hundred yards out.

Leader chanced another shot as he ran. Andrew quickly answered twice with no hope of a hit, just to make Leader stop and take cover, cover that Andrew would see. Immediately at the shots, Leader disappeared behind a thick oak beside the grass laneway.

Andrew lay flat, spread-eagled, preparing his aim, drawing a bead on the very edge of the oak tree. He breathed slowly in and held it, and slowly out, and all again, the relaxation exercise.

The width of the tree was three feet, giving Leader little room on either side. He would have to make a move. Training had taught Andrew to note how a shooter held his rifle. He had seen Leader shoot right. If Leader perceived his chances were equally good in both directions, which it seemed to Andrew it was, the odds were that he would either shoot from the right side of the tree, or run to the right. Andrew aimed twelve inches to Leader's right of the tree, his finger resting lightly on the trigger. He breathed deeply, evenly.

Several seconds passed. He saw a flash of color. He pulled the trigger. Leader took it in the shoulder, tumbling at the edge of the lane, grasping for his fallen gun.

Andrew steadied again. Leader was crouched low and swung the rifle around to aim. Andrew fired. There was a sudden jerk in the jacket fabric and Leader fell sideways.

Andrew glanced to the cabin for any sign of life. He quickly fired once at the cabin door and once at each of the two windows, shattering the glass.

He watched and waited. He glanced to Leader again. He looked to where he had last seen Madeleine. She was in cover.

He looked again at the cabin. If anyone was in that cabin, they would have joined the fight by now, well before now.

He looked again toward Leader. There was no movement.

He fired once more at a cabin window, jumped and ran a zigzag pattern toward Leader.

No reply from the cabin.

And Leader, he was stone dead.

CHAPTER FORTY FIVE

HIDDEN WELL IN the woods and at a safe distance to one side of the cabin, Velez and Nix, each wearing a black hood, two holes for the eyes, watched Andrew walking back from Leader's body. They knew Madeleine and Chris were in hiding at the edge of the woods at the rear, but too far away for Nix and Velez to do anything yet.

Nix whispered, "He's very good with that rifle. We have to wait for the opportunity."

They had arrived ten minutes earlier at the front road expecting to simply announce the code word to Leader and expecting that Andrew and Madeleine would have already been taken hostage and be safely squared away in the cabin.

But they had heard significant rifle fire as they approached the property entrance so had pulled over. They had come onto the property on foot away from the entrance for safety, making their way with caution through the thicker forest a hundred yards to one side of the lane. Moving roughly in the direction of the cabin, they had heard more gunfire. They had crept in concealment to gain a position where they could see what was happening, sorting out the players, seeing who was winning, and, unhappily, who was losing.

They realized they were now left to deal with Andrew on their own.

Nix carried a rifle, Velez a long barreled pistol. But neither was an experienced shooter. From very recent observation they knew better than to attempt any long-range gunfight with Andrew. They knew with a dreadful certainty that if they announced their presence with an attempted shot at this long distance, and missed, they would be in for a very bad morning. Better to wait for a surprise moment.

They watched Andrew slip cautiously into the cabin and come right back out again in seconds. They saw Madeleine and Chris begin running eagerly forward in the deep rear yard. Andrew met them half way. Chris and Madeleine hugged Andrew, and he them. They talked a few moments, and Andrew walked back toward the cabin, Madeleine and Chris staying where they were.

But still, he carried that rifle.

At the cabin he kneeled to examine the tall man with the arrow through his chest. He set his rifle down in the grass and turned the body over flat.

He then stood and walked the forty or so yards to the dead man in the grass near the outhouse. Nix and Velez tensed. Andrew didn't have his rifle. But he was still too close to it.

Andrew kneeled to the dead man, checked him over. Then he got up and began to walk back toward Madeleine and Chris, getting farther and farther from the rifle.

Madeleine let Chris run to Andrew and he scooped Chris up in his arms and kept walking toward Madeleine.

Nix and Velez waited and watched. Andrew was almost a hundred yards from them, and seventy yards from his rifle lying in the grass.

"We run straight toward his rifle," Nix whispered. "But we don't shoot until he's close."

"Let me shoot first. I don't want him dead," Velez said.

They broke cover, running hard.

*

Madeleine saw them first. "Andrew!" she screamed, pointing.

He turned. He dropped Chris and ran toward the cabin, toward his rifle, his only weapon.

It was a foot race, but Nix and Velez didn't have to get there first. They only needed to get near enough to him before he got to the rifle. At a close distance, they could safely wound and immobilize him.

As Chris ran to Madeleine she looked wildly about her for the pistol, realizing she had dropped it out in the tall grass when she had first pulled Chris to the ground, close to where the men were now running. Without a weapon she could do nothing but run to try to save herself and Chris. Terrified, she grabbed Chris's hand and raced towards the woods.

Velez fired once at the running Andrew and missed. But the second shot, when Andrew was just fifteen yards from the rifle, caught him in the thigh. He lost balance and tumbled, struggling on the ground, clutching his leg.

Guns pointed, Velez and Nix ran up, stopping a few yards from Andrew, fearing he might have some other weapon.

"Hands way out, roll over, face down," Nix shouted.

Andrew complied while looking anxiously to see where Madeleine and Chris were. He couldn't see them. He could only assume they were running deep into the woods.

Velez stood back, his pistol aimed while Nix walked close looking for a concealed weapon. He saw the empty knife-sheath at his back. Keeping his rifle pointed, Nix shoved his foot into Andrew's side, roughly pushing him over onto his back. Andrew moaned with pain, one hand reflexively going to his leg.

"Hands out," Nix shouted again, jabbing the barrel, checking him further.

Andrew couldn't make any useful move. His leg was limp, but he was certain the bullet hadn't hit bone. Blood ebbed slowly into the leg of his jeans, patching it darkly.

Satisfied there was no weapon, Nix walked to where Andrew's rifle lay. He grabbed it up and took it to a disused well some yards away, still watching Andrew as he did. He held the rifle over the well and dropped it in, a noisy clattering echo. "That's wreaked enough havoc today," he said.

Velez came forward and finally spoke to Andrew. "Well there you are, that little boy from so long ago."

He removed his black hood and tossed it on the ground. Andrew looked at him and saw he bore some resemblance to the latest forensic artist's depiction, but not enough to have ever found him based on that alone.

Still looking at Andrew, Velez said to Nix, "This is good. I'll stay and watch him while you collect the wife and kid. When Andrew sees them, he'll be more inclined to talk."

Nix removed his hood. He looked at Andrew's leg, noting the

blood seeping slowly into the jean fabric. "Lucky we missed an artery. You won't bleed to death anytime soon."

Andrew looked at Nix only a moment, then his eyes searched the woods, listening.

Nix said, "She can't run fast dragging a five-year-old in this swamp-filled property. And no place to hide, unless you want to flap around in the ooze for a while and hope I won't notice." He looked to Velez. "I won't be long."

Nix set off with his rifle, jogging through the grass yard toward the woods.

*

She didn't know how far behind the men would be. She ran ahead of Chris to pace him, to show him the winding path, to force him to go fast like her. His legs were so short and he was crying.

Immediately on running into the woods, she had heard the shots, two shots, but she hadn't seen anything. Two shots. Maybe… maybe Andrew killed them. One shot for each. He would have had to reach the gun first. And he would be running after her now, calling. She was certain she would hear him.

But she didn't hear any calling. She heard nothing, only silence. She sensed the worst. Two shots. One shot for each. It didn't seem likely.

Andrew…she felt herself screaming inside.

She had to think only of surviving now. Think only of that, saving Chris.

As she ran she swatted at leafy branches that drooped into the path blocking her way. "Hard, Chris, hard," she urged.

She didn't have the pistol Andrew had given her in the night. She had let him down. She had been careless, unforgivably careless. She could have shot at the two men as they were running toward them, maybe hit them, at least slowed them. Given Andrew a chance.

She realized she was crying. She could have saved Andrew.

She glanced back at Chris, his little head bobbing, his short legs pumping. Stop all self-recriminations, she lashed at herself. Stop thinking that way. Think only of saving Chris. That was all that mattered now, if she was very lucky. She had to get to the car on that back road. The keys would be in the car, or in one of the dead men's pockets.

Her feet pounded the winding slim dirt path, bog threatening on both sides.

Why had she been so careless with the gun? You were counting on me to help you, to save myself, to save Chris.

They were nearing an open stretch where deep swamp water lay on both sides, narrowing the trail to almost nothing for a hundred yards. She would be hopelessly exposed from behind. She looked back but saw nothing, heard nothing.

"Run, Chris. Run. Keep up."

They crossed the hundred yards and now Madeleine thought she heard something far behind.

Or was it someone calling?

Andrew?

She stopped and looked back, panting. It was nothing but a wind rustling marsh grass. Chris grabbed her leg with both arms and held it, crying, breathing so hard.

There were dwarf trees and bush ahead. It was sparse for as far as she could see. If the men got close to her, there was no place to hide anywhere.

She ran on, faster. Chris's legs were just too short to keep up.

His face was red and dripping sweat. He was soon far behind and calling. She slowed and reached her hand back outstretched, waiting for him to grasp it. She pulled him along.

She was too fast. In her speed his feet barely touched the ground. He lost footing and their hands separated. He fell and rolled, his leg hitting a jutting rock. He opened his mouth to cry out.

"No!" Madeleine censured and clapped a hand to his mouth. "Not now!"

She picked him up and he grabbed her, clutching. She carried him running for a full minute until she couldn't maintain her pace anymore. "You've got to run now. For dad."

He only cried more, and now she did too. She looked around and saw only impassable swamp. There was nowhere to hide, nowhere to run but on this trail. There was no other way out. They could follow so easily. They would be so much faster.

She looked back like a helpless animal with her innocent young, trapped and terrified.

CHAPTER FORTY SIX

"LAWRENCE IS IN my car trunk," Velez said to Andrew. "Dead, of course. He needs to be disposed of soon, so stinking hot out here."

Andrew looked away and rubbed his leg, hoping it wouldn't seize and render him useless.

Velez was walking slowly back and forth, keeping his distance. Andrew focused only on the woods, listening with every fiber, hoping with every fiber, that he heard nothing from those woods, that Madeleine would make it to the car in time and find keys. It was the only way. But he was filled with dread. He couldn't remember seeing her holding the pistol.

"In the trunk, like your father was," Velez said. "We've come full circle, you, me, your father." He paused and looked around, listened, then looked back to Andrew. "You know, you should know this, that when I took your father, I told him to tell me if he had told anyone what he knew. I told him that if he lied to me, held anything back, I would kill his son."

Andrew turned to look at him.

"Your father said he had told no one. I guess he didn't believe I would do it, kill his boy. And he was right, I wouldn't. I'm not a primitive. All this time I had believed he had told me the truth. But…I know now that he didn't."

Andrew watched him carefully. What was he saying?

"Let me tell you a little story about your friend Lawrence. He probably never told you that he got a fifteen-year-old girl pregnant when he was a cop, twenty-one. He arranged for an abortion, a back-alley kind, with a woman, Lucy, who he heard about, a woman I knew. She was charged before with doing an abortion but I paid off the right people and the charge got dropped. So Lucy owed me a favor."

Andrew listened, but his eyes still watched the woods.

"Lucy was no fool now. She wanted to know who it was who wanted her business before she would take it. She secretly learned Lawrence was a cop, found out where he lived. Like I said, she owed me a favor. She knew I would very much like to have something like this on a cop, an accomplice to a criminal offence. I had one of my people hang around her place the night Lawrence was to bring the girl. But he didn't show."

Andrew slowly shifted himself to take stress off the bad leg. All this was nothing he didn't already know. But…how did Velez know it?

"So my fellow took a drive to Lawrence's place to have a look. It was dark out. He saw some activity so he hid and waited. He saw Lawrence put a shovel in the back seat of his car, an odd thing to be doing. Soon he was carrying a wrapped white sheet with something long and heavy in it…like maybe a body."

Andrew began to put the pieces together. Velez had something much bigger on Lawrence than an abortion—the girl was dead, Lawrence had killed her, just as Lawrence had explained.

Velez walked slowly around Andrew, keeping his distance, keeping the gun ready. "Lawrence told me later it was an accident, but I don't know, maybe it was. He drove off with her that night like he was going to bury her, my guy safely following. But in the end he didn't bury her. He dropped her off at her house instead, a corpse, a jolt to the family."

Andrew rolled onto his good leg. He knew what was coming.

"When I realized Lawrence wasn't giving himself up, not confessing to the crime, I made contact with him, let him know what I knew, although we never met. I thought, though, that that might push him to the edge, make him confess his crime to his colleagues, take his licks. But it didn't. I had him. He was mine."

It seemed unbelievable—Lawrence had become an informer for Velez, all those years ago.

"We never met in person but we made an arrangement, and it worked out very well for me. He kept me one step ahead for a whole year, saved my bacon many times. He told me about the police trap in the Catskills, not that he knew about my intended ruse. His information allowed my escape, and my death. But, as another Buffalo resident famously said, 'reports of my death were greatly exaggerated'."

Velez squatted down five yards away, watching Andrew. "Maybe Lawrence told you that he left Buffalo after that, maybe feeling guilty. But, like everyone else, he thought I was dead. He went to college then joined the FBI, posted in Philadelphia. After a time he became the liaison officer between the Bureau there and Philly PD, which gets me to the point I was making earlier about your father saying he told no one what he knew. Not true. I learned last night that he told Lawrence."

Andrew registered the words. *All along, for twenty years, Lawrence had known it was Velez who killed his father.* All those times Lawrence had come to visit him when he lived with Grandpa, all the years in between, all the time they had come to know one another in the last month, all the talking they had done. *All along.*

"It was a shocker for me, too," Velez said. "I learned a lot last night. I learned that the morning of the day I took your father, your father had phoned Lawrence and told him what Macky had whispered as he laid dying—that I was alive, and more, that I was at the gala at the hotel. Your father asked Lawrence to say nothing, but that he come to your house that evening, work through a plan with your father to do a secret operation through the FBI away from any possible inside informants in the Philly PD."

Andrew shouted. "Are you saying it was *Lawrence* who told you what my father knew? It was *Lawrence* who tipped you off? *That's* how you learned? *That's* why my father died?"

Velez laughed an ugly laugh. "That would be terrible wouldn't it? No, not Lawrence, not as bad as that. I learned just enough from a police insider to make me suspect your father knew something, that as Macky lay dying, he had passed on something. I just couldn't leave that stone unturned. That's what made me come to your house, a hunch that proved correct."

Andrew closed his eyes. He didn't want to see this evil man. Anger boiled. But far more powerful was his ever-building dread for Madeleine and Chris.

"No," Velez continued, "Lawrence told me last night that

when your father told him, it was a genuine shock for Lawrence. He really believed I was dead. He told me he was preparing to come to your house that evening just as your father had requested, but then he heard the news of the abduction over the wire. He knew exactly what had happened. He said he got… 'weak'".

He had had a choice, and he chose to stay quiet, save himself. Andrew kept his eyes closed but his ears listened to the woods.

Velez said, "Maybe you've now figured his plan with you—his conscience slowly killing him, a burden he couldn't carry any longer. He brings you in, a skilled young fellow, but doesn't tell you everything, of course. Counts on having your cooperation because, after all, it's your father's killer you're after, an emotional attachment to the job like no one else would have. You would go outside the rules, you would keep things quiet. With his knowledge and his clues he calculated that you would find me, learn who I am, where I am. And then the grand finale—*he would kill me before I could ever reveal all I knew he had done*."

Andrew opened his eyes.

"Yes, Andrew, under a little encouragement last night, he admitted it all. He would kill me outright. No arrest, no trial, no risk of exposure of his past. He would orchestrate things so no one would look too closely at exactly what went down. I would be dead. And both of you would be heroes. But, as they say, the best laid plans..."

Andrew listened only to the silent woods. Nothing else mattered now.

Velez cast a long look there too, not speaking for many moments. Then he said, "Do you know what it was that gave me away to Macky that night at the gala all those years ago? My *voice*. I had had alterations to my appearance, of course, excellent cosmetic clinics in Switzerland, aided by hair coloring to make me look older. I wouldn't even know myself in a mirror. But you can't disguise your *voice*. I didn't see Macky at first. The woman I was with told me that a man who had been standing very near behind me had turned quickly in what seemed surprise to look at me when I was talking. She said he walked a short ways off but kept keenly observing me in odd surprise as if he knew me. She told me where he was. I got a passing look, saw it was an old employee of mine, Macky. He must have been confounded, believing I was dead. But you're still going to trust your eyes, and your ears. He had figured out my ruse. I got to a payphone by the washrooms, a quick call to Nix who was upstairs in a hotel room. My girlfriend soon gave Macky the eyes. He knew I knew. He fled, got six blocks before Nix got him. Nix thought he was dead. Unfortunately, not quite."

Velez looked at Andrew. "There it is, the whole sorry tale… triggered by that one small thing."

Andrew closed his eyes. A voice in a room twenty years ago. His father… and now his own young son, and his wife.

Velez gave a long sigh, suddenly weary. "A long night last night, wasn't it? For me, too, and for Lawrence. But I got what I needed."

*

Madeleine and Chris were slowing, exhausted.

"You can do it, Chris," she panted, but her own legs were like lead. "Be strong."

They were almost through the wide expanse of dwarf trees when it happened, someone calling. She stopped, looked anxiously back, hoping she would see Andrew. She couldn't see anything. Then a rifle CRACK. A tree trunk thwacked near her.

Chris cried out. She pulled him down.

Another rifle CRACK.

She could see him now, a small figure in the distance.

It wasn't Andrew.

An enormous weight crushed her. All the hope…gone. Andrew…gone.

She squeezed Chris and tears streamed her face.

But immediately she felt a powerful tide in herself pushing the other way. Anger, huge anger, welled. She felt its surging strength.

She glanced back and saw him on the move. She registered he was further back than she thought at first, a few minutes behind, maybe more. But he was now jogging, steadily, looking strong, the rifle held well up. He would soon catch up.

Her hand went out to Chris and she pulled him hard. "We've got to run so hard."

They crossed the final stretch of scrub and entered a tall-grass field. Ahead, at its edge, was the swath of real forest, thick fir trees, and she knew the road was just beyond that. The forest would provide some cover. "Hurry, Chris!"

Get to the car. Find keys. Get it started. Get away.

But Andrew…leaving Andrew…

They plunged through the open field, the stand of big trees getting closer, multiplying, the cover becoming thicker.

They were almost at the edge of the field, the road just beyond through the trees. Razor grass grabbed at her legs, again and again, the way it had last night. "Just about there, Chris," she panted. "Run, run."

And then she remembered.

CHAPTER FORTY SEVEN

NIX KNEW HE was gaining on them. He had stopped to take aim and fire, but only to scare them. He wanted them to stop running, to give up. But Madeleine seemed a more than determined woman. She had kept a pace with the boy he hadn't expected.

He rushed through the open razor-grassed field and entered the thickly forested area. He knew the road was close, just beyond the trees. If they got out on the road he would see them easily, the road straight and level in both directions. They would, instead, cross over into the next woods and be harder to spot. He sped up.

He heard a car engine start just beyond the trees. A car door slammed shut. Damn it! He would have to shoot at her now, plug the car repeatedly as it went. Maybe kill her. An easy shot, though, the road level and straight for a half mile.

He ran faster and saw the roadside coming up through the trees. He could hear the engine running but sensed the car wasn't moving yet. The boy was slower, holding her up. She was waiting for the boy. That was it.

As he broke headlong from the trees he saw the car wasn't moving. He dashed the hundred feet to it, his rifle aimed. She wasn't in the driver's seat. He glanced to the back seat. Nothing.

He looked up and glimpsed Chris well up the road, disappearing into the woods on the other side.

Then why was the engine running?

*

Madeleine stepped silently from behind a tree trunk thirty feet behind Nix. In her hands, pointed at his back, was the automatic rifle that the man had been carrying who had tackled her to the ground in the field of razor-grasses last night. She had remembered it only when she got close to that spot just now, remembered that when the man chased her, he had a rifle. But when she had fought, he had had to grab her with both hands. And when he picked her up, he had used both hands. And when he had dragged her, he had carried no rifle.

She had quickly found the rifle lying in the grasses beside a patch where the grasses were bent and flattened where he had overcome her and dragged her to the ground and they had fought. At the car she found the keys still in the ignition. She had told Chris to run and stay hidden until she called for him. She had started the car.

As a decoy, as a draw, the running engine had done its job. Nix was a momentary stand-still target, his back to her.

She squeezed the trigger. The gun jumped alive, jerking powerfully in her hands, the sound deafening. Nix was thrown forward against the side of the car, his body punched by the wild, crisscrossing spray, bullets ripping across the car as she couldn't hold her aim. She didn't know that the rifle would do that. Stunned at the clamor and the kicking recoil, afraid she wasn't hitting him, she kept the trigger squeezed, a full three second burst.

It finally stopped. Her ears were ringing. Nix, in bloody shreds, slid down the side of the car.

She stared in shock at him, her hand absently rubbing her gun shoulder. Then she snapped to attention and looked with sudden concern at the gun. Gritting, she pointed it at the woods behind her and pulled the trigger.

Click.

She pulled it again.

Click.

She realized she must have squeezed the trigger so long there were no bullets left.

She saw the butt end of Nix's rifle jutting from under his torn and bloodied body. She dropped her rifle and grabbed one of Nix's arms and, grunting, pulled him off his rifle. She picked it up. It was dripping with blood, bloodying her hands and shirt.

Gritting, she pointed it at the woods and pulled the trigger firmly.

Bang! A single shot. What? Not like a machine gun? She looked startled.

Angry, she pulled the trigger again. A single bang. Her eyes sprung new tears. She didn't want single shot. She was no sharp shooter.

*

Andrew and Velez had heard two distant single rifle cracks. Then later, a long burst of automatic fire, quieter, further away. And now two faint single shots again.

Andrew stared grimly in the direction of the gunfire. After a minute of silence, he turned to Velez with a burning hatred. He struggled to lunge at him but Velez stepped quickly back.

"I'll shoot!" Velez said.

Andrew fell, his leg giving out. His fists pounded the ground in rage. "I will kill you if it takes my last breath."

"Don't fret, Andrew. Nix is just scaring them out of hiding. You heard him, he wants you to see them again. He's just being enthusiastic."

Andrew squeezed his eyes shut, his heart bursting, his precious son, his precious wife. He felt he would explode. What had happened in that gunfire? He needed to stay alive until he knew the answer, to know if there was any hope for them.

When he heard the first two single shots, he knew they were from Nix because they were from a rifle, not from the pistol that he had given Madeleine. He knew its sound. But then later had been automatic fire, a long, long burst. Had Madeleine come upon an automatic rifle, maybe in the car?

Then had come two more single rifle shots. He figured they were from Nix's rifle. There were no shots from the pistol. Nix had survived the shootout.

Tears came. Madeleine had tried. But she didn't know guns, didn't know how an automatic rifle would act. But she had tried. Nix would have taken cover, let Madeleine empty her ammo, waste all her shots. Then…

The minutes passed like hours, ten… fifteen.

Velez had been sitting but now he was up, pacing again, casting looks towards the woods. "Your boy has slowed them on the way back."

Andrew raged inside, his mind barely controlled. He never looked at Velez. He kept watching the forest, listening.

At one point he half rolled to take some pressure off his wounded leg. As he did, and turned his head away from the forest a moment, his eye caught sudden movement in the grasses almost a hundred yards behind and to the side of him and Velez.

The wind? There wasn't any wind. A discrete set of grasses was moving.

He saw that Velez's eyes were on the woods. He looked at the grasses again and tensed.

In SWAT training they had learned to crawl, crawl through everything, flat on your belly, invisible. He had watched grass fields hundreds of yards away through binoculars, observing closely, seeing who could snake through the field without disturbance, and who couldn't, who would get shot, and who wouldn't.

The movement he saw now had the signature of someone crawling, someone without the least benefit of training.

He suddenly demanded, "Where did you put my father?"

Velez was startled. "So urgent a tone. You've already figured that out. So why do you ask?"

"*Exactly* where?"

"Is that so much a concern now?"

"I want to know."

"Back there in a bog, of course. Do you think I'm going to stroll you out there…for a quiet moment?"

Andrew looked angrily in the direction Velez had indicated for the distant bogs. He knew Velez was watching him. He avoided looking back at him.

A few moments later he glimpsed at the grasses again. The

movement, a swaying, was getting closer, now about eighty yards away.

Andrew pressed, "Tell me exactly."

Velez was impatient. "Oh let's wait for Nix. He'll find you amusing."

Andrew's heart leaped. A swatch of chestnut hair bobbed a moment over the top of the long grass. The hair progressed further sideways, moving to get more directly behind him and Velez.

He was utterly amazed. Madeleine knew nothing about guns, even hated them. But here she was. His heart beat faster.

He said, "I'm not afraid of death. In fact, I'm going to die happy knowing you've been beaten."

"*I've* been beaten? It doesn't quite strike me that way."

"Lawrence didn't tell you everything, then?"

Velez laughed. "Tricks, Andrew. I don't fall for tricks. Lawrence told me everything. I made very sure of that. Save your ingenuity so Nix can watch, too."

The grass stopped moving. She was now sixty yards out.

Andrew said, "Did you ever wonder what you did to me that day twenty years ago?"

Velez looked dismissive.

Andrew rolled lightly, squeezing at his leg to slow blood flow, his hand bloody, trying to manage Velez's attention.

Shortly the moving grasses were only forty yards out and Andrew began to calculate. What weapon did she have? His heart was hammering his chest.

Velez was five yards from Andrew. When Andrew looked at Velez he was able to see behind him into the grasses. Thirty-five yards out the grasses stopped moving. Still looking toward Velez, Andrew saw a long barrel ease up from the grass.

She had a rifle. He hoped she wasn't going to shoot from there. Thirty-five yards was still too far for her aim. She would probably miss with a single shot. Then Velez would shoot her. If it's automatic, the recoil would cause her to spray her fire everywhere and possibly not even hit Velez, but maybe hit him. Again, Velez would then just shoot her.

When she fires, do I stay down to avoid getting hit, or try to make a lunge, however feeble, for his gun? His only thought was for Madeleine. He would go for Velez's gun no matter.

Thirty-five yards. She seemed to be wondering, maybe going to prepare for a shot.

Still too far. Too dangerous for a miss.

But at thirty-five yards she would hear conversation.

Andrew's tone became taunting. "Do you ever think and feel, Velez, other than as a grasping, greedy fool?"

Velez half smiled. "Trying to redeem me? Rescue me from myself?"

Andrew knew she was crouched, maybe aiming. But she was still too far.

Velez was bemused but cast his look back again towards the woods.

Andrew caught her eye just a moment then looked at Velez. He began to shake his head unmistakably. "No, Velez, you're *too far* from redemption."

Madeleine hesitated, watching Andrew, sensing his meaning. She rose slightly and eased forward, the rifle see-sawing as she moved.

She was now thirty yards away. Still too risky, Andrew thought. She needed another few seconds, another five or ten yards. He rocked his body as if the pain had sharpened, grasping at his wounded leg, wincing. Velez watched him. Andrew hoped Madeleine had gained some few yards, but he dared not look.

Andrew suddenly cocked his head towards the woods and looked intensely as if startled. "I think someone's calling…*now.*"

Velez sensed something odd. He glanced behind and saw Madeleine twenty-five yards away. She pulled the trigger just as Velez's pistol arm spun toward her and fired.

Each missed the other.

But Andrew had lunged off his one good leg and now slammed Velez's gun arm making Velez's second shot fire wide. He threw a punch to Velez's face, snapping his head sideways, then fought to get his hands on the gun-hand to force the barrel down.

Velez was strong, his forearm moving under Andrew's clutch. The pistol cracked a third time, Madeleine jumping sideways as the shot walloped the ground near her.

Velez had two good legs for balance and footing to Andrew's one, causing both bodies to pivot wildly. Madeleine looked afraid to fire for fear of hitting Andrew. They bucked and jerked, the pistol swinging in an arc passing by Madeleine again, the gun firing once early, once late.

Andrew's strength began to tell. He got a death grip on the gun-hand. It was all he could do to keep Velez from shooting at Madeleine again. Velez punched wildly with one free hand at Andrew's head. Andrew forced the gun to rotate sideways away from the darting Madeleine.

Velez furiously head-butted as Andrew pried at Velez's fingers, gripping the trigger-finger, wresting it slowly away. He forced the pistol's barrel to ease around, coming between them.

Their faces were now inches apart, Velez raging. Their eyes locked and their bodies shook with their effort.

The pistol fired. They stayed deadlocked.

It fired again.

Distress came to Velez's eyes for several moments. Then the eyes steadied and focused hard on Andrew's. Through gritted teeth, Velez said, "that little boy…" and his hand weakly thrust once at Andrew.

The fire in his eyes suddenly died, and he fell straight back like a board, thudding the ground.

Madeleine grabbed Andrew.

He said, "Chris?"

She was crying. "He's okay, hiding. Oh Andrew, Andrew."

"Nix?"

"He's dead, too. Your leg—."

He saw the thigh of his jeans was fully covered in fresh blood from the exertion. He would do a tourniquet.

"It's okay," he said, hugging her, delirious in his relief. "Maddy, I heard all that shooting before. I thought you …and Chris…."

"I know, I know," she sobbed. "I didn't know how to use it right."

"Use it right?" He squeezed her. "Maddy, you used it right, very, very right."

CHAPTER FORTY EIGHT

FOUR DAYS LATER under a heavy gray sky, the bells at the Cathedral Basilica of Saints Peter and Paul tolled solemnly. Silent mourners spilled from the Cathedral's front doors, down its front steps and out along its sidewalks. Pallbearers carried Lawrence's casket to the rear of the hearse.

Andrew had been discharged from hospital the evening before. Gripping a wooden crutch, he and Madeleine and Chris watched as the casket was eased into position.

An FBI investigator from Washington HQ had come to the hospital and debriefed him two days before, astonished more than once as the narrative unfolded. Andrew's thinking and his feelings about Lawrence had swung like a wild pendulum, back and forth.

Lawrence had cared so much for himself all those years ago, placed himself so above justice and decency that he had failed everyone around him—the young girl, her parents, his colleagues, and… Andrew's father, who had trusted him, and him alone, with the secret that got him killed.

But he had also lived a life in deep anguish in consequence, forsaking human relationships like a penance, living his life alone, an island, striving to do his utmost to prosecute cases, making amends to society as he saw it, salving his conscience if he could, but ultimately failing in that, too.

But had he failed Andrew? Andrew had struggled with the question. Lawrence hadn't caused his father to die; his father would have died anyway. But he hadn't faced the truth and said what he knew, allowing the law to pursue Velez all those years ago. It would have answered Andrew's long held question, ending the torment of who, and why.

But…if Lawrence had spoken up, acted on what his father told him, would the law have been successful in finding Velez anyway? Velez had insiders. He would have been forewarned by them. He would know they knew his 'death' had been a ruse. He would have gone into hiding, and soon carried on elsewhere, his new appearance foiling discovery. He may have escaped forever, probably escaped forever.

Would his forever escape have been a worse torment than not knowing who, and why? Now both of those questions were answered, and Velez was dead, and his organization gone forever.

Lawrence's plan had held a much higher chance of success. And he died trying. He knew he was at supreme risk, but he didn't walk from it in the end. He wanted Velez dead, for himself, yes, but also for Andrew. He had also confessed much to Andrew, ready to take the consequences.

Andrew had also wondered what Lawrence contemplated in his dying hour believing that he had set in motion events responsible for the imminent deaths of Andrew and Madeleine and maybe Chris, innocents lost, an entire family. Surely his final hour was a hell.

Andrew had balanced his thoughts and asked the debriefing officer to seek approval from the powers that be to not reveal all of what Lawrence had done. He had too late in life confessed his actions, acknowledging himself to be despicable, but he had confessed. He had wanted to make amends, and he had tried, and that should never be denied anyone before their final day.

But he had failed. He had not found peace.

So he stood today watching a casket, not to honor Lawrence as others were who knew nothing of the truth, but to acknowledge the passing of a man who had suffered much in life, who, in the end, thought he was doing some final good, as he believed it to be, and risked all to do so.

The mourners stood quietly in observance as the hearse pulled away slowly from the curb. When it was half a block down, the crowd began to disperse.

Andrew felt a tap on his arm. "Andrew Locke?"

A gray-haired man with a smile offered his hand. "Jack Morgan. We spoke briefly on the phone."

Morgan was a lead investigator at HQ and Andrew knew he had reviewed the debriefing notes. "Yes, sir," Andrew said, shaking his hand.

"I haven't had the chance to congratulate you in person, Andrew. I want to thank you for the extraordinary job you did here, just extraordinary."

"Thank you, sir. This is my wife, Madeleine. I wouldn't be here if it wasn't for her."

"I've heard the whole story," he said, shaking Madeleine's

hand. "I'm deeply sorry this matter came to involve you and your son. You displayed extraordinary courage and action. The Bureau extends its utmost gratitude."

Madeleine gave a brief smile, a polite acknowledgement of kind words. But it was all an experience she wanted behind her. She looked down at Chris and took his hand and squeezed it. She looked up at Andrew.

He was watching her. He wrapped an arm around her and kissed her cheek.

www.ingramcontent.com/pod-product-compliance
Ingram Content Group UK Ltd.
Pitfield, Milton Keynes, MK11 3LW, UK
UKHW042004190726
13854UKWH00005B/2162

9 780995 287747